When We Disappear

When We Disappear

a novel by

LISE HAINES

UNBRIDLED BOOKS

Unbridled Books

Library of Congress Cataloging-in-Publication Data

Names: Haines, Lise, author.
Title: When we disappear / by Lise Haines.
Description: Lakewood, CO : Unbridled Books, [2018] |
Identifiers: LCCN 2017038279 (print) | LCCN 2017042748 (ebook) | ISBN
9781609531485 () | ISBN 9781609531478 (trade pbk. edition : alk. paper)
Classification: LCC PS3608.A545 (ebook) | LCC PS3608.A545 W48 2018 (print) |
DDC 813/.6--dc23
LC record available at https://lccn.loc.gov/2017038279

1 3 5 7 9 10 8 6 4 2

Book Design by SH – CV

First Printing

One should really use the camera as though tomorrow you'd be stricken blind. To live a visual life is an enormous undertaking, practically unattainable. I have only touched it, just touched it.

DOROTHEA LANGE

You have wakened not out of sleep, but into a prior dream; and that dream lies within another, and so on, to infinity, which is the number of grains of sand.

JORGE LUIS BORGES

In memory of

NORTON KAY

My father, my friend,
my heart, my guide

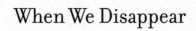When We Disappear

Mona

He shut off our alarm clocks, loaded his car, eased the hand brake out, and backed down the drive without turning the engine over. Richard, my father, was probably in Indiana by now. He had tossed his house keys on the counter as if he wouldn't be back. An envelope was propped on the kitchen table with a letter written to Liz, my mother.

"He didn't wake you? To say goodbye?" I looked through the blinds to see for myself that his car was gone.

His coffee cup stained the table, sugar sprinkled across it, wet spoon stuck back in the box.

"No, I guess he ..." She stopped when she opened the letter and began to read.

Next to the envelope was a coffee-table book, *National Monuments Across America*, filled with glossy color prints of Yosemite, Bryce, the Giant Sequoias, Niagara Falls. There were several Ansel Adams' black-and-whites. I used to pore over that book as if I were looking at shrines. We had talked about visiting monuments in one long vacation when I was young. He left the book open, weighing down the pages with our green carnival-glass salt and pepper shakers. Maybe that's how he was able to leave, thinking he'd return before long and someone would take that trip with him. My mother and I looked at the photograph of a herd of bison running across both pages, from left to right up to the edge of the paper like the edge of a cliff.

I tried to read the letter over her shoulder but she pulled it to her chest. Mom was in her mid-forties then, ran most days, drank little, never smoked. Now there were lines around her mouth I hadn't noticed before. Her eyes appeared smaller, as if they had sunk into her skull overnight.

The year was 2007. I was seventeen and Lola was three. Our plan had been to get up in time to see him off. She would have been fast asleep in Mom's arms at that hour. No one slept as soundly as Lola. Mom would have said goodbye for Lola, swaying her from side to side on her hip. I would have stood there for my mother's sake.

My eyes began to water, and the bison looked smaller, more like lemmings.

Folding the letter, she put it in the pocket of her robe. "He'll call when he gets to New Jersey."

"You aren't going to tell me what he said?" My voice began to strain, as if I had started running to catch up with his car.

"He had a hard time saying goodbye."

"You'll have to tell Lola."

"You aren't breathing right," she said.

"I'm fine."

"Hold on."

We had a drawer stacked with lunch bags.

When I was breathing in and out, filling and collapsing one of the bags, she said, "We'll go to the Art Institute today. We have a month left on our membership."

This was her solution to most things: lose yourself in art. But I couldn't afford to take off because my father had taken off. I was in high school, finishing the first semester of my senior year. I had three finals coming up.

"We'll show Lola the Thorne Rooms," she went on, in her spirit of repair.

Each of the museum's miniature rooms was decorated in a different period and style from the thirteenth century to the 1930s, the furnishings on a one-inch to one-foot scale. Everything was perfect, yet no one lived in any of those rooms. Or from the other side, the curator's side, everyone who peered inside was a giant and all of their imperfections showed. Mom had taken me there many times when I was Lola's age.

Once I was breathing normally, I said, "Maybe next weekend."

My mother held me and kissed my cheek. "Come upstairs if you need me."

Then she went off to turn on the shower in the master bath. Here she would break down. I walked in on her doing this once. She sat on the lid of the toilet, weeping under the sound of the shower, as if none of us would find out.

While I listened to the water run upstairs, I wondered if things might have been different if I had woken early and found him at the kitchen table, pen in hand, about to sign his name to the bottom of that letter. Maybe he would have gotten past the sadness of leaving her to leave her the right way.

Though I had stopped listening to his stories years ago, I would have listened to this one, even pulling a chair up to the table and turning off my phone. He would have started with a man taking off from the people he loved in difficult times, using great care in the way he invented this man, the look in his eyes, his rumpled clothes. Dad was an impeccable dresser then, so this last detail would have been his effort to set himself apart from the man he conjured. After a while Richard would have reached into his suit pocket to give me the handkerchief that was laundered and pressed for the road, trying to make me feel that things were going to be all right. This idea would have lingered in the light penetrating the blinds. But once he was gone, it would have dropped to the linoleum and left a mark as if a heavy jar had landed there.

The thing I couldn't say to my mother was this: Lola was too little to be left, and Mom wasn't fragile exactly—I never saw her as someone who would crack—but she was unprepared. And I really had no idea what he expected me to do about any of this.

I listened to the familiar thump in the pipes as the water was shut off upstairs. I went into my room. There I curled up and fell back to sleep, the only place where I knew how to cry openly.

After he left, we began to move around the house like dogs trying to settle, each of us showing the tension. Yet Mom continued to make him sound like the mail carrier that comes through. "I don't know a better man than your father," she said too often. There was a feeling that stood behind or off to the side of those declarations, something about his departure I couldn't name.

Lola began to hide things under her bed. Popsicle molds, favorite toys and clothes, small boxes of cereal, light bulbs, cotton balls, and photographs of him. She clung to us in ways she hadn't before. And Mom thought too much about the dangers that might befall us if we weren't vigilant, now that we were living alone. She watched an endless string of safety demonstrations online and wanted to reenact some of them with us. At least Lola was willing. I began sleepwalking again, and when I gravitated to the neighbors' dry fountain next door where they found me curled up in my pajamas, Mom worried about me walking into the street, and she worried about me being out in the cold, and she worried about the upcoming summer when the fountain would be full. She got her drill bits out and installed chain locks high up on the front and back doors.

I knew his going wasn't only about a job in New Jersey. She made a point of telling me he sent money every two weeks without fail. Though she never broke this down, the money was never enough. Once a week she talked with him by phone. I was convinced they were pretending at something. Mostly she talked to him deep in her room, sometimes in her closet.

When she emerged, Lola would get on. She could be very chatty, and Mom often helped her to say goodbye and let go of the receiver so Mom could budget and call next week. Once, Lola didn't like this idea at all and pulled so fiercely to keep the phone, it sprang back and hit her in the forehead. Mom sat for a long time with her, holding ice against a swelling bump, whispering and rocking her, and telling Lola everything was going to be all right. I described the scene to Dad because Mom insisted I keep him on the line—until she realized this was only making Lola cry harder.

Lola got phone shy after that, so he started sending her postcards. They came with pictures of fairgrounds or restaurants or caves—the kind of free cards advertisers give out where he found enough room to write around the pitch. Mom helped her start a scrapbook with the cancellation marks and smudged town names.

One of his letters arrived from New Jersey. That was his way, to send letters in blue ink. He didn't like the idea of email or texting. He laughed at social media, made stupid jokes about Skyping. I was about to throw the letter in Mom's bill pile when I realized it was addressed to me. It took me two days to open it.

Dear Mona,

Do you remember when you were a little thing like Lola, and Mom gave you her old Brownie camera? You wouldn't let anyone show you how to work it and before long there were dozens of black-and-white photos of shoes and ceilings and noses. She pulled a box down from her closet and searched around and handed you one particular picture she had taken and said, "I could show you how to put a ghost in a photograph." Your first lesson was on double exposures.

I've been thinking we're all double exposures in a way, that there

*are things we sometimes miss in the layers. What am I trying to say?
I know things haven't been easy between us for some time. But I was
wondering if we couldn't get a fresh start. Maybe if we wrote once a
week for a while and talked a little on paper I could get to know you
better. I'll begin with this letter and hope you drop me something, even
a sentence. I know you're busy.*

*Next letter I'll tell you a story about your Great Uncle Sorohan,
who could see through the layers, right to the bottom of your soul and
a couple of ticks further.*

Please take care of your mother and Lola, and know that I love you.
Dad

In my whole life I hadn't taken a single double exposure.

I went out behind the garage, where Mom kept her cleaned-out
oil drums for scrap metal. I set a small fire in one of them. I opened
a photo album I had started years ago. There was the picture where
he was guiding me on my first two-wheeler, one at the beach in his
swim trunks, one standing by a new car. I took them out of their
sleeves one by one and dropped them into the fire and watched
them bubble and curl at the edges.

A few days later I learned that he hadn't received his commissions
at his new job. Mom increased her part-time phone sales—pushing
her real work, her giant sculptures, off to the evenings, sometimes
late into the night. She had only taken that job as a stopgap right
before Dad left, while her résumés and applications circulated in a
shrinking job market. Now that selling ad space was the big thing
in her day, Lola and I weren't supposed to pick up the landline. If
she had to go out or use the bathroom during her shift, she called
another salesperson by dialing a code into the phone. I recall one
conversation in particular when Mom switched to speakerphone so
she could fold laundry before starting dinner. She hugged Lola, who
was lingering in her arms, and handed me the shoe-tying board so

we could continue the lesson they had started between calls. Lola quickly pulled it out of my hands, saying, "I can do it myself."

"Okay, I think we're all set. I'll repeat the message," Mom said after a while. She rolled a pair of Lola's socks while she reviewed her notes. She had learned early on that if she got the message wrong, it came out of her pay. In a flat voice, at a good volume, she said, "Quote: *We met in the best of times, you made it the worst of times. You're a total witch, Debbie, and I hope you and your whole family go to hell*. End quote. You want this to appear in Friday's paper, in the *Personal Regrets* column in twelve-point type, inside a bold box, to run for six days. Wednesday will be the last day it will appear unless you call in on Tuesday by noon to extend the ad."

"I didn't say *witch*. Who says *witch*?" The guy's voice boomed out of the speaker. "That's *bitch, bitch. Bitch* with a capital *B*."

My mother stood up, and a dozen pairs of neatly tucked socks left her lap and bounced and rolled across the floor. She signaled to cover Lola's ears while she struggled to turn off the speakerphone. But Lola broke away and chased the socks, kicking them here and there as I pursued her.

"The newspaper has a policy against—" Mom began.

"Just tell me what it's going to cost to get the fucking message I want in the paper."

Lola stopped, and her eyes got wide. She was alert to the tone or the word or both.

"Even if you understood Dickens or the French Revolution or why they stormed the Bastille ..." Mom began.

The guy hung up. With intense jabs Mom punched in the code on her phone to signal for another customer service agent to pick up. Then she looked at me and said, "God help me," and went off to the downstairs bathroom to soak her face with a hot, dripping washcloth over the sink.

Mom introduced her latest safety demonstration when Lola was away at an overnight. I was watching The Giant Gila Monster on TV, getting ready to go out. Mom called me into the kitchen. She stood by the stove and handed me a box of wooden matches. She wanted me to start a stove fire so she could show me how to put one out.

Glancing into the living room, where the TV was still lit up, she asked, "*What* are you watching?"

"It's about a big lizard that terrifies a town in Texas."

Mom began to say something, but maybe she thought better of it. She pulled a cast iron pan off its hook, got a high flame going, and when the pan was hot, she dropped a tablespoon of bacon grease into the center and then another. We watched the fat turn transparent with small bits of black in it. "Once the grease starts to smoke," she said, "I'll give you the signal."

"I have to finish getting ready," I said.

"If you're alone with Lola, you need to know how to do this."

I had started to live more out of the house than in, so my mother liked to snag me whenever I landed. The thing was, I had made hundreds of meals for Lola. They were never complicated. Lola liked pasta, macaroni and cheese, apple slices, carrot sticks. Mom just wanted the world buttoned down because none of it was anymore. Sometimes it seemed easier to go along.

Taking a match out of the box, I held the red tip against the striker.

"Ready?" she said. She was in a heightened state now, apron sash tight, straight dark hair loose around her shoulders, her eyes large and bright. She put her hand on the paper sack on the table like an actor in a public service commercial. "In case you have to put a fire out while you're cooking, it's always good to have salt at the ready."

"Got it," I said. My mother began to tug at the white string at the top of the sack. I saw that everyone was already at the sock hop and the Giant Gila Monster was headed their way.

I didn't see that the string wouldn't budge. She told me this later.

I did, however, clearly hear my mother say, *Now.*

She meant *Now* as in *Now ... if the bag won't open, you might need to get a pair of scissors.* But I was sure I heard the signal, so I lit the match and it left my hand and arced toward the pan at the same moment she turned away from the stove to look for those scissors, her hair flying out in a wide circle.

I saw a blue flame surround her head like a crown of stars, and I heard her scream the same terrifying scream a wild peacock will make out in the dark. I had a great uncle who lived near wild peacocks, and as the fire danced along my mother's head and I stood there paralyzed, I heard that exact sound leave her throat.

In a sudden flood of safety memories, I knew to grab a jacket off the back of a chair and cover her head, holding it there until the fire was out, holding my mother until the flames were gone.

We took a taxi to the hospital because she was afraid of the cost of the ambulance. I was the one who cried, apologizing in a soft whisper, thinking her ears had been burned. She seemed to be holding her breath while she patted my leg to quiet me.

Once the examination was done, the ER doctor shut his eyes for a moment as if he were pulling up thoughts from a dark cave. He said my mother was a lucky woman. "You'll have some scarring on the back of your scalp," the doctor said, opening his eyes again and indicating places around her head while I held the hand mirror. "But much of your hair will grow back and more or less cover those places."

My mother flinched, and he said, "You might have been facing the stove," as if he thought she would do this again.

That's when I realized how easy it is to burn the house to the ground with all the people in it because you're trying so hard to prevent disaster.

On the ride home she asked me not to tell my father, like we should be worried about protecting him.

For weeks afterward a vision of that crown lit up my mind, sometimes during the day but often in the middle of the night. It was the pain I felt over what had happened, of course, but I was sure I had also seen a drawing or painting of that halo. When I searched online, I found *Our Lady of the Apocalypse*.

I recalled that a photographer friend of Mom's had given her a coffee table book filled with shots of Virgin Mary statuary. Locating it in the shelves of art books, I read that he had spent months traveling around the States following a path of closing parishes. He would set up his camera the day before a church was going down and shoot those ethereal figures, many already pulled from their pedestals. Some had crowns on their heads, some with stars. There were hundreds, maybe thousands of abandoned Marys with missing noses and arms and heads. On her worst days, I think that was exactly how Mom saw herself after my father took off.

I went begging and Geary, my old photo teacher, hired me to help in his darkroom. It was my job to set up lighting and backdrops in the studio, order supplies, catalog, and make deliveries around the city. He and his wife, Lettie, had only one car, so this often meant public transportation.

One delivery was to a fashion photographer on the near west side named Nitro. He did some of his own fine art prints but relied heavily on Geary for the fashion stuff. I was supposed to call if Nitro gave me any shit. Before I could find out what Geary meant he got a call from his wife. So I left and rode the L and when I leaned my head against the train window, I heard the wheels on the tracks sounding: *Nitro. Glycerin. Nitro. Glycerin.*

A guy in his late thirties, wearing jeans and a white button down, met me at the door to his loft. He had two controllers in his hands. *Halo* was on a big monitor across from his couch. Looking a little embarrassed, he said, "Just setting up some new equipment."

I held out the two black photo boxes, one stacked on top of the other.

"You're from Geary's?" he asked, making a study of my face.

I looked down at the boxes, Geary's studio name and address typed right there, and looked back at him.

"Halo?" he asked, taking the boxes.

I shrugged and he handed me a controller.

He wasn't very good at it. I had to keep explaining how the controls worked. Or he was good at it and just wanted to sit close to me on his old leather couch. He put his hand on my knee and I took it off. After I beat him at the game too many times I got up and looked around.

Nitro had photographs of his parents on one wall, their faces blown up so big you could drift into them and feel like a speck, like a bug in their eyelashes. Nothing flattered, nothing pulled back. They reminded me a little of Mehdi Bouqua's stuff, a street photographer working out of LA. On another wall Nitro had seven shots of young gang members in the city. He used backlight and fill, and somehow this made them appear as if they were about to ascend into the sky in a threatening yet childlike moment. They sat on beat-up playground equipment in a city park and I realized what he was after. "You like William Blake, his artwork," I said.

He looked at me as if to say, *What kind of creature are you?* I could hear that word *creature* in his thoughts. "Yes, very much. *Pity*. I think that's my favorite. Do you know that one?"

"I like the really blue version at the Tate," I said. Not that I had been to the Tate but my mother had an art book of Blake's work with four versions of *Pity* compared side by side, and I tended to remember things like that.

"You want to stay for dinner?" he asked.

"I should get back." Looking at some of the fashion work spread out on a long table, I asked, "You date any of them?"

"Used to," he admitted.

"I'd never get attached to you the way they did," I said.

He laughed and asked, "Why's that?"

"Because I don't give a shit about immortality."

"Stay for dinner," he said. "We could talk about your dreams." He nursed some kind of tenderness as he coaxed. Dream analysis was a party trick Nitro performed. When I questioned his ability to make interpretations, he said his mother was a psychoanalyst.

I got my jacket on and wrapped my wool scarf around my neck, and in an odd moment I let him knot it and throw one end over my shoulder as if he were dressing me for a shoot. He came very close like he had an impulse to kiss me but he pulled back at the last moment, which told me he was probably used to this kind of seduction. I took off and got home in time to read Lola a bedtime story.

I made another delivery a week later and when he opened the door I saw cheese and bread and wine arranged with a bowl of fresh dates on his coffee table.

Each visit got a little more elaborate: the four-course meals, the special selected movies, hookahs with full bowls.

I began to go over there once a week to deliver myself.

Nitro and I played a lot of *Call of Duty* after I got him started. We racked up kills and we began to photograph each other clothed and naked and standing in front of a large mirror embedded in a piece of architectural salvage—from a convent bathroom or an Irish bar—he couldn't remember. We stretched out on his bed and along his kitchen counters and dining table and sink and bathroom floor and fire escape and in front of his giant windows at night and we had unadulterated sex.

But that's not why I fell for Nitro. It was watching him burn and dodge in the darkroom, the seconds of exposure, the way he cropped an image. Sometimes I sat on a stool to watch and sometimes I put my head against his shoulder for a minute, and he would tell me how long to make the exposure, and we became inseparable until the timer went off.

I guess I amused him at first. There was a lot he didn't ask me directly, so I photographed what I thought was a lack of questions in his face and he photographed the questions in mine. He loaned me cameras and tripods. We smoked too much pot and he bought me eye drops and mints so my mother wouldn't quiz me when I got home. He asked what I liked in my omelets. We talked about lighting techniques. His loft became that place where I could say anything, do anything. That's how it worked.

He had a four-year-old son and an ex-wife. A model. They lived in France and Nitro saw his boy three or four times a year. He said he'd be going over there soon. I waited for him to beg me to go. And then I saw two tickets, one his, one with a woman's name. I assumed she was one of the flawless women.

I cried on the way to the L going home, but I figured that was something about modern love. It wasn't about him. It really had nothing to do with him.

He told me many times he loved the way I looked: unaltered, pure, almost virginal. But after he took off on his trip, I began to think about legs and arms and bracelets. About jackets, perfumes, stockings, the things he caught with his lens.

I pushed my way into Neiman Marcus, just taking a cut-through in the mall at first, until I saw this blouse. I was sure he would like it. I tried it on in the dressing room and cut out the device on the bottom hem that sets off the store alarm with the manicure scissors in my makeup bag. It was cream-colored silk with a pointed collar that felt right to the touch. I was surprised at how easily I walked out of that store and how I enjoyed the breathlessness. At home I cut off the bottom and used my mother's sewing machine to rehem it.

The day after his return he looked at the delicate custom buttons open to my waist, smiled, and said, "Sabrina." Then he had to explain that this wasn't about another girl. He was thinking about an old movie in which the chauffeur's daughter, played by Audrey Hepburn, suddenly becomes a woman out of Paris *Vogue*. I was pleased and didn't care that in his hurry the fabric ripped where I had stitched it. Something had changed.

I began to clip the kind of jewelry that sits out on counters. I knew it would be easy to take a jacket or scarf holding a place in a movie theater or coffee shop, but I understood his tastes, and this meant small acquisitions from particular stores. I walked away in a handsome pair of heels, leaving behind socks and beat-up footwear on a showroom floor one afternoon.

"You have to figure this out," he said later that day when he realized what I was doing. He was staring at my heels. I pulled away and sat up in bed. Neither of us had had the patience for the buckles. "There's someone you're trying to rattle."

Rolling onto his side, Nitro lit a cigarette and I watched the smoke drift, looking for that point where it disappeared. The ceilings were twenty feet high and the late afternoon light poured in through the long sash windows. His loft was part of a converted candy factory taken over by an artists' cooperative. There were marks where giant copper vats had been strapped to the floors.

"Rattle?" I said.

"By getting caught eventually." He picked up my phone and began to flip through my photos. I tried to grab it away, but he got playful. I decided not to make a deal out of it so he'd stop. He paused on a shot of my parents together at a restaurant. I had used a high intensity flash so they looked half there and kind of shocked.

"Nice framing," he said. "So your mom thinks he'll be back?"

I don't know why this was sitting in his foreground now. His cheeks were pitted and this made him look rough at times. He told me once that he couldn't stop scratching when he had chicken pox as a kid.

"She's waiting for him, that's all I know."

"They don't do well," Nitro said, lost in his own meditations. Then he looked over at me and began to blow smoke rings as if I needed entertainment.

"'They'? Who doesn't do well?" I asked.

"*Left* women. You know, when children are involved."

I felt my blood pick up pace. "He was out of work for a long time," I said. "And then this job turned up in New Jersey. I wouldn't call that leaving her."

"You don't have to go to New Jersey to sell insurance. Besides, if this was strictly about a job, you wouldn't look troubled."

"You think I'm a child," I said and pushed into his stomach with my elbow to reach the bedside table. I pulled the last cigarette from his pack and grabbed the lighter.

His father, who had died of lung cancer, looked down at me like a dark cloud from the wall. I lit up, inhaled, and found out how light my head became on tobacco.

"Maybe you're thinking about your son, about the way *you* left *him*," I said.

"But I didn't," he said, clearly pained now. "She left me and took off for France. And in the French courts there was little I could do."

"Who did you take with you to Paris this time?"

"An old friend, a photographer."

"Someone you see from time to time?"

"You're making too much of this."

"What does she look like?"

He hesitated long enough to realize I'd persist. There were

some pictures on his phone. She seemed rather plain, wore almost no makeup. Certainly there was nothing about her clothes to draw him in.

"What type of photography? Show me."

"You aren't going to let this go, are you?" he said. He got out of bed and took my hand. I was a little wobbly in the heels. He guided me over to a set of large flat drawers. She had her own drawer. I didn't. I didn't have a drawer. She was a street photographer. I wouldn't say she was better than me, just different. It almost looked as if she had posed her subjects, certainly they were standing still in their settings, and she took her time to frame things. I was more abrupt, more into movement, light, and emotion. I didn't mind that someone was lopped off or caught at a funny angle. I liked to shoot people before they had time to think, to respond.

She was thirty-five, he told me when I asked. They had seen each other on and off for years. But things weren't like that anymore, he said. I wasn't sure I believed him.

I closed the drawer and worked on the buckles and left the stolen heels by the door. I got dressed, and all the time he watched me. I turned my phone on again and began to flip through my mother's messages. There were seven.

"You understand they arrest you if you get caught," he said, circling back to my small larcenies, pushing away from his.

"I've already got a mother," I said and held up the phone with her texts stacked in a heap.

"If you need money, all you have to do is let me know."

But I was already working on other ideas. Not clothes.

Pushing in, he offered to give me a ride back to Evanston. I took the L.

Of course it had to be that night when the bill went online breaking things down in preparation for my first year of college. I didn't tell my mother and called a financial aid officer the next day.

"Things have changed," I said.

The woman waited as I told her my father had moved away and wasn't sending much money before she launched in. Maybe the AC units were broken in her office that day or she was working from home and a cat was gnawing at her toes or she just didn't like the sound of my voice. Whatever it was, she got merciless about the college's funding distribution practices, the limits of federal aid, how far from extended deadlines I had drifted, the effort they had put in to *arrive* at a good package for me, as if her entire office had traveled for months in a desolate country to reach me. Finally, she suggested I consider delaying admission for a year. I could reapply for aid next winter. "You might need to submit an updated portfolio," she said, topping off my empty glass.

"That can't be right," I said.

"You'll want to check with the department."

"There's a small fortune in photographic paper, chemicals, the time it took to—"

"I just wanted to give you a heads-up," she said in her monotone.

"Your head's up your ass," I said and dropped the phone into its charger.

A few days later, when Mom asked for my password to get on the site to see where things stood, I said I was taking a gap year. She pushed back hard, but when I said I wouldn't budge, that I wanted to work at Geary's full time and save up money, I don't know, maybe she began to accept the logic in it.

In the letter I wrote to the department I said I would be traveling during my delayed year in order to photograph national monuments that were sinking into the earth along with the reputations of our best educational institutions. Later, I regretted dropping this into the mail slot and then I had to call and ask them not to open the letter, a second would follow, and so on.

From the glossy postcards that continued to arrive every two or three weeks from Dad to Lola, I began to believe that if everything else was going to hell, our father had plenty of beaches where he roamed and that the skies were always blue.

You should see the ocean, he wrote on one card.

You should see how broke we are, I almost wrote back. How Mom doesn't sleep anymore, how she worries about things you can't imagine.

Mom held up a copy of *The Secrets of Car Flipping.* I didn't realize at first that she was saying she had to sell the station wagon.

"When I went to that retraining session at the newspaper," she said, "I met a new hire named David, and during the break we talked cars. He just called to say he has to sell his father's van to help pay for his dad's home health care. David had his mechanic check it out, and he says it will run until Armageddon."

That's one of those statements you have to think about, but I'm not sure my mother did, given her worries. David drove over to our place the next day so she could *give the van a spin.* He had hair popping out of the edges of his long-sleeved shirt, cuffs and collar, like a physical manifestation of the energy exploding from his psyche. His father, he said, had babied the thing.

"He'll only sell it to someone who loves it as much as his father did," Mom told me after he was gone.

"And?" I asked.

"Well. I could haul an awful lot around in something like that. He said he'd give me an exceptional deal and he offered to pitch in over the next year, change the oil, replace the belts, that kind of thing."

"Was he hitting on you?" I asked.

She reddened, and I felt certain some flattery had been involved. "He showed me a picture of his wife and kids. He has a son your age and ..." She stopped and said, "He's going to list it next Saturday."

Over the week, she hesitated and worried that the van would be sold out from under her while she hesitated. She read something in *Consumer Reports* and talked to her bank and her brother, Hal, who wasn't all that encouraging but didn't have any other ideas. He wasn't a car man by nature.

"What do you think?" she said, circling back to me.

It's not like I knew what she should do. We were both in shock about having to sell our wagon because it had felt so safe driving Lola around in a Volvo. But it was time to get over it and stop asking people. I told her this and she went for that van as if she were leaping from a high-rise, convinced someone would bring out a net if the sidewalk got close.

Fourteen days after we got it, the van sprang an oil leak, and that hairy guy no longer answered his phone. Was it possible he wasn't actually employed by the paper? Was he just there at the training session to sell someone a bad vehicle? Was this a business venture or a lark? Did he sell other goods as well? Broken radios, busted dishwashers, books with their front covers ripped off?

Mom was too exhausted to puzzle this out or to track him down, and it probably wouldn't have done much good if she had. She began to use cans of this additive to patch the leak. By then we had two leaks, maybe three. When she fired the engine up it smelled like something was burning or dead. The undercarriage dripped and black oil pooled everywhere we parked. Before, when she picked up Lola from a play date, Mom used to pull into her friends' driveways, but now she made a point of parking on the street—sometimes on the other side of the street or down the block.

Another letter arrived.

Dear Mona,

So I said I'd tell you a story about my Uncle Sorohan, my mother's brother. I knew him during his carny years, but before that he was a roustabout with a circus, when he was even younger than you are now. Uncle Sor had an old fedora he never took off, even in the tub and even when he went to bed. His face was deeply lined from all the cigarettes he smoked and years of being outdoors, and he was a hardworking man but also a true romantic.

He often stayed for a night or two if he was on his way through town, and one time, I must have been five or six, he drove a flatbed to our house with a tall wooden cabinet painted red and roped in the back so it stood straight up and down. The cabinet had a few crude paintings with oriental dragons on one side and a woman in a kimono with a strange stare painted on the other. In the front was a door. I guess it was inevitable that a boy of five or six would get curious, and so after dinner Sor found me in the flatbed, trying to peek inside the box.

You know my father drank rashly, and he had worked himself up and warned my uncle at dinner that he better get that thing out of the drive early so he could move his patrol car sitting in the garage.

When Sor found me up in the flatbed, he climbed up and opened the door to the cabinet and asked if I'd like to disappear. There was a makeshift seat inside, like a phone booth without a phone.

"Where would I go?" I said.

"That's the question. Where do we go when we disappear? I believe I disappeared into the circus, but you might disappear into the police force where your father hides out if you aren't careful."

"No, where do I go if I disappear in the box, Uncle Sor?"

"Oh, the box. You go somewhere else. I'm not really sure. I hear it's quite pleasant, but I wouldn't recommend it for everyone. The last man who tried it stayed away for years until a magician came along with the right spell. When he tumbled back into the box finally, and his wife asked where he had been, he seemed too happy to speak. Here, help me with these ropes."

Soon we had the magic disappearing box out of its anchors and I was helping him bring it into the house. It was surprisingly light. As soon as my father saw it, he blew up at my uncle for being a bad influence and stirring up one kind of trouble or another. My mother did what she could to calm him. But Uncle Sor just ignored my father the way he always did. He directed me to turn to the left and then the right and watch the top stair so we would clear the bannister. We put the box at the foot of my bed.

"I'm going to leave this with you for a while," he said. "Now, you need the spell so you'll be able to come back if you try it out and there are no magicians around." And so he gave me this: "Upon the brimming water among the stones are nine-and-fifty swans."

I heard the basement door slam, and I knew my father had gone down to the family room, where he had built a saloon and where he would drink, mumbling to himself, and fall asleep with his head on the bar, hating the world. My uncle went down to the living room to sit with my mother and talk in whispers—I imagine trying to convince her again that she should leave my father.

The next day my uncle was gone before dawn and my father went off to work and my mother made me lunch and I was off to school. It was the following weekend my father went out with his buddies and came home stinking drunk and went after my mother and me as if he were invading an enemy camp.

After my mother had given me a cold compress for my face and after she had taken her quiet medicine, she stretched out on her bed with her own ice pack. I went back to my room and got inside the box, and that's when I discovered the trapdoor. If I lifted up the floor using this tiny bit of rope in one corner, I could crawl into a box in the bottom that had air holes drilled into the back.

It took me a few years to understand that the spell was one of Yeats's and that my uncle had built the box with his own hands to a purpose. I discovered I could curl up and hide out when my father was hunting me. He would open the door in the midst of bellowing and tearing things up around my room, but that was about it. He probably thought a disappearing box was too easy and simple-minded a place to hide. After all, he was used to working with professional criminals. I only wish that I had had a disappearing box for my mother.

The summer I joined my uncle on the carnival circuit, my father took an ax to that thing and started a bonfire with it. I imagine he had found out about the hiding place.

It's always been my Uncle Sor I've wanted to emulate, never my father.

Before I close, your mother tells me you've decided to take a gap year. I hope you know I'll be excited to hear your plans. You have a good head on your shoulders, Mona. It's not a bad idea to build up some savings, but if you look at internships, we'll have a room for you once we find the right place here. Public transportation is pretty good and we'll make it work.

Love,

Dad

Sometimes I think my father's drive to New Jersey, away from us—perhaps especially from me—began when I turned nine and started to assert my independence, speaking up in ways I hadn't before. When we bought the house he worked longer hours and I had things to do with my friends on the weekends. I got used to Mom filling the spaces and became less interested in what he had to say. He became fragile if I was busy and didn't have time to do something he hoped we might do—bowling, batting practice, miniature golf. As I pushed further into my own life, he appeared sullen or withdrawn. My mother understood life and art and what we're here to do. He understood insurance.

I think he tried again to be this imaginary father when Lola was born. But once you carry a lack of confidence, it's hard to hold a baby in your arms without thinking you'll drop her.

After that we barely spoke at all.

Richard

I wrote something out to Liz at the kitchen table so she wouldn't worry, and left half the money I'd gotten from the ATM. I slipped my car key off the ring. I knew Mona needed to sleep and Liz would insist she get up to say goodbye, and that would stir some new rancor I'd have to carry with me to Newark. Lola, who was the soundest sleeper, would be a sack of potatoes in Liz's arms.

So I went back upstairs and instead of waking her I watched Liz in the circle of closet light. She was curled up with one hand tucked around her right breast, her hair spread along my pillow. This was the picture I would take with me, always wishing to crawl back into that one particular moment. I shut off the alarm.

Lola was in the little-girl bed I had assembled that week, out of her crib now in her own room. I stroked her hair and watched her breathe. I worried that she would grow too quickly while I was gone.

Downstairs again, I put my palm against Mona's door and thought about turning the handle. Mona is a sleepwalker. She has a way of finding disturbances in nights the rest of us find calm. Maybe you could say that about the daytime too. With any luck she'd forgotten to set her alarm, consciously or unconsciously, the way she sometimes did, counting on Liz to wake her. I thought it best to let her be.

That morning became the coin toss. Daily I've wondered if waking my family up before taking off would have landed us differently.

With the suitcase in the car, I hoped to make it to New Jersey without spending a night in a motel. I had a blanket and pillow in the back if I needed to pull into a truck or rest stop. I let the handbrake out, and the car rolled down the drive.

I made good time all the way to Pennsylvania. The weather held, but the highway gradually filled with semis. I looked at pictures of donuts and office supplies and sweating Coke bottles on side panels for miles. It became harder to pass them, and then if I did, it was only to get wedged into another cluster of giant trucks. Reaching a rest stop, I grabbed a coffee and studied the Pennsylvania map, deciding on a rural route for the next leg.

I was fifteen minutes out on that two-lane highway when I saw a great plume of smoke—a cloud so long and thick it arced across the sky. Later I would try to tell Lola over the phone that it was like watching the tail of a giant cat. The smoke came from a tire graveyard set on fire, the rubber bedded down in gullies, pushed up ridges and thrown down over every slope. My windows were up, but the car filled with the stench.

A woman stood by her car on the shoulder making big, sweeping motions with her arms, appearing and disappearing in the smoke. I didn't want to lose time, but I had stopped many times with Uncle Sor to help a stranger when we were on the road together. It's what you do. Pulling ahead of her, I parked and got out and walked back to her car. She was midway between Mona's age and Liz's. She had a beautiful face torn up by acne and some kind of trouble. Her hair looked as if a fury had driven it straight into the air. There was a message on her T-shirt, but I didn't want to stare at her chest. The backseat and the passenger side of her car were full. A small dog carrier sat on a pile of magazines in the front seat. I looked to see if there was a flat, but her tires were fine. "I have a few tools in my trunk," I offered.

"The engine light wouldn't go off, and I thought I had another can of oil. My sister lives a few towns over. Give me a lift?"

"Sure," I said without asking *which way* over.

"I think someone can come back and tow it. Let me grab some stuff. I'm Linda, by the way."

"Richard. You want to call them? I have a phone," I said.

She fished hers out of her jeans and held it up, saying, "I think they do better with surprises. All I need is to get turned down because they have to think about it." That's when I read the message on her T-shirt: *Hold your own ... if you go limp.*

I thought Linda would just take a suitcase and the dog with its small, rhythmic yips. But she kept moving through that coil of black smoke to get more, and I kept helping. "I heard it's been burning for days," she said, looking out to the hills. I set the crate in the footwell behind my seat.

There was a toaster oven, three sets of hot rollers, and framed posters of drag race cars. She wanted the magazines. I pulled my collar up and tried to breathe through my shirt when my hands weren't full. Finally we were back on the road. "It's a straight shot," she said.

A fine rain began and picked up pace, but that did nothing to the reek of burning rubber.

She said, "You ever been betrayed?"

I figured she mostly wanted to talk about herself. So I said, "You?"

"By my own son. The older they get, the more they think they know, right? Snooping in your drawers, your pockets, listening in on phone lines, seeing what they can pry loose like they want to know who you really are when all they're up to is finding a way to get back at you about one thing or another. I was sure my son was out with his friends when I was on the phone, you know, breaking it off with this man. It ripped me pretty bad because I thought we might have had a chance in this sick world, but I told him I was staying with my husband for my son's sake. I was going to keep putting up with the drinking and the hunting even when it wasn't the season and his damn meth cooking in the basement like I'm supposed to spend my nights waiting to blow up while I'm making supper. Anyway, my son came up to the kitchen just then and pulled the phone from my grip and hung up the receiver. He said he was going to tell Willis, that's my husband, his father, when Willis got home from the gun show. So I just loaded up the car. No reason I should get a beating for staying loyal, you know? I've been beat enough."

A loopy kind of fatigue took over as I watched the wipers clear a path through the rain. I hoped Linda would keep me alert with her stories over that stretch of green hills dotted with cows and farm equipment.

When I felt she was waiting for some type of response, I said, "So you're saying kids have no respect?"

Under the quiet tones of a talk radio station I had forgotten to silence she said, "You making fun of me?"

"No, I just … I think you're right. The older they get, the more damage they can do."

She didn't say anything to this, and I couldn't help but think about Mona. I often wondered how much she knew at seventeen, what things she recalled and what things she had decided to let go of. She was in her own world most of the time, but that didn't mean she didn't surface when she wanted to. And though I always asked, half the time I didn't really know where she went at night even when she told me, or who she was dating, or what she spent her time photographing. She didn't show me the way she showed her mother.

Liz subscribed to this psychology magazine, and she once read aloud to me from an article on secrets. It said that keeping family secrets is as common as getting up in the morning. I asked Liz what she thought, and I was surprised when she dropped the magazine by the bed and said, "I think telling secrets, well, some secrets anyway, can be more harmful than holding on to them." I didn't say anything, and right after that she shut off the light and we went to bed, much as I couldn't sleep thinking about this idea.

"You imagine you'll go back?" I asked Linda. "When things calm down?"

"You must be crazy," she said. Then she released her seatbelt and shifted things around and got her dog out of the carrier. He was a scrawny, trembling thing without much hair, and she placed him under her sweater, right over her belly, where he settled. She called someone on her phone and said she was a couple of miles away and to meet her at the diner.

When we pulled into the parking lot, there was a man idling in a pickup painted flat black, with rims the size of Pennsylvania. He was smoking a joint and just sat there, not helping, while she and I loaded her stuff onto the bed in the rain. I didn't know if this was a brother-in-law or her boyfriend or what. She didn't make any introductions. When we were done we covered her wet things with a blue plastic tarp he had up in the cab. But as soon as they pulled away the tarp flew up into the air and landed in the lot, and they didn't bother to circle around to get it.

I stood there in that desolate country, the rain coming down, wondering how I was going to put things right with Mona. I wished in that moment that my Uncle Sorohan was around. No one had a better sense about people than he did and what kind of secrets it's best to keep. I didn't know how long Mona would keep hers.

Uncle Sorohan was a professional guesser on the carnival circuit and that meant he could tell your age within two years, your weight within three pounds, your birthday within two months. If he guessed wrong, he handed you a prize. But he rarely guessed wrong. He told me once I would wander. I never imagined this would be away from Liz and the girls.

Sor hired me to help out the summer I turned sixteen. Guessing had him on the road from one end of the country to the other, early spring to late fall in an old Chevy, and he said he liked having someone along. The Chevy pulled an Airstream with a special rig off the back that hauled a giant scale. He always got us to the next show before the break of day, nursing a flask.

The first time I saw his booth in a midway, it looked like a cartoon with question marks dancing at its edges. It was painted red and yellow, and it looked as bright as a burning city. Centered at the top was a sign that read, *Fool the Guesser*. Stuffed animals hung in clusters and were perched on shelves at the back. The Howe industrial scale verified his accuracy. "You have to know who's going to put their money down," he told me, "and who's going to be a repeat customer, and who's going to grab their friends and bring them back here thinking they'll cheat you."

In mid-July, after being on the road for six weeks, we stopped outside Chicago, a few towns over from where my family lived. It was one of the bigger carnivals where we had a weeklong stint. I didn't even tell my parents we were in town, I was so happy to have my freedom. Sor let me try my hand at guesswork but I kept handing out prizes. Finally he said, "Guessing someone's age within two years means two years on either side of the year they were born in, so you're giving yourself a five-year span to work with. It's not that hard." Once that sank in and I discovered where he hid the flask, I began to relax.

He helped me understand bone mass: how a lump of fat in the upper arms will tip the scale, something about weight lifters and their light heads. He showed me how to assess pockets filled with keys and wallets and how a pair of work boots can be loaded with steel. "Look for yellowed fingers and stained teeth," he said, pointing out particular lines in a face to show me the way a smoker could throw me off on age and how heavy coffee drinkers lose water weight and get a sunken look in their cheeks.

I thought birthdays were the toughest, but he said, "In time you'll start to see the sunny disposition of the summer baby, the spectral look of the autumn born, the rapid talker of spring, the perennial sadness of winter's child. I have books on Chinese face reading, body language, palmistry, and clothes psychology and fabric composition. You're welcome to borrow any of them."

His favorite author was Sir Arthur Conan Doyle, and each night he read one of Sherlock's adventures aloud to me from his bed as if I were a young boy. He slept on two facing couches that pulled together in the trailer, and Sor's deep voice drifted over to the nose of the Airstream, where I bunked. He had a fedora he never took off, even when he slept.

"You'll just know. You won't have to think about guessing after a while. I'll admit there's a letdown to seeing what's behind the curtain, Richard, but you'll get over that and find other kinds of letdowns waiting for you," he said, and then he laughed.

While most people who came to that carnival outside Chicago thought he was paying a quick compliment and taking their tickets, he was reading them to their cerebellums. One day as two girls were eyeing the booth he nudged me and said, "Your turn."

They were about my age and one had a high laugh, a smile that showed her full gums, and a body as thin and light as smoke.

The other was the beauty with true brown hair pulled into a ponytail. She wore a short skirt with a tank top and gym shoes. She didn't use a lot of makeup and had a way of sizing up every last thing around her. When her eyes mirrored the streaming, flashing lights of the park, she made all the other carnival goers who had come from the city look dull and habitual.

She was holding a paper dish with a sugary lump of fried dough when I blocked her path. "I can guess your weight within two pounds," I said.

"Before or after I eat this fried dough?" she said, staring me down.

"Both," I said.

"But can you tell the hour of my birth?" she said, looking smugly at her friend.

"If you tell me your name," I said.

Sor coughed to let me know I was heading out on a fragile limb. The friend tugged at her arm, eager to push on. But the beauty laughed and said, "Elizabeth. Don't forget to include the time zone."

I knew from taking tests in school that it was better to fill something in than leave it as blank as my mind was at that moment. And I knew from Uncle Sor not to overthink things and that sharp-minded types are often born in the late hours of the evening or early morning.

"Eleven thirty-three p.m. Central Time," I said. "If I'm wrong, I'll hand you a prize." Her friend gave me a sour look. "I'll give you two prizes," I said, and Sor spit on the ground.

Elizabeth knit her eyebrows together, and then something seemed to change and she looked at me with a kind of wonder I wish I had a photograph of and said, "Aren't you clever? Only off by a minute. Eleven thirty-four."

I wanted to ask if I was really all that close when she said, "If you guess my phone number next time, I'll let you take me out." And then she and her shadow were off in the direction of the Tilt-A-Whirl.

"She'll be back tomorrow without her friend," Uncle Sor said. "Make the most of it. We leave in two days. And before you ask, no, that's not her real birth time. She's more like two in the morning. Maybe a painter. I'd say ceramicist, but her hands weren't dry."

That was a Friday and we were folding up Sunday night. I sat by the front of the booth on a stool all Saturday and waited. I looked at every face that went by. I didn't wander off to get lunch and I skipped dinner until Sor brought me some. I doubt I peed all day. By late Sunday afternoon I decided my uncle was crazy and I had been an idiot. I considered leaving him halfway through the season to head home and face the regimented life my father was pushing. He wanted me to follow in his bootsteps and become a cop.

Just after the evening lights came up and the music whirred louder, Elizabeth walked up to the booth in a blue dress with her hair halfway down her back. She didn't make me stand around guessing. Instead, she let me take her on all the rides. We had swallows from my uncle's flask and we made out behind the haunted house. She told me she was going to study art in college.

I was thick with love as I unrigged the Chevy that pulled the trailer and drove her home. We stopped five times to make out along the way. Just before we got to her house she made me pull over and handed me a slip of paper and opened the car door and ran down the block. In the light from the radio I saw that she had written out her name and phone number with instructions on when not to call so her parents wouldn't interfere.

My uncle looked over at me as I folded and unfolded that paper late that night. We were in the car, hauling the trailer and the scale and my lame heart down the highway. He reached over and handed me a stuffed animal from one of the open boxes in the backseat and said, "She took her sweet time showing up, so I was off by a day. But I always pay up."

I worried that she'd pick me up and put me down. But she found ways to see me until we graduated, and I began to gain confidence in us. Eventually we made it into the same state college. She was accepted into other schools, better schools, but exerted her will so that we would be together.

When she became pregnant with Mona, I dropped out. That was our junior year. We went through some tough days, her mother crying on the other end of the phone, family members on both sides convinced we had screwed up badly. I told them Liz was going to stay in school no matter what and she would go on to graduate school because there was something godlike in the way she could sculpt.

I learned to take any kind of work I could get, stocking shelves in grocery stores, hauling drywall around, wiping down cars at the carwash, hosing out port-a-potties. But for all my efforts, I wasn't earning enough to support a family of three. I was sitting out on the back porch of our tiny apartment one night in the miserable summer air, halfway through a pint, when Liz called me into the bedroom.

She was naked and six months pregnant. Our fan was broken in the corner. She asked me to get undressed and lie down beside her on the bed. I thought she wanted me to make love to her and I felt the whiskey travel to my groin. But she said, "Wait. I have to talk with you."

And like most things where Liz was concerned, I went along. She asked me to close my eyes. "Lie still," she said. So I did.

I broke into a sweat and she blew lightly on my face. "Now I want you to think about the things you know how to do best in all the world—no matter how small."

I laughed, and she said, "No, *that* will be your reward. Now clear your mind. Let things just drift through."

"I can change the oil in the car."

"Okay," she said earnestly. "What else?"

"I'm still pretty good at math. Percentages."

"Keep going."

"Map reading," I said. "I've always been good with maps."

"Yes."

"I think I'm a little drunk."

"You're not getting off that easy," she said.

"I can … I can guess your weight within three pounds …"

"And my birthday within two months. So you can read people," she said.

"I don't know that I've read *myself* very well," I said.

"Pity fest tomorrow. Stay on track."

"I miss that old guy."

"You said Sor taught you how to tell if someone was sick and if they had money and …"

"And if they'd lay that money down."

"All right. Good with percentages and maps, able to read people and see if they're sick or not. I don't know about the oil change. But you can tell if they're going to pay up. …"

I could see her mind racing. There was a long silence, and I'm afraid all I could think about were the little sounds she made when I drew into her.

"Insurance," she finally said. "You could sell insurance. Quick, open your eyes."

Before long her hair was falling around my face, her swollen belly moving back and forth over me, and I realized, in that way that I try and think of other things when she's getting close, that she was right. It did seem like the kind of business where the more you could read someone, the richer your rewards.

Few things have come quick and easy in my life but

twenty years later I was able to say we had a decent house in a pleasant neighborhood with a couple of fruit trees and a garage that we turned into Liz's studio. She got all the way through graduate school, often with Mona on her hip. Her work showed periodically and a couple of the largest pieces sold—they were awfully big and expensive to make and move, so we were patient.

Our daughters, of course, were the real things. Lola was full of spunk from the start, walked early and could climb just about anything. She has her mother's persistence, her eyes and her ruddy Irish skin. Mona made me think of a young Elizabeth Taylor when she was young, with intense dark eyes and hair. I'm afraid I've worried too much about our sleepwalker, though. And she only made it worse by staying up half the night talking with friends, but Liz told me I should leave her be, she'd grow out of it. She has her mother's artistic nature, so maybe Liz read her in ways I couldn't.

When I got laid off, I thought the world was over. I couldn't find another spot anywhere. Employers wanted the younger guys. Suddenly I heard from an old friend who had been with the firm years back, a guy named Phil. Phil was the regional manager at a company on the East Coast now. We had known each other pretty well at one time and that meant he understood my record, my ethics, and what it is to support a family. He offered me a job in New Jersey.

Liz and I talked about it over several days. The plan was to let Mona finish out her year since she was a senior in high school. This would give Liz time to finish up a couple of her bigger projects and organize. Mona would go off to college and Liz and Lola would move to New Jersey. This would put Liz close to the New York market. She seemed ready to take this step.

Things made sense until I woke up that morning, the car packed for the trip.

When I think about that moment, I wonder what I was driving away from. I knew I was letting my family down, that I was all out of magic. Or I had the kind of magic that turns bad.

Mona

Mom removed one of the grilled cheese sandwiches she'd built into a mound. She cut it into fours for Lola who was watching a show in the other room.

I asked my mother if she and Dad were still together. "I'd rather know," I said.

"Did he say differently?"

She knew he was sending letters to me and she had tried not to probe. In the past, she simply reassured me. I watched her pull another sandwich from the pile and quarter it without really looking.

"He makes it sound like you and Lola are moving to New Jersey *imminently*. But *imminently* has been going on for months. And if he isn't sending enough money, what are you moving *on?*"

She looked out toward the yard where one of her sculptures sat. She had been with my father since they were teenagers.

"He doesn't fly in to see you. He doesn't send you tickets to see him. Don't cut my sandwich," I said.

She looked at the pile and stopped. There was only one whole sandwich left. She took a measured breath. "We're trying to save for the move."

"There's something you aren't saying." I picked up my photo bag, about to leave.

"Wait, you haven't heard my news. You remember my friend Tom Watts—the one who does the ceramic pieces with those incredibly thin walls? It looks like he's convinced an editor at Architectural Digest to attend my opening. With a photographer. I think our luck is turning."

I just shook my head.

"I know. You don't like the idea of luck," she said.

"Not really."

"I'll do the eighth pour," she said, setting her jaw. "I won't leave anything to chance."

"I wasn't saying … I just meant you've worked really hard. It has nothing to do with luck. This is such good news."

"I'll feel more confident if I do the eighth."

This meant she would have a new bill to pay at the metal forgers. Her sculptures required jumbo flatbeds, blankets and drop cloths, spools of industrial rope, crates and commercial cranes to move them. When I brought this up, she said, "Things have a way of working out."

The night of the opening, she appeared to be right. Golden lanterns hung in the rafters of the gallery. They reflected my mother's work in a striking way, magnifying everything she imagined to be true that night. She sold two of the smaller works within the first hour and had promises for more sales, the gallery owner taking a deposit on one of the largest pieces for a corporate client. A favorite of mine appeared in the magazine. We weren't on solid ground yet but we could see solid ground floating out in front of us.

But this was 2007, and shortly after the magazine article appeared, the gallery called to say the corporate client felt it was prudent, based on current market indicators, to hold off acquiring any new art at this time. The subprime market was buckling. The economic crisis had begun. She received a kill fee. And like that, the gallery owner began to express doubt about selling her work. "Maybe when the economy picks up," she said.

Mom had several pieces of mid-century modern furniture that she began to sell off. One Italian chaise, an Aalto, drew down two thousand dollars. After the new owners left with it she went up to her bedroom to lie down. The chaise had been her grandmother's.

In time we were turning and looking before taking a seat to make sure a couch or chair was still in place. She embellished the story of *Goldilocks and the Three Bears* to keep Lola from worry, saying, "The *chairs* are out for *repairs.*"

I was out roaming one evening with a 28mm lens on my old digital SLR. When I came in and started up the stairs to the second floor, I heard Mom on her speakerphone. I assumed she was talking with Dad. The light from her bedroom pooled on the carpet in the hall and I sat down near that pool and listened. Lola was already asleep.

It was her brother, Hal, the high-end banker who sat on several boards, drove a Mercedes or two and fed regularly on pate. She often expressed her confusion that they had been raised by the same parents in the same house.

I was about to get up and head to my room when I heard him say, "I've gone over that."

"You can't be serious," she said.

"Have I ever not been serious?" he asked.

Maybe he meant to say, *when giving advice.* But Uncle was a cheerless soul, and his second wife, Margaret, was worse. My mother choked up rather than answer.

"This is about the housing bubble," he went on. "You need to sell the house and find some practical work while you can. If things go as badly as some of us think we could all be underwater. My money's tied up or I'd buy one of your objects to help out. You know, if Margaret had any eye for art."

Normally my mother would have said, *One of my objects?* in a pointed way. It troubled me that she had gone mute.

"You're absolutely certain?" she said finally.

"Have I ever not been … ?" That unsaid word filled the house like a gas leak. It was a good thing we had learned to avoid matches.

Mom met with a Realtor a few days later, set some potted plants in bloom around the front steps, and trimmed the hedges. Our property was a little odd, and Mom wasn't sure how the sale would go. The small house had once been the butler's quarters on a large estate, but it and the tall barn-like garage that could store up to six cars had been split off and sold as a parcel years ago. She decided to keep the price low. The crash wasn't in full play yet, but she wasn't taking any chances. After paying off two mortgages, we leased an apartment in Rogers Park in a far northeast pocket of Chicago. Without a proper space to work in, it was clear that she would have to quit sculpting cold turkey or find someone to lend her studio space. She made a stream of calls. It was unfortunate that she worked so large. Mom said something romantic to me about the benefits of *a fallow period* though I saw her smart.

We left our keys in the kitchen where Dad had tossed his.

The new place was a one-bedroom apartment at the top of a three-story walkup. There were six apartments in all. The L ran along the back side of the building causing a noticeable trembling and a high, piercing sound every few minutes, and the parks appeared to be full of junkies. She had looked everywhere. It was either this or head into a spiral of credit card debt.

"You're taking the bedroom," Mom said as we looked around.

Standing by the bedroom window, I could see the faces of passengers looking our way as if they hoped to catch someone fighting or hooking up or breaking down or shooting up. But I didn't complain about the location of my room. I would be the only one with a bedroom door. "Lola gets the living room," she said. "And I'll take the dining room. I can use the highboy and the two Japanese folding screens to make a little privacy."

I was having a hard time hiding my anger at all this sacrifice. "I'll take the dining room," I countered. I turned to face her but she shook off my signal.

By late afternoon we had looked through all the boxes marked *Lola* and hadn't found her dolls. Starting down the stairs to check the car, I stopped when I saw a guy backing out of one of the two first-floor apartments. He was pulling a T-shirt over his head, clearly in a hurry to be somewhere. When he turned and saw me, the voice of an old man came from inside the apartment.

"*Ajay! Ajay!* Do not forget to lock the door!"

It wasn't the work *Ajay* had done on his body that pinned me to the stairs. I didn't care about things like that. But it was like bumping into someone with the same features as a lover or old friend—he had a familiarity I didn't know what to do with. He smiled and I found it hard not to smile back and that made me feel even more peculiar.

Returning upstairs, I told Mom I had forgotten the keys and would go down again shortly. I mentioned seeing one of our neighbors—this guy on the first floor who seemed nice—and then I got back to work.

I was surprised when she brought him up late in the afternoon. The weather was burn-in-hell August. We had no AC, and we hadn't found the box with the tower fan. She kept saying, "Maybe the movers stole it." And probably by the time we were completely unpacked there was no other way to account for the missing items. She had found the movers on the cheap. But I doubted a tower fan would have done much good. The heat from all three floors rose steadily and came to a dead stop in our unit.

As I unpacked Lola's picture books, I lingered over one I had read to her a hundred times, *Bye Bye, Baby: A Sad Story with a Happy Ending*. Lola was on her raw mattress on the floor, dropped into a steady nap. We were still looking for her circus bedding. She told us she wouldn't sleep on anything else. I had no idea how we were going to get the bed frame assembled. It was one of those Swedish products with a million pins and bolts and one small Allen wrench.

Mom stood in the opening to the dining room. I looked up at her face, streaked with sweat. No one had alerted us that the super would leave old food crusted in the refrigerator and cabinets, rat droppings under the sink, a broken toilet roll and towel bar in the bathroom. All of this, Mom said, was to be taken care of along with the promise of fresh paint in all the rooms, and we got none.

She too had run into the first-floor neighbor on one of her trips up and down.

"He has the look of a drug dealer. Ignore him if he tries to talk with you. Avoid any eye contact."

"That sounds kind of ... racist," I said.

"Don't go there," she said. She knew I was trying to drop this guy as a subject, but her face lit up. "We're in a high-crime area, that's all I'm saying."

"But this is where we live now," I said.

"But he's lived here longer," she said.

I could almost see her brain fuel up, logic peeling off like broken heat shields. Putting the last stack of books on the shelf, I looked at her as she began to arrange T-shirts and pants in Lola's drawers. Each time she folded an arm or leg, it was as if she were trying to get an unconscious child to move her extremities. I knew how she worried for Lola.

Just then I saw Ajay outside. He grabbed a large bottle of detergent from a pickup truck and walked around the side of the building.

"Eighteen shootings last year," she said. "I won't tell you the number of stabbings."

"We have an understanding," I said.

The understanding went like this: I would do my share of housework, help with Lola, and pay for some of the utility bills—at least my phone and data use—while I saved up to move out. She would pay the rent, buy the groceries, and so on. Meanwhile, I would keep my own hours, set my own rules.

"Well yes, but ..."

An elevated train went by, and I shouted, "I'm going over to Howard Street for ice!" I knew I'd get no argument. The refrigerator had been unplugged when we arrived, and it still wasn't cold enough to make ice cubes. Grabbing my wallet, I fled.

I stopped outside the basement entry on my way. The air that came up through the doorway was remarkably cool. Going down the concrete steps, I walked through clumps of lint and dust.

Ajay stood in front of a bank of coin-operated washing machines, about to pour his detergent into the cap. When he looked up I saw the blue liquid ribbon over his hand before he realized what he was doing. He shook his head, smiling to himself. Rubbing his hand on the clothes, he said, "I'll be out of here in a half hour. The third machine is a clothes shredder by the way—skip that one. I'm Ajay."

I stood there for a while trying to figure out why it was so pleasurable to throw him off guard. I came closer and saw that the clothes in that one washer were so thickly coated in blue detergent now there would be an overflow of suds down the washer and across the floor as soon as he got it started.

"How many quarters does it take?" I looked at his eyes instead of down at the slots. There was that peculiar sense of intimacy.

He reddened a little and broke away to wash his hands in the sink. "Eight for the washers, at least four for the dryers."

Then I heard him say, "And you are?"

But I was already halfway out the door and didn't turn around.

You do something weird one day and there's no way to follow that except to get weirder still or stay out of sight. So I avoided him. And that had nothing to do with my mother.

He called out to me a couple of times in the weeks that followed and I almost stopped to talk. I thought of telling Nitro about him, but it took a lot to stir Nitro.

I met Cynthia Carshik when I returned from the store that first day. She was sitting outside her apartment on the stairs, moving the air around with a paper fan. The large window on the landing was open. The humidity was awful but there was a breeze.

"See that," she said, pointing outside. I looked out at the massive dark cloud over Lake Michigan.

"It followed me home," I said.

"Then you've brought rain with you. Thank God." She introduced herself and said, "Hell of a day to move."

"Any chance you have a can opener we could borrow? We haven't found ours yet."

She loaned me hers along with a cooler. Then she offered me a cold beer and told me about the people in the building. I took a seat at her kitchen table.

"Ajay lives with his grandfather on the first floor. He graduates from architecture school this spring. Women love him by the way. He had a girlfriend for a while, but he dropped her. He seems pretty serious about what he's doing. Oh, and the iron gates and the sheet metal and pipes in the basement are the grandfather's. You'll notice them when you're trying to get to the washers and dryers sometimes. He doesn't like to have anything disturbed. If you ask him to move a fire grate, he'll stare you down. But the next time you go down to the basement every last thing will be swept and stacked. He has a small welding business with a partner, so he tidies up when the work goes slack, not before. Though he seems to be working less now.

"Across from the Kapurs is a man named Neil and his wife, Rabbit. They're tattoo artists. The guys in the apartment next to me are probably going to be evicted next month, don't ask. And the old woman who lives next to you, all her mailbox says is *Lily*. You'll never get her to talk. You can look her in the eyes and shout, 'Good morning!' and she'll look right through you. And no, she isn't deaf. I'm pretty sure she lives off Social Security or disability. You'll see her wander around the neighborhood with an old camera. I'm sure she doesn't have any film in it."

"No film?"

"She just seems like that type."

Cynthia was twenty-two and worked at the comic book store on Howard. She and I were the same height, close to the same build, listened to a lot of the same music and were nervous driving cars. I swallowed my fears to get Lola around, and Cynthia mostly clung to public transportation but kept her mother's old car running. We had both had scarlet fever and liked to watch silent films. Cynthia smoked herbal cigarettes and had done insane things.

Her bedroom was directly below mine, and she had converted the walk-in closet between the dining room and bathroom to a tiny bedroom for those occasions when her musician boyfriend Luke's three-year-old son Colin visited. There were Cubs pennants on the walls, lion bedding on the cot, a small nightstand with a lava lamp. All the hangers had been removed from the bar, and there were board games and plastic tubs full of toys up on the shelf. She had hoped he would stay over more often, that he or Luke would settle in, but Luke had taken off for New York with his collection of guitars and amplifiers just before we arrived. She said she had a recurring nightmare that went like this: "Luke returns for a visit from New York and we get into bed that night. The Ravenswood train makes its approach along the building and suddenly the cars jump track and drive into our bed, taking him out but sparing me. The last person who had your apartment said sometimes my screams were so loud the sound shot through the radiators," she said, apologizing in advance.

I said that if I heard her scream, I would take something, a book or cup, and tap on the pipes so she'd know someone was there. She said she would do the same for me, anytime.

Before I dropped off that night, I thought about what holds us together. When I was little I could almost see the cord that stretched between my parents. He would stand behind her while she sat at the dining table, and he'd put one hand on each of her shoulders and rub her muscles and she would look content. He was doing well, selling plenty of policies. She was sculpting. Mom and he would make a point of dressing up and going out one night a week. She often wore full skirts cinched in at her tiny waist, and just before they left the house he would ask her to turn in a circle to show off her outfit, commenting on her legs as the skirt lifted in the air. He wore nicely fitted suits and ties, and his shirts always looked new. They were a handsome couple.

Maybe the cord frayed when she began to outpace him. She continued to work part-time to help with the mortgage since her costs as a sculptor were so high but often found ways to do this at home. She had become, however, a sculptor with gallery representation. And he got a new boss and began to feel pushed around at work. She did her best to hold him and the life we had together, but then his job disappeared. My mother told me losing his job was like a picture he kept folded in his wallet that he transferred from one outfit to another. Every time he paid for something, every time he'd think about what he was doing, where he was going, he'd see that picture.

It didn't help that she liked classical music and stayed up half the night looking at images of art while my father spent increasing amounts of time watching crime series and the kind of talk shows that turn into brawls. As things ground gears, the volume cranked. I heard Mahler's Eighth Symphony at earsplitting decibels while some sister's boyfriend's lover's husband went down with a sonic boom before a live audience.

If relationships split along certain lines and we tend to fall out on one side or another, I knew my side. Sometimes in those days I got in bed with her and we watched a stream of visuals on her computer well past midnight, or drifted into movies, while he pitched about on the couch with his shows. We preferred stuff flooded with one brand of love or another, even airless romances that bring the wind back up into your throat, and the French films my mother adored where little happens.

It's possible I was waiting for them to fail. By the time I was in seventh grade, somewhere between a third and half of my friends' parents were divorced. Some should have been but weren't. And statistically, I read in one of my mother's magazines, half of the group that was left cheated, and half of that half felt they were doing more than their share of the housework and child-rearing or missing out on their real ambitions. Halve the last bit again and there was a small collection of funny people left to dodge inevitable heartache.

There were two couples. A friend named Deena who had two moms, both doctors, and though I didn't spend a lot of time at Deena's the moms seemed to be in decent sync whenever I dropped over. And Joe's parents, the first to get a jumbo flat screen TV. We used to pile into their house on weekend nights. When we weren't watching a movie or playing a game, pictures of the family would come up on the screen, the father's arms around the mother, the mother's arms around the father. They weren't little people by any means. They liked to eat and have all of us for barbeque, baked potatoes with sour cream, garlic bread heavy with butter, and so many beverages stuffed in the icy cooler you could float away. They rarely raised their voices except to call out for more sauce or napkins. Even their kids said they just worked somehow.

When I realized I could only find two larger-than-life couples in the whole lot, I guess I lost faith in the idea.

At school the boys I knew were friends mostly and we traveled in packs with the girls I knew, and I watched them hook up and fall in love or the other way around. They broke each other's hearts in the middle of movies, over cheap meals, on the phone, in fragmented texts, by ghosting.

My friends said I was too shy, that was my problem, but there was a boy who ran after me into Lake Michigan once and tried to tug my bathing suit off. Another one kissed me in a locker room as if I were a sport he had to win. I had crushes and months of sadness over a third guy but mostly I watched everyone else travel around fortune's wheel, getting snagged and ripped on its nails.

When Nitro came along, things made their own kind of sense. I didn't want to be a couple, at least on the conscious side, and neither did he.

That made it extra strange to wake up one morning curled in front of Ajay's door in my pajamas. Mr. Kapur, his grandfather, stood above me. The morning light was coming up from the entryway. I had no idea how long I had been lying there.

I had mostly seen Mr. Kapur in passing, and he had one of those faces. Wiry and strong, he could have been fifty, but he could just as easily have been seventy or even eighty. He wore the same kind of jeans I had seen him wear each day on his way to and from work. His shirts were neatly tucked in and buttoned to his knobby throat. He was a welder by trade, and I sometimes imagined he and my mother might sit around talking shop.

His cowboy boots, in a state of high polish, were inches from my face. A sailing verbal assault began. "Get up, get up, get up! Do you have no shame?"

I worked my way to a seated position.

A crush of Hindi words followed as I brushed a layer of grit from my face. I asked him the time.

"What time is it? What time?" he mocked. "Six a.m. precisely. You would like the weather report now?"

"How long have I been here?"

"I am getting ready for work, going down to get my newspaper, and the girl from upstairs asks me this as if I have been standing outside my apartment all night long to see if some lovesick person will wander by and ask for a detailed report on conditions?"

"Lovesick?" I said with a laugh. I got up and took a seat on the stairs, too wiped out to make the climb to the third floor yet.

"My grandson is not a movie personality, and I am not the morning news station."

"Your grandson is not ... ? I don't have any interest in your grandson." It's possible I reddened a little but if I did he didn't seem to notice.

"What is wrong with you then? Making a spectacle of yourself."

"Sleepwalking," I said. "Sleepwalking is what's wrong with me."

He softened a little and said, "Then you have a nervous condition. You should see a doctor." Leaving me for a moment, he went into the apartment and came out with a blanket that he draped around my shoulders.

I was going to say something about the uselessness of doctors but decided to drop the subject. Just then the low sun rolled further into the lobby and hit the hall window on the landing between the entry and the first floor, the reflection beaming directly into his face. I thought that's why his eyes began to fill.

"Are you all right, Mr. Kapur?" I asked.

He looked disoriented.

"Mr. Kapur?"

Stepping out of the beam of light, he seemed to consider me anew. "Are you not the girl from upstairs? If you are going for your newspaper, you should wear a robe," he said. "Did no one raise you correctly?"

"I ..."

"It is a matter of common decency," he said. Then he got his keys out and quickly disappeared into his apartment. I wondered if this was a one time incident or if his condition was progressive.

We rarely saw Lily, the woman who lived next door to us. She would leave her apartment once Lola and I were out of the house and Mom had gone on the clock with her phone sales. She returned before Lola's afternoon pickup and long before I got home. It was almost as if she wanted to avoid us. Mom saw her figure from our living room window. She wore an old hat and coat and beat-in flats. She always had a camera with her and this made me think of the ghost images she must have inside. So far none of us had come face to face with her.

Though Mom often lost herself in her work, she was by nature gracious and warm. She liked to extend herself and offer help where she could with old people in particular and had volunteered at the senior center in Evanston for many years. Placing a plate of fresh baked cookies by Lily's door one day with a short welcoming note, Mom hoped to strike up a conversation. The plate sat there untouched until Mom removed it, worried about drawing vermin.

One morning Mom got curious and, purposefully breaking her routine, stepped into the hall when she heard Lily's door open. Lily was a tall woman, and she looked weary, my mother said, her face deeply lined. She had a Rolleiflex on a strap around her neck. Lily looked her square in the face, coughed as if Mom was a small bone to get out of her throat, and hurried back into her apartment.

It was sometime later that Mom agreed to accompany Lola's class on a field trip, and I came home early with a migraine. My head was splintering as I got to the top floor. I noticed Lily's door was ajar. I waited for a moment, trying to figure out if I should do something, but finally decided she'd be annoyed if I knocked.

All I wanted was to lie down with a compress and sip a cold Coke. If I got a dose of medicine quickly, I might avoid a forty-eight-hour siege that would include a light show and severe vomiting. The bottle of medicine was empty. I called the doctor's office where we had gone for years, and they agreed to send a prescription to the pharmacy near our apartment. I rang Cynthia to see if she was willing to pick it up, but she was out. If I rested, even for a moment, I would be down for the day. Somehow I walked over to the pharmacy on Howard and got my pills and walked home.

When I returned Lily's door was still open. I thought about my own grandmother, my mother's mother, and what it would be like if some neighbor ignored a warning sign of a stroke or a fall. Knocking a couple of times, I got no answer. I stepped inside and found a small table and a chair set by the window, looking out toward the lake, the wood floors bare, no other furnishings.

Maybe it was the sparseness, but everything felt still. I called out before I entered her bedroom. A single bed and a small dresser stood watch. Her kitchen seemed to hold only the most essential items. No framed artwork or family pictures. Nothing on the walls. She had the same built-in shelves in her dining room, but where our cabinet doors had panes of clear glass she had backed hers with dark fabric.

The starburst effect from the migraine began, and in that awful glow I thought I must be hallucinating when I found rows of camera bodies and lenses inside the cabinet. A couple of old Kodak Brownies and a Rolleiflex 3.5T, along with a 3.5F, 2.8C, and an Automat. She had a Leica IIIc, an Ihagee Exakta, a Zeiss Contarex and a slew of other SLR cameras. It was impossible that all this beautiful machinery—a collection of cameras that might have taken a lifetime to build—was housed next door. I examined a few and though none had film, the mechanisms worked perfectly. I wondered if she counted out her wealth with regularity, sitting at her little table.

The halos of light grew worse, and I hurried now. The bathroom was, for all intents and purposes, a darkroom with an enlarger, trays and chemicals, though I did find a hairbrush and a bottle of shampoo. Lastly, I pulled back the set of curtains to the walk-in closet slowly so the sound of the metal rings moving along the pole wouldn't peel through my skull. Inside, hundreds of neatly stacked print and negative boxes lined both sides with an open stepstool in the middle. Against the back wall the boxes were almost to the ceiling, each one clearly marked with dates and subject matter or location. I pulled one print box off the top marked *Downtown, 1965.*

The work was tender then gritty, cold-eyed then heartbreaking and almost uniformly luminous. Blacks were true, deep black, whites crisp. I pulled open another box and another. I lost track of time and place and even my head seemed to throb differently in those moments of discovery. Weegee, Dater, Cunningham, Bresson somehow all resided in her images yet she was her own photographer. Lily was her last name. Her first name was Anna.

I thought of Nitro, how much he would love this work.

Over decades she had taken photographs of people in every social class along with self-portraits, often in mirrors and windows, some of them of her younger self fully nude. As far as I knew, Anna Lily was unknown.

I heard my mother and Lola on the stairs, talking as they

climbed. Then our front door opened and closed, and the TV went on with a kids' show. I put everything back and at the last moment grabbed one box of negatives marked *Arlington Racetrack, 2002.* I could never steal anyone's cameras. But if I borrowed a few of her negatives and prints for my own small use and returned them.... I felt far more nervous with her negatives than I did when I'd stolen a two-thousand-dollar pair of shoes. Before I left I made sure everything appeared to be undisturbed.

I gave myself a minute, tiptoed down and walked up the last set of steps, and arrived at my door, where the pain in my head finally blossomed. Once I was inside, Lola rushed to tell me about her day at the Aquarium while my mother said, "You're home early."

"I have to lie down," I said and held up the prescription bag. Mom swung into action and got me a compress and a Coke over ice and asked Lola to start her homework at the kitchen table—she would fix a snack in a minute.

I got on my computer the next morning and discovered in the world of photographs published, shared, pilfered, over saturated, distorted, lost, retrieved, and made to express every sentiment on earth, there was nothing by a photographer named Anna Lily. Not a single image.

I was mulling this over when I realized my mother had placed a new letter from my father on my desk.

Dear Mona,

When I first got to New Jersey, I found a shortcut to work. This took me by a tract of upscale homes without personality and a stretch of manicured park that no one seemed to use. Eventually I got to a long row of estates that made me think I was driving through a Hollywood set. My boss has his home there and his pool, his tennis court and his little stable—most of which he doesn't use because he goes to clubs for these things. Each day I was left with a feeling that my temporary world, in this 1950s motel room with its hot plate and view of car dealerships, was rather small.

It was the motel owner who suggested another route and something I might do if I was willing to leave earlier. The next week, instead of turning right at the main bridge I went left and this took me by small brick homes built in the 1940s, most of them well kept, the lawns trim. And then the sad places began, the abandoned houses and the ones where people can't keep their porches repaired, the windows from getting broken, and the nails in place. This is where a line of men wait, hoping to get day labor. And this is where I was instructed to stop.

I went over to a food truck. Later in the day this truck will sell burritos and pulled-pork sandwiches and icy drinks to men and women who work downtown and line up halfway down the block for tasty home cooking. But in the mornings the day laborers, who are mostly homeless and might not eat otherwise, are given a hearty meal. I was welcomed by the owner, who provided all of this food on his own dime with only a small fund his church had set up. And so for forty-five minutes I helped wrap the food and hand each man a meal so generous he could eat some for breakfast and save some for lunch and get through.

Honestly, I think it's getting me through the days.

I miss all of you deeply. I am sorry that coming home has been delayed so long. Your mother's probably told you by now that I am still waiting on my commissions. Maybe the boss had to build a new swimming pool this year. I'm sure things will be straightened out soon. Please try not to worry.

Love,

Dad

I began to look for something I might send in return. Some message to let him know how I felt about his rules to live by. He probably had a new home in New Jersey with some girlfriend and her kids. Because once you've lied, especially by omission, you can always lie again. It's like stealing. The difference was, I knew when I stole.

Then I found it. Mom got the paper delivered for free because of her ad sales. They stacked up by the kitchen door until we took a bunch down to the trash. Right there on the top, on the front page, was a full-color photograph of a car accident that had happened on Lake Shore Drive—two cars smashed together as if they had been propelled by anger. Emergency vehicles with their lights, stretchers, bodies in braces, blood on the asphalt. I got one of my digital cameras and shot this image. I downloaded it, cropped it to remove the caption and ran it out on my printer on the kind of paper stock that makes a good postcard. On the back, all I put was my name and address in the upper left-hand corner and his name and address in the *To:* space. I stamped it and went downstairs and dropped it in the mail.

He had a talent for metaphors. He could tell his own story.

After that his letters stopped.

Richard

I found a bare-bones motel in Newark owned by a man named Leon. He was in his late forties, never shaved with accuracy, and each day he wore a different T-shirt from an '80s rock band. Down in his office he had thirty-three glass tanks filled with snakes. He told me the number before I thought to count them.

I put in a clean effort at work each day and always stayed late. When I got back to my room I threw something in the microwave and looked at the traffic going by the dealerships and the pancake house across the road. Sometimes I'd put on my sweats or shorts and go for a run out on the side streets—I'd have to drive to find those. Liz had packed a copy of *Siddhartha* in my suitcase, by a writer named Hesse.

The Buddha on the cover kept an eye on my screwed-up life from the bedside table without breaking his gaze. The long unemployment, my family back in Chicago, the house gone. He probably didn't miss a thing. When Liz pushed a book my way I assumed she was sending a message of one type or another, so I began to read *Siddhartha*. It's a little flowery but here's how it starts:

In the shade of the house, in the sunshine of the riverbank near the

*boats, in the shade of the Sal-wood forest, in the shade of the fig tree
is where Siddhartha grew up, the handsome son of the Brahman, the
young falcon, together with his friend Govinda, son of a Brahman.*

I liked that he was a falcon. You have to respect the raptors.
They're unapologetic about their jobs. They have a fearlessness,
something that helps in my line of work. The more I read, the
more I thought Liz wanted me to see this rotten business of being
so far away as a journey, not a punishment.

Going downstairs to stretch my legs, I saw Leon in his office,
lights blazing. He was up feeding his snakes. Mona had sent me
a disturbing postcard that had come that day and I couldn't stop
thinking about it. Two cars in a terrible collision on the Drive. I
had gone right out and bought a pack of cigarettes after work and
started smoking again.

I seized on this opportunity to have a conversation. The bell
rang over the door as I stepped inside.

"Hey," he said.

I returned his greeting, and then I looked at the rafting
brochures, the parasailing adventures, the hot-air-balloon rides.
From the corner of my eye I saw Leon watch me, and I stopped. I
wasn't sure what to say. He went back to the business at hand and
dangled a squirming white mouse with red eyes by its tail as he
opened the top of the first boa constrictor's tank.

"Do you have a hard time feeding them live things?"

"My last girlfriend asked me that. She was on the Christian
side, so I said, 'Your god does it all the time. Storms, floods,
earthquakes—gobbling up people right and left.'"

"I'm not sure I ..."

Suddenly the boa struck and coiled around the mouse. I saw a
back leg twitch, the other precisely pinned. Awful way to go.

"So you think of yourself as a god?" I said, hoping he recognized my humor.

"You'll have to ask the ladies," he deadpanned.

I had run into a woman a couple of nights earlier when she was getting out of a Lexus and I came down for ice. She rang the office bell and Leon let her in with a kiss on the mouth of some duration. She wore a black raincoat and flip-flops as if she had rushed out of her house to be with him. I wouldn't have been surprised to discover she wore a shorty nightgown beneath her coat or nothing at all.

"Each one of my snakes is named for an ex-wife or girlfriend. Hedy, she's my boa. She likes it when I call her Hedy Lamarr, the way my girlfriend did."

In the months I had roomed there I had seen a dozen women come and go in succession, and maybe there were more snakes crowded into the tanks.

"You're a romantic," I said.

Leon laughed. Then he asked how things were going back home, and I told him something about Liz and the girls. It wasn't exactly that I couldn't open up to someone at work, but the guys there had been together for a long time, and they thought of me as the boss's friend because the boss had taken me out to his country club three or four times. But the new golf clubs he'd pressed me to buy sat unused in my room.

"Describe your wife," Leon said, "as if I'm a chauffeur picking her up at an airport."

I didn't go on and on but I did mention the way she tied her hair up in a ponytail, the fine hairs at the back of her neck curling without effort. "Sometimes I'll see her in the backyard looking over a new sculpture, her hands fixed on her hips, her spine nice and straight, the light filtering through the tall elms to rest on her shoulders. It's a beautiful thing to see her like that, to see just how alive she becomes." I finally had to stop.

Leon couldn't believe how long Liz and I had been together and that I had only been with one woman. I think he saw me differently then. Not the lonely man passing through but someone who had roots. Balled up roots, I admit, but eager to be planted in solid ground again as soon as she was ready to join me.

"I met someone recently," he said.

"It looks like you're running out of room for tanks."

"This one's different. I'm trying not to screw it up. Maybe you'd be willing to offer some advice," he said and dropped another mouse to Hedy. "Hey, why don't you come over for dinner tomorrow night?"

"Don't you think she'd rather see you alone?"

"No, no, Sybil's the social type. Always likes to have people around."

"I should probably work," I said.

"On a Saturday night? I'll meet you over there. Around eight." He drew a map. I folded it and put it in my pocket.

The next night I showered and shaved and put on a pair of chinos and pressed my shirt on the bed with the iron Leon loaned me. I saw him drive off on his motorcycle and I noted the high school kid sitting in the office minding the front desk when I left.

I parked on the street. There was room in the drive at his girlfriend's but I wasn't planning on sticking around too late. I recognized the woman in the raincoat when she came to the door, only she wore jeans and a light top now. It fluttered with her movements in a nice way. She looked as put together as her house. From the entryway you could see all the way to the back where giant picture windows and sliding doors looked onto a pool glowing with submerged lighting. The first thing I thought when she took me into the living room to introduce me, Liz would love this place. Just the artwork alone. I recognized a couple of the artists, though I couldn't call up their names, and a set of chairs was from that designer Aalto who did the chaise lounge Liz inherited from her grandmother.

Leon stood by the empty fireplace with a drink in his hand, elbow on the mantle. He had shaved down to a fine stubble and his hair was pulled back. Wearing a pressed white dress shirt, he was transformed from the wastrel owner of a rundown motel to the lord of the manor. Sybil introduced David Fong and his wife, Amanda—two young retirees from the high tech world who had moved back to New Jersey to care for Amanda's declining mother. Sybil and Amanda had gone to one of those Ivy schools together. I had the sense that Edie, a lean woman with large green eyes and a soft bob, had been invited at the last minute, or I had, to fill out the table. I pegged her for a shy woman who might have trouble making conversation over dinner despite her boldness in not wearing a bra.

"This place is remarkable," I said after Leon handed me a glass of chilled wine, saying it was a Chardonnay he liked from the Russian River in California.

"Show him around while I get the hors d'oeuvres set up," Sybil said to Leon.

There were five bedrooms and seven bathrooms, and as he took me through I realized the closet off the main bedroom was larger than both my daughters' bedrooms put together. I'm not sure why he wanted to show me this but he treated me like a potential buyer who wants to look inside every space. There was a game room, a wine cellar, and a viewing theater in the basement. We took seats in the four rows of highly padded chairs that swiveled and rocked back and forth. A large screen rose and lowered, Leon at the controls.

"How did you and Sybil meet?"

"She's on the board of a lion rescue organization. I went to this event a few weeks ago and that was it."

"What on earth am I giving *you* advice for?" I asked.

"The problem is, I've lost all my hesitancy. Like we're listening to 'Eight Days a Week' on a loop, and I know eventually we'll have to face the fact that there are only seven. I haven't met her kids. They're grown but none of them live in the area. I don't know if she has to have all this luxury to be happy. I don't know. Don't you ever get frightened when things look too good?"

I wanted to say that that wouldn't worry me right now. "What about her ex?"

"She lost her husband five years ago. Attacked by a lion when they were helping to tag a pride."

Maybe this is what happens to the rich. Their little passions tear them apart. Liz likes to make fun of the fact that they all want their kids to take ballet and painting and learn a musical instrument and act in a million school plays and concerts but they're up in arms if their kids grow up and want to do these things as careers. But that wasn't the subject at hand, and Leon seemed sincere in trying to sort things out.

"I know when I met my wife, I thought the world would split in two if I couldn't be with her. Everything else … the rest didn't matter though maybe it should have," I said.

He patted me on the back, like we were beginning to understand something together, even if we weren't entirely. "Let's get you topped off," he said, and we returned to the living room. It had been a long time since I'd seen such a spread. Liz and I used to have big potlucks with our friends at the house, back when we could supply all the wine, the juice and stuff for the kids, the coffees and desserts, the liqueurs she liked to serve at the end of the night—when things were the way they were supposed to be.

This whole business—the house, the art, the lap pool—I knew

this was what Liz had imagined for herself. It's what her parents and grandparents had seen for her. The bright wrap. The things I wished I could give her.

After we talked about pool filtration systems—Sybil wasn't sure she was happy with hers—and munched some of those hors d'oeuvres Edie and I were asked to sit next to each other at the table. It wasn't long before our conversation became more of the intimate, whispered kind than talk of the public business at hand. I didn't think I was the cause, but maybe I lost track. In any case she seemed eager to draw me in. I watched Leon and Sybil as they entertained, the conversation dipping between endangered species, conservation, new forms of media, how these areas overlapped or might, kids, travel. I kept up where I could.

Too early into the evening I had begun to see them as potential clients, and that made me think about the commissions I wasn't getting paid at work, and maybe I drank a little to stop those thoughts. It's possible I had a forlorn look, like a guy who needs to be rescued, because suddenly Edie reached under the table and put a hand on my leg. Not down by the knee but up high as if she were about to slip something inside my pocket. She was talking about this course she was doing on meditation and breathing techniques, and she had a particular, maybe you'd say expensive glow. Her eyes appeared to soften each time she engaged me. Several times she grabbed my leg when I laughed.

I could tell Edie was one of those women who have regular facials and massages, get waxed and have filler injections, do Pilates and long workouts with personal trainers. They have their therapists to absorb the shock of life—every fold and quirk and fear her heart and mind could ever hold—so that she will never know a moment alone or unchartered, so that she will be kept at a consistent temperature like the wine down in Sybil's cellar. She was on one side of a wall and I was on another, and I knew the sound thing was to keep it that way.

I reached down and put my hand over hers to gently remove it, but she turned her hand inside mine and squeezed my palm as if she had been waiting for some kind of gesture from me and took this to be it. I eased my hand out and picked up my knife and fork like there was an urgency to cutting the small potatoes on my plate. She smiled and coughed into her napkin, thinking, I guess, that we had set something in motion. Then she leaned in close to my ear.

I felt each word separately, the way her breath worked against me, when she said, "Do you feel anything about Buddhism?"

I almost laughed because I didn't understand how a question like this could seem so intimate and uncanny instead of annoying. Happy for this small piece of good fortune, I said, "I've been reading *Siddhartha.*"

"I read *Siddhartha* floating in an inner tube in the Bahamas," she said. "The whole world opened up."

"I've been thinking about what it says about journeys."

The minute this was out of my mouth I wondered if I had betrayed Liz, if she would be hurt by my telling something I could attribute only to her.

"Yes, yes, exactly," Edie said.

So we talked for a while about journeys. I didn't go into my family's trials, my lost job, and so on, but I did let myself get a little philosophical the way Uncle Sor sometimes got and maybe for him it was about trying to fit in as well. I probably came off sounding lofty, and maybe I made up a thing or two in that way you have to embellish if you want to have any kind of stake in honesty.

"I'd like to show you something," she said. And then she turned to Sybil. "I have to show him the new painting. We'll be back to help with coffee."

"Take your time," Sybil said. "All I have to do is flip a switch and it's ready." It's possible she winked at her friend. But it might have been the pool lights playing with my vision.

I followed Edie down a long hall. I'd like to say I knew where that hall was going from the first tour but my head was lighter now that I was standing, the wine moving through my system. And there were a number of doors and passages. I know we went up a set of stairs and then a second and found our way to a room at the very top of the house with a slew of windows, like a widow's walk, only bigger. You could see the lights of the city.

There was a low table draped with a cloth. On top were a couple of golden bowls, a candle, fresh flowers in a vase and a photograph of a man in an orange robe. There were cushions to sit on, and I assumed this was where Sybil and Edie sat and meditated, or at least thought about doing that. Off to one side was a daybed. On one wall was the painting. It was done mostly in reds so dark they were almost brown, and the figure was a little hazy.

Edie slid the rheostat up a notch, and I realized it was an image of the Buddha. I stood dumbly there, my head in a fine spin, when the lights dimmed again. Turning around I saw that Edie had opened her blouse. She slipped her arms out now and let it drop to the floor. I whispered, "Probably better if we don't." But I'm not sure she heard me.

She loosened the drawstring on her pants until they dropped and she stepped out of them. I was stunned to see she wore no lingerie at all.

In the months leading up to my departure, Liz and I had felt crushed by events. I thought we would make love the night before I left since we hadn't in a while, well, several months, but she didn't reach out for me. And I didn't want to upset her or be met with rejection. We talked after I was gone and we both regretted not getting past a new kind of shyness that had settled between us.

Edie walked over to me and touched my face. Her hand was warm. When I started to say something she put an index finger against my lips, and then she began to unbutton my shirt.

"Maybe we should go down for coffee," I said, as if this might put me in a sober state or make her clothes fly back onto her body.

"There's time. It only takes the flip of a switch," she said.

"Yes, but ..."

When she reached for my zipper I took both of her hands in mine. I couldn't see her full expression in the light. I asked her to talk with me for a minute. We sat down on the daybed. One side of her hair dropped in front of her face and she didn't pull it away. Edie was a fine-looking woman, and I stopped finding the ways that she was foreign to me.

"I have a wife and two daughters. Back in Illinois."

"Sybil told me. Divorced, one son in high school," she said, fixing her hair behind her ears. "My husband cheated on me with my best friend."

"That's awful."

She became still. Maybe she studied our hands.

"Sometimes I think about the way everything can change in a second," I said.

"I've had my tubes tied," she said in the sweetest way.

"No, not that, it's ..."

"Oh. Oh, God. Where's my head? Sybil must have condoms stashed here and there," she said. She was even more nervous than I was, stretching to look in a drawer behind her, her torso elongated, her pelvic bones outlined in such a way. She found nothing. Sitting upright again, Edie said, "It's been a long time since I've had to worry about stuff like that. Only divorced a year now. Too wrecked by it, you know? She thought ... Sybil thought ... we might get along. She said she thought you had been alone for a while."

"I haven't completely expressed ..." I tried again.

She reached for her drawstring pants. But instead of putting them on, she held them loosely in her hands Her shoulders rounded forward, her arms bent so they rested against her legs. "This was a bad idea."

I took her in my arms and rocked her a little, and we stayed close for a while. I don't know if anyone makes the perfume that filled my head. I think it was just Edie. I can honestly say I wanted this woman almost as much as I had wanted Liz when we first met.

And this made me think about Liz going out to see friends. Someone might hit on her. She could easily meet any number of men through the gallery. She would have plenty of chances if that's what she wanted. I thought about lines—crossing them, drawing them, erasing them, drawing them again.-

I pulled back a little and touched Edie under her chin. I kissed her face, and then I cradled her so that she would lie back. I told her, "I can't make love to you the way I wish I could, but I want you to know how beautiful you are. How truly beautiful."

I did things that have always pleased Liz, without going too far, without letting her take me. I don't know if this makes me less of a man or more of a good man. Probably neither. But by the time Edie was at rest, I don't think I had crossed the kind of line where I would need to make a confession or carry around a belly full of guilt. My pleasure had been in feeling her pleasure and in keeping true to Liz in the most fundamental way.

We took turns stopping in the small bathroom down the hall, and then we went downstairs and downstairs again and appeared by the lap pool, where there was a line of lounge chairs and where the others had gathered. We received a couple of looks, and I was handed a slice of cake.

I drank some coffee and waited until I felt my departure wouldn't be awkward. Then I shook hands all around, thanking the hostess for the evening, the wonderful meal, the good company while my head continued to swim.

Edie offered to walk me out, so I helped her with her coat.

She leaned into me by my car. "I'm expecting you to get in touch," she said. "I mean, we can just talk. Everyone needs to have a friend or two out there."

"I'm probably the last person you want as a friend right now. My family … just today … I mean, I think my daughter would just as soon see me dead."

She looked at me with care, and then she lightened and said, "The nineteen-year old? That's rebellion."

"I think it's more about debts I have to pay."

"We all have those in one way or another."

I gave Edie a final kiss and got in my car.

As I approached the motel the lights from the car dealerships streamed across my windshield, reminding me of everything I could have: smooth lines, big offers, newness. I was dopey from wine and shouldn't have been on the road at all that night.

The next day I went into the office determined to talk with Phil about my commissions again so I could get Liz caught up with some of her bills and go home and see my family—everything else could wait. But before I sat down my old friend and boss eased back in his chair and with precise aim shot me out of the sky. He told me about this other fellow who was coming back to work—to my job.

"What?" I said.

"He's been with us a long while, Richard. We didn't think he'd make such a quick recovery. Or that he'd recover at all. We'll get a check to you right away with two weeks' severance."

This other fellow, I would learn later, was his brother, who had been on an extended trip. Maybe it was around the world. I heard he went to Prague, Barcelona, Dublin, Reykjavik, Morocco and Istanbul, as if he was throwing darts at a map—probably on my commissions.

When I pushed back Phil said, "I'll write you a good recommendation. You shouldn't worry about that. But now that all the stats are in, I don't know that insurance is the place for you anymore. It's possible you've lost your touch."

I reminded him, though it was absurd that I had to, that I had more sales than anyone at the firm that quarter.

"Figures were inflated. I'm working with a new accounting firm now."

"No matter how you cook the numbers, I haven't seen a single commission."

"The check will take a day or two to cut." He extended his hand and thanked me for *pinch hitting*.

"'Pinch hitting'?" I said, letting his hand waver there.

"The bottom line is, you didn't make it through the first year's probation. It happens," he said.

"You stated, emphatically, that the probationary period was three months. You congratulated me on passing the mark. You took me to lunch that day."

"I'll have my secretary send a copy of the internal memo related to this," he said, egging me on. I knew if I punched the guy, everything would be lost.

The check arrived a week later with my regular pay less expenses. When I called the payroll person she ran down a list of *expenses* that included paying to have the name changed on my door and my parking spot.

When I asked where my commission check was, she said I'd have to talk with Phil. But Phil and his financial manager and then the payroll person stopped taking my calls. I contacted an attorney to see if she'd take my case on a contingency basis. After we talked at length she did a brief synopsis for me: The firm had the right to create a probationary period; I had no documentation on the length of this period; I had been laid off my last job, and that would provoke an inquiry; even if I won, there would be costs and court fees and the lengthy business of petitioning and reviewing documents; and Phil's company could appeal. I tried two other attorneys and got the same basic story. Finally I decided my time was best spent landing the next job and getting to work.

I sold the car and put the funds in the bank and wrote out checks to Liz, stretching the money as far as I could. Now that I understood Leon's situation, I asked him, man to man, if he would let me owe him the last month's rent. I was out every day looking for work by then, but I was behind on rent. He said he had decided to sell the motel and that he didn't care, honestly. He was heading to Kenya soon with Sybil. Then he said something I wasn't expecting. "Edie has an empty guest house. That's all. I just, well, I think she wanted me to tell you, so there you are."

The idea of going home a failure, well, Liz had enough worries on her hands. She had moved out of Evanston into the city, renting a small apartment with the girls. I thought about looking it up on Google Earth, dragging the small person icon until he stood in front of the entryway, but I couldn't.

Mona

To prevent Lola from being entirely uprooted when she began kindergarten, old friends in Evanston, the Halyards, agreed to say we lived on the top floor of their house—as far as Lola's school was concerned.

"For play dates, she can go to friends' homes," Mom said.

"She'll want to have her friends over," I said.

"I know, but I'm in school. People understand hard work, right?"

"Do you want me to say something or just agree?" I asked because by then I had no idea. She looked heartbroken.

"Maybe for today just agree," she said. After a serious talk with a career counselor Mom had signed up to become an X-ray technician. It was a training program where the hospital picked up most of the bill. When she first got her acceptance letter, she sat us down and said, "In two years' time I will be a well-paid technician, and in an economic downturn the medical industry is still a pretty safe bet."

"People have to get sick!" Lola said with enthusiasm.

My sister and I listened as Mom talked about the human body and the importance of good imagery until she ran herself out and was saying something, maybe it was about the luminous quality we have as people. But that whole X-ray thing ... we no longer had any of her sculptures where we lived. Sometimes we got in the van and drove to a location where we could see one of them, and all of us choked up.

She was determined to help pay for college and said getting this credential would allow her to pitch in. "Next year," she said, "the FAFSA will look completely different, the financial aid package a whole lot better. It's going to happen."

But the small things, the day to day, seemed to overtake her at times. "I don't know how I'm going to get you back and forth from work and Lola back and forth from school and take all these classes," Mom said, considering her schedule now.

"Just drop Lola off at her school and pick her up from aftercare. I'll take the L." Mom seemed to forget that I had been working out my own transportation for a long time now.

"What street would you walk down to get to the L?" she asked.

"From work?" I shrugged. "I don't know."

She tried again. "If there was a tornado warning, wouldn't it be better if you took the same route home from work every day so I'd know how to find you?"

"Before I'm sucked up into the sky?" I asked.

"Be nice," she said.

"It's winter. We don't have tornadoes in winter."

To avoid a fight, I agreed to walk down Church from the studio daily, ritualistically. Not that I planned to do this. But what neither of us considered at the time was that anyone wanting to follow me, anyone keenly interested in my movements, could figure out where to find me during the work week, under the weight of my backpack, earbuds in, oblivious.

I was nineteen then and still saving everything I could to travel over the summer with my cameras. Geary kept telling me there was a story to tell in the country's economic wreckage. I worked as many hours in his studio as he'd give me to get to that wreckage. The minute I walked in the door to the apartment, I hit household chores to get those out of the way early unless I was catching the last of the day's light.

Glancing out our front windows now as I made Lola's bed, I saw the holiday lights edging a window across the street and an electric menorah glowing from another. An abandoned shopping cart with its wheels off and a car engine sat in a driveway mounded with snow. I got out one of my SLRs and put the telephoto on. I could see the television show the couple in the stucco house across the way watched. Sometimes when I walked by their apartment I heard actors firing guns at one another that sounded a lot like the real gunshots we heard in the neighborhood. Three or four times since we had moved in the cops had pulled up outside their building, lights flashing. Cynthia said those were domestic battery calls, though I had never seen anyone being hauled away, so I had to take her word for it.

Ajay came into view and began to pace by the snow-buried cars. It had to be thirty degrees out and he was in an open shirt and down vest as if he couldn't feel a thing. Most of his tattoos were the kind you'd see at a big water park on a hot day. A tiger, some words in an Asian language, a knotted symbol—maybe Celtic. The ink I was curious about was on one arm, covered by the shirt he buttoned now. I had seen it more than once in the hot weather. It was a name surrounded by wings: *Constantina*. I found myself repeating that name like a song I couldn't shake. Of all the women who came around looking for him, I hadn't figured out which one was *Constantina*. There was one woman in the early fall who had appeared in electric-red shorts and tight athletic tops. She used to take off with Ajay when he went on his daily run. They followed the line of the lake and often headed into Evanston. I knew from the times

I passed them in our van that they probably did eight to ten miles before he came home slick with sweat.

She didn't last long. Maybe they were just friends. Maybe they moved at a different pace. After a while, I assumed she wasn't the reason he had gone under the needle.

The other women wore tight pants, leather jackets, short skirts, bulky sweaters, high tops, strappy sandals, scarves in their hair, short, sleek cuts, and long, complicated dos with rhinestone bobby pins. They pulled at his arm, wanting him to go somewhere, and when he wasn't in sight they leaned on the bell, letting their cigarette butts and gum wrappers drop to the floor of the entry hall as they waited, so the rest of us had to wade through their trash. I wondered if Ajay cared about any of them.

I noticed he wasn't very good at answering when this one woman with a tight updo and short, thin jacket drove her fingernails into his doorbell. And Mr. Kapur couldn't stand it if she showed. If Ajay went outside to talk with her, his grandfather would yell out the window in a quick string of Hindi. And once, when his shouting was ignored, as it sometimes was, I heard his grandfather slam a window so hard the glass shattered. Somehow she didn't fit my image of Constantina.

Ajay stopped pacing now and drew his hand along the crown of his head, back and forth a few times. I couldn't tell if he was concerned about something or if he just liked the way his bristly hair felt against his palm. I thought I knew what it would feel like if I were to touch it.

"Dinner!" Mom called from the kitchen.

"You go ahead. I'm not really hungry."

Just then Ajay looked up at our apartment as if he knew I was watching. I switched to continuous shooting mode for a few seconds and let my camera rest. He went back to pacing.

"It's going to get cold!" Lola called.

It was hard to refuse Lola. I came into the kitchen, kissed her on the cheek, and poured one cup of coffee for me, one for Mom. She had her laptop open. "Sorry," she said, blowing on the cup. "I have to get this one in tonight."

School had turned her into *The Living X-ray*. She was able to recite the names of all the bones of the body in under three minutes. And when she was really on, she could see right through you and read you like a piece of film held up to a light bulb.

She spent her evenings in a world marked by lung spots, broken tibias, and damaged skulls. One doctor gave her nothing but troubling images to consider. She would point to something, a tumor or a node, and make predictions about survival rates. The ones of babies, I couldn't look at those. With her fingertips she scrolled her computer and suddenly smiled to herself. Then she remarked on the kind of fracture she was looking at as if the whole world hinged on the way things break instead of the simple fact that they were broken.

She wasn't sleeping much anymore. I knew this because I was up most nights listening to her not sleep. She would get so worn during the day she wouldn't bother to put on makeup, and her hair was a mess where once it had been washed and neatly brushed each day. I saw that it had come undone from the rubber band that she had taken off the morning paper. I was tempted to reach over and pull that band out the rest of the way and hand her a comb, but it was hard to know what was holding her together at that point. I didn't want to pull out a lynchpin.

Looking at the wooden sticks on Lola's plate, I saw that she was on her third corn dog. She squatted in her chair instead of sitting, the way she did sometimes when she had growing pains. That winter the pain moved up and down her legs, and she often asked me to rub it away. I thought at first this was about sadness, about not being with friends enough, and maybe it was in part, but then I saw that her appetite had become ceaseless. And when I measured her against a doorframe, she was taller.

Leaning over the open page of a library book, she was so intent on finding one little man among thousands that she hadn't stopped to eat the French fry she held, coated thick with ketchup. I was about to caution her when hundreds of Roman warriors were suddenly buried alive. I grabbed my napkin, but she pushed my hand back. "I almost have him," she said without taking her eyes from the page. Later I would rub the ketchup in to make it look like blood spilled in all that Roman chaos. Mom didn't need the cost of replacing a library book.

"Found him!" she said, beaming her flashlight into my eyes. I guided it out of range, having lost track of the number of times she had looked all the way into the back of my brain with that thing. Lola had developed some of Mom's impulse for worry by then, and I know she looked with that flashlight for signs of imminent departure.

"They *all* have striped hats," I said, studying the illustration, trying to imagine if he was even there. She pulled her wool scarf up to her nose to indicate that I was out of it. I wondered if this was how, in her mind, she looked for our father. Keenly, precisely, without rest.

Waiting until the elevated train passed and the cups hanging from hooks stopped swaying, Mom said, "That's definitely a compacted fracture." She shot me a look of satisfaction. And then she returned to us and said, "No dinner tonight?"

"I had a late lunch," I said.

"Be a love and get the mail, would you?" Mom touched my hand.

I don't know what it was about that building and its capacity to take on discarded things. When I got down to the entryway I found a large planter with a dead rubber tree and a stack of old *Spy* magazines—stuff no one had the inclination to move in or out. No bikes, though. Bikes were stolen quickly. That happened to Lola the first week we moved in, though Mom had a solid cable fixed around the frame and a floor-to-ceiling pipe in one corner. She promised to replace it as soon as the spring hit, but Lola told me in confidence that all the money would be gone by then. She must have heard us say too many times that we couldn't afford something she wanted. I explained that I would give her my birthday money when I got it from our grandparents and uncle. But Lola was a girl of unshakable beliefs. A thousand ways to break a heart.

Ajay was still out in the cold, sometimes stretching his arms out as if he were limbering up for an athletic event. I watched him for a moment through the glass door, and then I jammed my hands into my coat pockets. I'd forgotten my keys. Before I could buzz upstairs, he spotted me. My body locked as he came inside and the cold air swept the entry. Bits of paper danced around his boots and came to a stop when the outer door finally shut.

"Any good mail?" he asked, rubbing his hands together, finally showing he had to warm up. I dreaded that someone might see the envelopes printed with *Second Notice, Third Notice, Delinquent.* I pulled my gloves from my pockets as if I needed them.

"We didn't get our mail today," I said. But when I followed the direction of his gaze I was reminded that our mailbox had diamond-shaped cutouts in the little door, allowing anyone to see when it was crammed full, as it was now. I honestly didn't know why he cared.

I considered the smallest tattoo on his chest. A goddess of some sort, she had four arms, two hands raised holding flowers and two with coins raining from her palms. A couple of weeks earlier I'd had a dream about her, though she had only two arms. She stood in my room in her sari and gave me a long look and then she started to talk, but too low for me to catch the words, like a movie with bad sound. I had the sense that she was trying to warn me about something. As I began to wake I realized her voice was the voice of someone on the television in the dining room selling fall blouses or false houses. It was three a.m., and my mother had dropped off. They were always trying to sell her things she couldn't afford while she was unconscious.

"Why does she have four arms?" I asked, nodding toward his chest.

He laughed and said, "The better to hold you with, my dear?"

"That work on your girlfriend?"

I've had my share of lucid dreams, and often in that state I can manipulate how I move, what I decide to do. I can drop into water and start swimming, turn a car around and drive off in the opposite direction. More often I take to the air. Yet for all this fluid motion, I know we are as earthbound as rocks. We are self-contained and tough as hard apples.

An odd thing occurred, however, standing there with Ajay in that freezing hallway. Something I hadn't experienced before. I felt somehow tugged from myself, drawn out little by little, as if I possessed a lighter body inside my solid one. And that lighter body eased into him the way two chemicals mix in a darkroom tray. I found myself breathing with him as if I were held for a second or two in his ribs. I stood inside him, following the stream of thoughts soaking his brain. A lot of those thoughts were about trying to keep me from leaving and going upstairs.

Thinking back, it was like those light-headed moments brought on by skipped meals or too much sugar and coffee that became a habit in those days. Maybe the sensation lasted longer than I imagined. I'm not sure. Time had a way of distorting when I was around him.

The next thing I knew he was shaking my hand and introducing himself again, as if I hadn't heard him that day in the basement. I did the same.

Despite our clumsiness, I began to see how my head might rest in the crook of his shoulder, what he would say to me the first time he cut himself open to reveal something he tended not to talk about. He looked at me as if we were working off something inevitable. I drew my hand away.

"What makes you think I have a girlfriend?" he asked. "Because I don't … have a girlfriend."

"How about keys? I left mine upstairs."

He seemed relieved that I had a mission for him. Unlocking the door, he tried to hold it open for me, but I'm used to making my own way through doors, so we had a funny exchange. "We called the super, by the way. About the hot water," I said, starting up the stairs.

"We did too. Then my grandfather pushed me out of the door half dressed to keep an eye out for the guy so I could help him find a parking space. I tried to tell him he's been working here for years. But you can't tell my grandfather anything until he calms down. I moved home to help out for a while. He's gotten too forgetful."

"I hope he's okay."

"You know." He shrugged. "You planning to be around for a while? I mean, living here?"

"Probably 'til the start of summer."

"All right," he said. We were almost in front of his apartment door. Here he moved ahead of me. Taking hold of the banister with one hand, he braced his other hand against the wall, gently blocking my way. "Listen, I was going to ask …" but he stopped and seemed to change course, "if you keep your sister away from the park down the street."

"We go to other parks," I said.

"Good, that's good. Look, if there's anything I can ever do. You know, change a light bulb …"

"I think we've got it down with light bulbs," I said, finding it tough not to laugh.

Days later I found the woman his grandfather couldn't stand waiting in the entryway to our building. She wore that same thin jacket, as if she was confused about the season. Her hair was up in a topknot. She pulled the door open for me.

"Do you live here?" she asked before I was halfway in.

I nodded and went over and got the mail out.

"I'm looking for Ajay?" It was odd that she stated this as a question.

"I'm afraid I can't help you."

"I'm Constantina and ..."

"You're his tattoo," I said, locking the box again.

She took off her jacket and pulled her right sleeve up to show me a bird in flight in blue ink. "It's a *jay*," she said, as if I might not get it. She asked for something to write on. I guess we should have supplied a dry-erase board for his callers. I watched as she rummaged in her purse. On the floor was a flyer for a new pizza place. I picked this up and handed it to her.

"So you know him," she said and got out a pen.

I began to understand Mr. Kapur's troubles here. "You're his girlfriend?" I said. She looked away. When she didn't answer, I said, "You all set?"

I'm not sure what I had expected Constantina to be like. Anna Karenina with piercings had gone through my mind. In any case, I thought she would be older. But she was just this woman, probably in her early twenties, not very lean or wan or Olympic or hard-looking. Just a woman willing to trust anyone to get a letter through to a guy—as if he were a soldier at the front. I couldn't say I understood the war at the time, what was at stake. I told her my first name when she asked and said I had to get upstairs.

"If I write a note to him will you give it to him?" On one edge of the flyer she started to compose her thoughts. "If I leave it in the mailbox or under the door, his grandfather will get it."

I wondered how long she had been waiting for someone to come by, if she had asked anyone else. She reached out and took my arm now. "For love's sake?" she said.

"Have you tried calling him?"

"I think his phone is dead. I'll write quick."

She went back to composing. I would not have trusted me with her love. But then there's a name for a condition where you're unaware that you're unaware. Cynthia liked to use words like that now and then, but she did crosswords. Anyway, I think Constantina had that. Everyone does, I guess, about certain matters.

I noticed the cheap jewelry around her neck, the battered character shoes. It was this lack of anything else, the fact that she was just a woman sick with love, that made me feel sorry for her. I waited while she scratched something out and then while she started over. Once she was done she folded it into a funny shape, as if she was doing origami for the first time, maybe so I wouldn't open it. As soon as she handed it to me, I unlocked the inside door.

"Can you put it in your pocket so no one sees?" she asked.

This seemed extreme, but I stuffed it in a jacket pocket and said, "Good luck. I mean, with everything."

She left quickly, and I assumed this would be the last of her. As I passed Ajay's apartment on my way upstairs, I put my ear to his door. I didn't hear anything except water running in the pipes, a sound that could have come from any of the units. It was hard to say if he was home. On the next landing I pulled the piece of paper out of my pocket, unfolded it, and read.

Ajay~ I have to see you. At my aunt's for a few days. Call me. Forgive me. Call even if you can't forgive. I'm cut to shreds over you. ~Constantina

I tore off the thin strip that contained the message. What was left—the greasy-looking pizza slices photographed in full color and all those great deals—I let drop to the landing.

Then I ate her note. Slowly. While I trudged upstairs.

I thought of going down to Cynthia's that night to tell her what I'd done. That I had consumed another woman's love, that I had eaten her sorrow and maybe her best effort to patch things up. She might be able to tell me why. But I didn't go. Lola had dropped off, and Mom stirred for a moment when I snapped the lock open but went right back to sleep. A train went by and I went into my room and put Coltrane on low, Constantina's love still swimming in my belly.

I made a couple of prints from one of Anna Lily's racetrack images. She had spent time at Arlington. I was intrigued to see how she ignored the rule of three. There was a feeling of movement in many of her images, though the people tended to be still. Whether she shot a simple ticket window or a hot-dog concession, a man's hat pulled down or a woman looking up at the board to see what she would bet on, everything she shot felt essential and a little mysterious, as if she was giving you the start of a long story. She photographed the privileged in their smart outfits and reserved boxes. Their faces nicely shaded, money in good supply. Her lens had a way of respecting them while exposing them, as if she had pulled down their pants in public while highlighting the beautiful fabric and stitching. But the depictions of the desperate characters captured me the most. Here were the gambling addicts, the people out on the hard benches in the sun tearing up tickets, the ones who stayed at the bar too long. One man looked like my father. But he was in the background, turned away.

I had Lily's printed versions for comparison. She had a particular way of burning and dodging that I was trying to understand. I took them over to Nitro's to get some technical advice. As soon as

I pulled them from the box, he wouldn't stop talking about them. Finally, after asking me when I had taken these shots and talking about a couple of ways I might reprint them, he took my hand and we went over to the long, flat drawers where he had shown me the work of the woman he went to Paris with. He opened the third drawer from the top—the one above hers—and removed whatever was there and placed Anna Lily's work inside. He assumed they were a present. I removed them just as carefully and put them back in the photo box I had brought them in.

He gave me a funny look and suggested I soak while he finished something up. His tub, sitting out in the middle of his loft, accommodated two. The word MARAT was painted in dashed black letters along one side. Here I soaked and watched him through a pair of binoculars as he worked. He put down his mat knife and came over to where I bathed and slipped the strap of the binoculars over my head. He placed them on a table, undressed, and got into the other end of the tub. I watched his penis bob in the water.

"You look sad today," he said. "How can anyone look sad who's just shot the best photographs of her life?"

"They aren't mine. I was just printing something, playing around."

"Who's the photographer?"

"Never mind."

"Okay."

He lay back and cradled me in his arms so I'd open up a little. He had a boyish, lean body and it was a little difficult to get comfortable against his ribs, even in the water. But I imagine some of Freud's patients complained about the scratchiness of the rugs on his couch.

"I had a dream I keep thinking about."

"Tell me," he said.

"When we lived in Evanston my mother's sculptures used to spook me at night, the way they mirrored the house and the workshop and anything that moved across the lawn. We had a lot of rabbits in our neighborhood, and their reflections would suddenly loom up in the metal like a funhouse mirror. Now I just miss them, the sculptures. In the dream I was standing in the yard again, surrounded by her towering work. Our lawn was covered with seedpods, outdoor furniture, and bicycles left out. I could feel the wet grass soaking my feet and the bottom edges of my pajamas. Then all at once I took off into the air. Moving above our house, arms outstretched, my clothes fluttering against my body. I was far above the sculptures, above the troubles."

He asked me to turn around so he could wash my back. I did this and crossed my arms and put them along the edge of the tub, resting my forehead there.

"I felt ... lighthearted."

"Headed?"

"Yes, light-headed, lighthearted—flying dreams are like that for me."

He kissed the back of my soapy neck and slid his hands around and cupped my breasts. But I wasn't feeling that way and turned, nudging him off, rinsing his soap away.

He lay back again at the other end of the tub.

"Ajay was in the dream."

"Who?"

"This guy who lives in my building."

"You haven't mentioned an Ajay before," he said, looking concerned.

"He's on the first floor. I hardly know him. But in the dream I felt as drawn to him as I do to gravity."

"You should probably stay away from this guy," Nitro said.

"But it wasn't even about him, really."

"Then why was he in it?" he asked.

I didn't know why I played these games with Nitro, but I did.

"I've been sending my father postcards. Did I say?"

"I thought you weren't talking to him."

"Each one is a tragic accident. Some are quite bloody."

My head began to feel too light, the water too hot. Maybe I should have eaten lunch. "If I saw him tomorrow," I said, mumbling to myself, "I might turn him in."

"For what?"

I thought over the possibilities. "For each time Lola goes without."

"Do you think you're his tragic accident?"

"I don't know what that's supposed to mean. Just fuck me so I can go home. I'm going to be late for dinner."

He held on to both sides of the tub and pulled toward me. "You said they were pretty young when they had you."

"You're driving me crazy," I said and pushed him away.

"I'm sorry. Wait, stay."

"Call your girlfriend up. Ask her to stay." I got out of the tub, water sheeting off my body onto the floor.

"She's only a friend. You're ripping my heart out of my chest," he said.

Richard

The dollar store was in one of the older malls in Atlantic City where I got hired to work 28 hours a week. I thought I'd find something better than I could in Newark. But the job market got pulled into the pit along with all those foreclosed homes, so I worked at the mall as a stopgap.

I stood at the register ringing people up, sometimes glancing at the nail salon across the way, watching the two Vietnamese women filling tubs, turning on back massagers, and bending over tough feet. But mostly I kept my head down and sold plastic butterflies with suction cups on their abdomens, pill containers marked Sunday through Saturday, ketchup and mustard squeeze bottles, and enough wind chimes to fill the whole world with the sound of tin striking tin.

Some men browsed the store, and they tended to buy small electronic things, but most of the shoppers were women. A lot of them collected Social Security, and you could see where hair dye needed a fix or their plastic purses or shoes were cracked along the seams. Plenty of mothers came in with their kids and bought toys stockpiled from China, many with unknown safety records. I was asked to come over for dinner or meet up somewhere for a beer when I got off work by a couple of them, but I always said I had to get home to my wife and kids. Night after night I started to dial Edie's number but stopped short.

I didn't have enough to rent another place, but it was a mild winter. I lived out of a backpack I got at a secondhand store. I bought a cheap sleeping bag and pad, and I used the alarm clock on my phone. Most nights I walked until I found a safe spot to shut my eyes. Some nights I spent in Laundromats.

I thought of Mona sleepwalking at night, wondering what she was trying so hard to find, scared half to death that she'd leave their apartment building in her sleep. Before I left Newark, I got more of her postcards—terrible images that kept me from getting any rest.

There were homeless shelters, but I heard about stabbings. I also got wind of the city's habit of rounding people up and dropping them off in other districts like those no-kill rodent traps where you drive to a park in someone else's neighborhood and let your rats go. I couldn't be certain that this was true, but I wasn't about to take a chance, so I did my best to stay out of sight. Someone pointed out a soup kitchen.

I was as hungry for home as I was for three solid meals, but I knew I had to be patient. I wrote long letters telling Liz I was still with the insurance company, only they had made a severe reduction in my hours—and I was doing some traveling, widening my area. She wasn't a letter writer, but together, over the phone, we got angry with the bastards. I got her to agree that I should hold on as long as I had work, at least for now—see if I could pick up something else to supplement the income loss. Sometimes it seemed she had given up on me, but then she'd say we would get through this just like everything else. I should have unraveled the shame and just told her.

Standing at the register one day, ringing up customers, I heard my phone go off. Tina, one of Uncle Sor's kids, had left a number for me to call. She was only a couple of years younger than me, but we had never met. I called back on my break, sitting on a bag of Styrofoam peanuts headed for the recycling center, wondering if I had lost Sor along with everyone else. I had not been good about keeping in touch.

"Elizabeth gave me your number," Tina said. "My father wants to see you. He's going in for open-heart surgery on Monday. Quadruple bypass. Can you go down and see him?"

I swallowed hard, thinking about the old guy. Tina was calling on a Thursday, and once I got off my shift I had to be back at work on Sunday, and I had just wired my paycheck to Liz. "I really don't know how to say this, Tina. Your father ... I love your father. But I've been hit by hard times. I don't even have the bus fare right now."

"I see. I understand. My husband and I talked this over just in case. We have airline miles saved up, so we'll get you a plane ticket. I've done this before with my kids. My dad really wants to see you, Richard. I live in Oklahoma, and Linda is in Los Angeles. We'll be there next week for the surgery. But I'm afraid no one will be able to meet you at the airport. My mother doesn't drive."

It stung me to think Tina was doing for a grown man what she had to do for her kids. But she read out the schedules and said she would make arrangements. I went to my locker as soon as I was off work and took everything I had to the Laundromat and used the one-hour cleaners next door for my suit. I grabbed a shower and shave at the city rec center, where I had gotten to know one of the evening guys at the desk. I had offered to look over his insurance bills for him once and told him how he could save a lot of money each year. He let me use the facilities if I came in during the last hour and was quick about it.

When I got on the plane I was drowning in a black suit that had once been tailored to my body. But I had held on to a belt, and that kept my pants on.

By four in the morning I landed in Florida and took a bus to Clewiston, a former sugarcane town with an area of four and a half square miles. I've never slept so hard as I did on that bus ride. For months I had lived with the knowledge that a cop could drag me out of an abandoned structure or alleyway and throw me in jail for vagrancy or that I could be rolled or stabbed or God knows what—I'd heard all sorts of stories.

I awoke to find a text from Edie. She wanted to know how I was doing. She wanted me to come visit. She wanted me to know that she had me on her mind. I realized she had sent this note late at night. I didn't like to text, but I didn't want to use up my phone time and I didn't want her to feel sad about getting in touch. I sent her a quick note saying I was seeing my uncle in Florida and would call when I got back.

In Clewiston I found empty stores, overgrowth, and endless humidity. I rolled up my suit jacket, placed it at the top of my pack, and hiked from the station. The sky was loaded with clouds that grew both dark and bright at the same time. The asphalt was hot and shimmered, and the smell of tar made my empty stomach queasy. I kept to the sidewalks and shoulders as much as I could so the tar wouldn't burn into my shoes.

I stopped at the small clapboard house with a screened-in porch and low fencing. The garage door was open, and there I could see his old carnival booth knocked down into sections, the bright red standing out against the long, flat green and yellow landscape. It rains a couple times a day in Clewiston, and as I stood there, overcome with memories, the sky let loose. Two hounds ran toward the gate and started barking, and a man emerged from the screen door, letting it flap shut behind him. He called to the dogs to quiet down.

"There you are," he said. And then he shouted into the house, "He's here!" Running toward the steps to keep the rain from ruining my suit pants, I was startled by how much he had aged. His cheeks were fat and thick with lines, and his belly pushed out. A newer hat, like the one I recalled, sat on his head. He shook my hand. The warm, leathery grip had turned soft.

"So glad you could make it," he said and opened the screen door wide. I was about to set my backpack down when he reached to take it. I didn't let it go at first, worried about the strain. But he pushed against my arm so I'd release the pack and swept it into a back bedroom, saying, "Go on into the living room."

Aunt Alma embraced me for a moment, touched my face as if she was blind and hoped to learn my features. "What a fine nephew I have," she said. Alma was a short, solid-looking woman with large eyes and uneven pigmentation. Dark cloud shapes seemed to float over the land of her lighter skin. She wore a skirt, a hand-stitched blouse, and several strands of beads. I guessed she was in her late sixties like Sor. "Bathroom's halfway down the hall to your left. I set out a washcloth and hand towel."

Once I had freshened up, I joined them, and Sor said, "So you finally got to meet Alma." He put an arm around her waist and kissed her cheek with tenderness. I expressed my pleasure in getting to know her and asked about my cousins.

"Tina works as a bookkeeper. Linda has the good life." Alma raised one eyebrow. "I think she sits around the pool too much, but Sorohan tells me I'm just jealous."

When they set out platters of food, they wouldn't let me help. I was told to sit at the head of the table and wait. Across from me was a television and over this a picture of Jesus. Dish by dish, a great meal appeared. Homemade enchiladas, tamales, chile rellenos, chicken mole, rice, beans, tortillas, and salad. She must have cooked for two days. Alma said, "Welcome." Then she did a blessing, and we dug in. I ate with my head down, not letting a thing in the world distract me, even the intense spiciness of the food. Finally Sor reached over and touched my sleeve, saying, "She'll fill out your clothes if you aren't careful."

"I couldn't slow down." I laughed. "That was too good."

"And for dessert …" Alma said. She reached over to a bowl of fruit on the credenza, plucked out an apple, and drew a paring knife from one of the drawers. We watched as she made a slit near the stem. I thought she was going to pare it so that the skin formed one long, circular slice. I had seen my mother do this many times when I was a boy. Instead, Alma made a second slit, a third and fourth, and so on, gradually lifting off minuscule sections of peel as one might make an intricate carving on a pumpkin. We were quiet as she worked away. I had tried one of those professional carving kits that came with the miniature tools one Halloween to impress Lola and to entice Mona to join in. It was good that Lola was such a tiny girl and that Mona was too busy to care. I had no skill whatsoever and should have left the carving to Liz.

"Alma used to be with a small circus," Sor said. "An Italian man, a roustabout, taught her, and he learned from his grandmother, who had been a fortune-teller. The knife has to be kept particularly sharp. I bought a knife-sharpening wheel for her one Christmas."

"Best present I ever received," she said.

When she was done she handed me the apple with a face. It was my face but aged too much. It was a bitter face I hoped never to own. She didn't see the man who had attempted over the years to stay young and fit, the energetic optimist hoping to please his wife and daughters, to always do well in insurance and keep on course, to pay the bills and load the car for vacations and clean the gutters out in the spring. This man wasn't evident in Alma's carving.

I praised her skill but felt undone when she told me to eat the thing. I didn't say that the apple frightened me, worried that eating this fruit would somehow make the picture come to life inside me. Finally, hoping to avoid a fuss, I bit into the eyes and nose, taking out half of that face, and swallowed hard. I had fallen into magical thinking being around Sor again.

I hoped we were done, but Alma reached over and took another apple from the bowl. This one had a brown spot. Again we watched her carve. When she was done she set it on the table so that the face confronted me. I wanted to imagine it was someone else. Liz, perhaps. The young Liz I met when I worked for Sor that summer—I would have felt comforted thinking over that time. But I was looking at Mona's face. The rotten spot covered her eyes like a dark mask with holes cut out.

The heat of the food sitting in my stomach traveled into my skin and blanketed my entire body. "Who is this?" I asked Alma, as if I might hear something different from her.

"That's the truth teller. Now, go sit on the porch for a while," Alma said.

I felt disoriented, barely able to hear what she said next until she got to "Just don't let your uncle drink too much. The doctors want him strong for the surgery."

This was the first time any of us had spoken of his heart, and Sor's response was to pull a bottle from the liquor cabinet and set up three glasses despite Alma's grimace. He poured one drink for Alma that he left on the table. I offered to help with the cleanup, but she shooed me away.

It was still light out, and the humidity rose up, building into fresh clouds. Sor and I settled on the porch, and the dogs got up and shifted but seemed content to guard the house in a dog stupor. Insects sounded in the fields. A few other homes were spread out along the road we had come down, with another road off in the distance. "Alma has a small business selling dollhouse furniture," he said. "And that's doing well enough. She has a good eye and sound business sense, and we own our house outright." They kept a vegetable garden going all year, and Sor said once he was on the other side of this medical business he could always pick up some kind of work.

"You worried?" I asked. "About the surgery?"

"Alma has a friend, a nurse over at the hospital. She thinks I'm in good hands. We'll see what fate has to say about it."

My uncle stretched his legs out, took a pack of cigarettes from his shirt pocket, and offered me one. I thought about saying something. *But what do you say to a relative you haven't seen in over twenty years?* It's not like you can start lecturing. Maybe if I were going in for a quadruple bypass, I'd want a cigarette. I lit the match.

"What was that business with the apple?" I asked.

"I'm guessing it looked like someone in your family," Sor said. "Maybe someone who has some truth to tell you."

"I don't know about that, but it looked like Mona."

"Alma must have found a photograph in your wallet."

I reached for my back pocket.

"It'll be on your nightstand in the girls' room, don't worry."

"My aunt pickpocketed me?"

"Did I ever tell you about Rubber Woman? She was with the first circus I joined."

"I don't think so."

"She liked to tell the audience that mystics had hypnotized her and turned her bones to rubber. I had never seen a better contortionist. Truth was, she was double-jointed and knew some yoga. But I kept thinking there was something more. Then someone told me. She had had two of her lower ribs removed."

"You're making that up."

"And the man with ten thousand eyes. I told you about him, right?"

"No." I laughed.

"He stood in a spotlight in the middle of this stage set up in a big old sideshow. His assistant blindfolded him and asked three people to come up and check that the blindfold was secure. The lights dimmed and the room filled with eyes, faintly glowing eyes everywhere. He had an assistant out in the audience who asked people to hold up certain objects or photographs. He described them with accuracy."

"That's just hidden microphones."

"And the eyes?"

"Monofilament."

"Wrong era."

"Wire or string, I don't know."

"Ten thousand eyes on wire or string that you don't see when you enter the tent? Eyes that open and close?"

"Good old smoke and mirrors."

"Okay, so Alma pickpockets you when you walk through the door, and she works with the pictures in your wallet when she's in the kitchen, and she listens to everything you're willing to divulge about your life, and she studies your physicality with great care, and she looks at the suit you're swimming in, and she thinks about your age and the gray that's taking over your hair, and all the while you think she's just serving up enchiladas and making small talk ..."

"Exactly."

"What I'm saying is there's all of that and there's the part I can't discern, no matter how many times she does it. She might have cut Liz's face into the apple or Lola's. But she knew it had to be Mona's. And by your reaction ..."

I took a long drag and watched the smoke sit in the heavy air for a moment.

"Your wife says you're working for a big insurance firm up in New Jersey."

I watched a car go past on the distant road. "That's right," I said.

"But we both know that isn't so."

I felt a little winded when he said this and tipped my whiskey back. He filled my glass again.

"You're standing all day and walking all night," he said, eyeing my shoes. "And you're feeling sick and lonely for home, and what's worse, you're starting to feel sorry for yourself. I'd take you on the road with me, but I think those days are over." He grew quiet, and I knew there was more. "Your real concerns aren't about money, are they?" he finally said.

I laughed. "Sor, I—"

"I know you aren't making ends meet. But you've been wrestling with something else for a while now. You might as well tell me."

I didn't know what to say.

"You might think that summer when we were on the road together was a small thing. But to me it was like having a son around. I love my girls, don't get me wrong, but I always hoped we'd have more time to spend together, you and me."

"It wasn't a small thing, Sor."

"I'm waiting, then."

"Not that I believe any of this circus magic."

"'Course not," he said and took a sip of whiskey.

"Mona and I became distant long before I left—well, she did anyway—and I think that's had an effect on the marriage. Mona's a serious sleepwalker. With Lola to look after and Liz's work, I know this business of staying up late worrying over Mona has frayed her nerves." I shifted in my chair and considered the sudden drop in light, the cars on the road turning on their headlights.

"Your mother said you walked in your sleep for a while."

"I don't remember that," I said. "Huh. You know, we keep thinking Mona will walk out the door into traffic."

The outside light came on, and we heard Alma's footsteps. Moths began to circle the light. She set out food and a fresh bowl of water for the dogs. They rushed to greet her, and then she went back inside. We heard the clatter of dishes and water running in the sink.

"Mona and I were in a car accident when she was nine. Liz needed us out of the house for the day, so I took Mona over to the racetrack with me. Just something to do. She loved looking at the horses. I hit a long shot. So I took her out for burgers and a malted to celebrate, and we headed home. She was sitting in the front seat when it happened. I think the impact scared her more than anything. But since we weren't really hurt I told Mona it was probably best not to tell her mother, that it might upset her since Liz was pregnant. Mona seemed to understand."

Sor topped off our drinks again.

"It wasn't long after that that she began to sleepwalk. And then she just pulled away. It was all about her mom and her friends— everybody and everything else. ... I was patient. But she never changed back."

He looked at me like I had left something out. But that was Sor, always lifting up rugs, looking for more. "I can tell you, from raising my own girls," he said, "that they can make a turn at a certain point, either toward the father or mother. If it's the mother, they start mimicking and looking for secrets and advice and ways to be—even if they fight with their mother. They're a tribe, and we're not members. It's possible you've let this worry take over without realizing it."

"Maybe you're right," I said.

"It's easy to think that everything around you is about one moment, one event, but you know life isn't like that. You need to be strong for your family, Richard, clearheaded. Tell me what happens when Mona sleepwalks."

"She gets up in the middle of the night, and sometimes she just goes into the hallway and stares at the photographs there. Sometimes she goes into the kitchen. I mean, she did when we had the house." I began to feel a relief, talking with Sor. I let the whiskey ease my way. "She starts a funny conversation with herself, and at first I tried to answer, but they say not to wake a sleepwalker, so I just listen and watch to make sure she's okay and that she gets back into bed. I've asked if she remembers anything, but she just shakes her head. Liz says Mona *flies* in her dreams. You know, like flying through the air. And she claims she wakes up in a new spot from the place where she fell asleep."

"I loved a woman once who flew at night ..."

I gave him a look, and he laughed.

"You can be as skeptical as you want, but that won't help you understand your daughter. I read a good deal on this subject at one time. In fact you might say I made a study of it. I learned that some Tibetans believe in mystics and *dakinis* that move across the sky. And some Native Americans and Hindus, they have flyers. Now, the Babylonians ..."

"The *Babylonians?*"

"They thought we had a *light* body that could slip out of our *heavy* body," he said, tapping his chest to signify what he meant by heavy. "And that light body just takes off into the air. There's a whole world of people who believe they can fly from one place to another, dreaming or otherwise. Some of them end up in the carnival or circus. You know, they have a hard time fitting in the everyday world."

"Okay, I'll bite. Where did this girlfriend of yours go?"

"Her name was Donna, a real sweet woman who worked with a stage magician. We spent a couple of winters together. She helped me make the disappearing cabinet for you."

"Ah, the cabinet."

"A few states over her mother had been placed in a convalescent home—she had Donna pretty late in life. The sister lived nearby, so her mother was looked after, but Donna couldn't get back there very often. So Donna would fly off and sit with her mother at night. She told me when we were breaking up that she sometimes visited an old boyfriend she couldn't get over. I suspected as much, but what can you do?"

I really loved this old guy.

"On one of those nights I happened to reach over, and she was gone. I checked under the bed, all the closets. The windows were locked, and the front door had a chain lock in place. She had told me if this ever happened—if she went missing in the middle of the night—I should go back to sleep and not worry. But I couldn't. I drove around the neighborhood for an hour or more and came back and checked every corner of that house again, securing the chain lock. I stayed up on the couch into the early hours. When the sun came up I was about to get on the phone and call her friends, call the police. Then I heard someone in the bedroom. There was Donna, sitting up in bed, still in her nightgown, cheerful as ever."

"I swear you make this stuff up," I said.

"If you're struggling, maybe you'll appreciate this one since it was documented in a famous journal. I have the issue if you need proof. A man in Ohio left his body one night and *projected* himself into his mother's living room three towns over. He saw her watching a television show, and it was the very first episode of a new series. A while later he woke up back in his body in his own house, and he called his mother and described everything that happened in the show and what she had for dinner and who she talked to on the phone. And every last thing he described was correct."

"He could have watched the previews," I said. "And maybe she ate the same meal every night and the only other person she talked to was her cousin who called at the same time day in and day out."

"I don't think you ever really got that carnies, circus people—everyone from the grinders to the joeys to the bally—we're a different breed. We depend on that one thing that can't be easily explained. We feed off it. That's our stock in trade. Just like any artist out there. That's the thing you were drawn to when you met Elizabeth. And now you have a full-grown daughter who sees the world differently than you. She's probably got as much wonder as your little one—even if she has some bitterness or anger. Her real world is about mystery. She hasn't shut down. Not yet anyway."

I felt stung by his last remark and tried to shrug it off. "Most mysteries can be figured out," I said.

"I would give anything to send you back in time so you could watch Michelangelo paint the Sistine Chapel." Sor rose to his feet and then stopped for a moment as if there was a pain shooting straight down through him. "So, I should demonstrate how to operate our crazy shower before we hit the hay."

I followed him inside. It wasn't just the reversed hot and cold knobs. Sor had to show me what to do with the giant insects that had come up through the drain. "Welcome to Clewiston," he said as he dumped them into a bucket they kept under the sink filled with some kind of noxious liquid.

Sor and Alma turned in early, and I did as well after a very short shower. There were pennants and trophies and photographs from my cousins' high school years in the bedroom where I slept. Both twin beds sagged in the middle. I picked the one closest to the window. There wasn't any AC.

It was strange to be in a bed in a bedroom. I had planned on writing a letter to Liz, but it felt as if a lifetime of fatigue pulled back the covers so I could slip in. As soon as I turned on my side and got comfortable, a breeze picked up for the first time all day. My door opened slightly and just as quick it clicked shut. Open, shut, open, shut. I couldn't move to do anything about it. I couldn't even open my eyes. Then I was out.

I woke in the middle of the night when the door banged shut. It was so loud it felt like it slammed inside my head.

I sat up and there was Mona. She was floating in the air.

The walls, the bedding, even Mona and the dress she wore—everything was blue. She hovered there with her hair and dress fluttering, wind traveling through the room. She was barefoot and looked tired, as if she had come a long way. I felt certain she had something to tell me. I waited. She began to open her mouth. I waited for that one thing. But then, before I could reach out and stop her, she disappeared.

I couldn't sleep the rest of the night.

Mona

I often looked out at the trains, at the platform lights that mesmerized in order to get to sleep. As I drifted one night I saw a man on the tracks.

Maintenance crews went out to check ties and repair sections of rail, but I had never seen them work solo. Then I got it, the vest, the way he stood, the shape of his head with that short-cropped hair. I turned the music off and sat up. I grabbed my camera with the telephoto.

Maybe Ajay had climbed up the support beams, if that was possible, or jumped off the platform onto the rails. There was the third rail of course. Just looking at the warning sign between the tracks made me uneasy.

On the other side of our walled yard was an underpass. In the daylight you could see the shimmer of broken bottles, the husk of a TV, old mattresses, and snow heaped up on the western side, pushed there by the wind. At night the underpass was pitch black, as it was now. The trains came every five minutes or so, but I wasn't sure when the last one went through the side where he stood. He looked directly at my window.

I turned my bedside light on, shot out of bed, and made big arm movements, trying to get him to move off. He waved back, as if he thought I was saying hello. I felt the vibration and saw the lights of the northbound train. He was on the northbound side. It was still far enough away, but he wasn't looking at it. I tried to get the window up to shout to him, but it was stuck, ice built up around the bottom edge. I was frantic to pry it open, pulling and pulling on it.

I heard a scream and looked up again. Maybe it was one of those false sounds produced by the train, the way you can hear the phone ring when you run a blow dryer, but he was gone. The train was passing through that same section of rail.

I rushed downstairs and knocked on Cynthia's door. I found her with a plastic bag on her head, dying her hair again. I grabbed her by the arms and said, "He's been hit!"

"Slow down. Who's been hit?"

I pulled her into her bedroom. Raising the blind, we peered as far as we could see in both directions. "Ajay."

"You didn't actually *see* it happen, right?"

"He was standing out on the tracks. When I looked away ..."

"See any trains stopped? Hear any alarms? Sirens?" she asked. "It's a big deal when they hit someone. You'll know, believe me," Cynthia said.

The radiators were banging hard, the heat dizzying.

"You sure?" I said.

"Yes, I'm sure."

In the kitchen she grabbed a burning herbal smoke out of the ashtray and took a drag. Studying me for a moment, she said, "What do you think he's up to?"

Another train passed, and I looked at a cluster of Hummels as they quavered on the shelf next to the sink. Cynthia was big on those figurines of children that hang out laundry on clotheslines, glide in skates, swing baskets on their arms. I think she liked the idea that they came close to breaking from the vibration but somehow endured. She still hoped to have her own child with Luke or at least share Colin, his son.

"Just steer clear of the grandfather," Cynthia said.

"I'll be gone by summer. Besides, Nitro keeps me busy."

She gave me a sympathetic look. "Nitro."

"Yeah, well ... ."

Cynthia nudged a slim book across the table. It had a plain black cover and gilt edges. "Better look through the section on dream analysis. Nitro's been messing with you. When I read it I realized Luke is the train in my nightmares."

"And that makes you the tunnel?"

"Riotous," she said.

Opening the cover, she thumbed through the pages, then read aloud, "An *astral body* is something like the vapors formed by a pot of brewing coffee. The aroma travels into the room, and if there's an open window, it drifts away. The secret is in learning how to open the window."

"What if your window is frozen shut?" I said.

"Exactly. I've tried every damn exercise in the book."

"And?"

"I tried the one where you walk through walls."

"You're cracking me up," I said.

She handed me the book again. "Flip to the back."

"You were trying to get through lathe and plaster?"

"I tried levitation. I even tried the one where you project yourself into a cemetery."

"Calvary?" I asked. Mount Calvary was our neighborhood cemetery, around the curve on Sheridan, separating Chicago from Evanston. My father's parents and grandparents were buried there. You could see one corner of it from our front windows.

"I wanted to go to the one near Luke's apartment in Brooklyn," she said. Then she took the book out of my hands and pitched it across the room. Her eyes began to swim. "Children. Children are natural flyers in their dreams," she said and broke down a little.

But the cooking timer went off, and she pulled herself together and said, "I'm thinking of going pink this time. You know, that *Lost in Translation* look."

"That was a wig," I said.

"Oh, I caught up with my boss. He's going to talk with you about the job as soon as he picks a day for you to come in. You should go online and learn every comic book figure that's ever lived. I'll send you some sites."

"I know how to run a cash register," I offered.

"Tell him that, and make your eyes big and dark like you're starving for something, maybe conversation. He loves women who are capable but bereft in some way."

The timer went off, and Cynthia said, "I better get this dye out. A friend of mine had all of her hair break off when she left it in too long. We could watch that ghost-hunter show, and I could make a fresh pot of coffee when I'm done. It might help you sleep. Does me."

But I was too tired to stay up to get tired in order to fall asleep.

The show we sometimes watched was about people chasing ghosts or other *disembodied entities* around abandoned prisons and hospitals and old hotels. The hunters tried to spot them with ultra-violet equipment, laser beams, and EMF meters. Sometimes they talked cruelly to the spirits to get them to move a chair or blow cold air down someone's neck. That's how they provided *solid proof* to the home audience that entities were present. Members of *the team*, the hunters, shivered and leapt around and wedged themselves into narrow crawl spaces where rusting pipes oozed foul-looking stuff. Sometimes a team member became so agitated and frightened he'd yell, *Holy shit!* or *Crap!* And that was bleeped out. One guy was known to run like a chicken with his head cut off when he got scared. Always good for a laugh.

The ghosts in my life needed no detection equipment. They were all out in the open. I liked that my father's disembodied spirit hovered far away. The ghosting of my mother was a different matter. When she had her studio she used to come in from the workshop after a couple of hours of welding or burnishing with that look of deep contentment. Sweaty and flecked with grime or metal dust, she would grab a cold drink and get right back out there. After Lola became a toddler and napped less often, it wasn't enough to have a baby monitor. Mom's time was more cut up, but she often set up little projects for Lola in her playpen in the studio while she sketched and planned and worked on grants or artist notes, as she had with me. She gave to us and to her work in a way that was unlimited.

But in the Chicago apartment she became little more than raw, chafed energy, and I sometimes felt I was walking through her to get to where I needed to go. I worried that she would get worse if she couldn't find a way to sculpt again.

When I got upstairs and glanced at Lily's door on the way to mine, I thought about her negatives and how I needed to find another moment when both she and my family were out.

It was almost two in the morning when I pulled my covers off the floor and settled in. I watched YouTube videos of teens jumping down between subway tracks in New York City and scrambling back up before the trains arrived at the stations. I guess this had become a thing. But Ajay was older and didn't strike me as a daredevil. He was taking care of an elderly family member and going to architecture school. You can lose balance or fall or get pushed, but he had been right there, across from my window, waving. I turned into my pillow like a dial clicking one more notch toward sleep.

Usually if Mom couldn't sleep she waited out the night with a pillow slumped halfway over her head, or she turned the TV on low or ate something while staring at the sink. As she nudged my door open now, I watched the photos I had pinned to my wall, each with a single pushpin, lift and settle in the draft. My mother stood there as if she wasn't sure of her purpose. I couldn't see her face that well in the platform lights. I reached for the bedside lamp, but she said, "Please don't."

"Did you catch another mouse?" I said. We had had a steady run of rats that she preferred to call mice. I had gotten pretty good at placing smears of peanut butter on traps and setting the wires. Those were the only times I saw her get out of control. The last time she caught one she went on and on: *I can't believe I'm making you and Lola live in a rodent-infested apartment by the elevated trains. I can't believe ... I ...* It seemed more productive after that if I set the traps and emptied them when necessary.

"No. I hope we're done with them for a while," she said. "Were you down at Cynthia's?"

"I couldn't sleep."

She drew the desk chair over. I watched the light on her face from the L. It made me think of the light from an arc welder, only softer, the way light can hit a face in old movies. She rubbed her lips with one of her thumbs, and I knew she had something difficult to say. I should have taken a picture of her like that. I should have blown it up to understand what I couldn't know. Because sometimes, even when she told me what was going on, I was certain there was something else sitting just behind that admission, something hidden behind her bones.

"The newspaper is folding. I didn't want to worry you and Lola.

But I found something else. Another job." She had been trying to get a spot at a gallery for a long time, but her face didn't reflect art gallery or a sense of relief. "I'm going to be cleaning out foreclosed homes. They're called *trashouts*. You know, go through, get rid of any furniture, arrange to have appliances bolted down, repairs made, that kind of thing."

We both knew what *that kind of thing* was: every last piece of crap someone losing their home was happy to leave for the lending agency that had fucked them over. It was the kind of garbage one cooked for the banks, for Wall Street. It was the trash too many of us wished we could deliver to their doorsteps. I had read that some people left messages written in their own excrement on the walls on their way out.

When I saw her face change in that light, in that lousy blue light, I realized I had to be careful with what I said.

"You might as well hear all of it, but don't tell Lola, not yet. I'm taking a leave of absence from school." She ran the flat of her hand over a stretch of sheet, like this might iron something out. "I have to build up our reserves."

"Don't do this," I said. Then I mentioned her brother. Surely Uncle Hal could loan her enough so she could stay in the program.

"Maybe if it were just Hal by himself, I don't know," she said.

This was the way we talked about his second wife, without using her name. "They own *three* homes," I said. "They go to Europe every spring, Aspen every winter, and they own how many Mercedes?"

"I don't know," she said. Looking at the clock now, she began to rub my arms, as if I were cold. "God. And you with work tomorrow. Everything okay there?"

"Yes. And I'm getting an interview at the comic book store."

"Just don't overdo, you promise?"

"I'm fine."

"I love what you did with this print," she said, nodding toward one of Anna Lily's photos I had forgotten to put away.

She had this saying when the worst events hit: *At least I'll get a sculpture out of it.* And maybe that's when she was at her most beautiful—when she poured everything she had into her art. She had the capacity to let almost everything else flee from her when she worked, like a flock of birds rushing out of a canyon. I hoped she would say that to me now, but she was probably too tired.

"It's a friend's work. I was just thinking about her dodging technique."

"She's crazy good like you."

I shifted against my pillow, and before I had a chance to, she brought the covers up along my shoulder line and kissed me goodnight, which she hadn't done in years. I said without hesitation that I loved her, and she said the same thing to me.

Mom had an alarm clock that began with a low-pitched tone and gradually emitted a piercing noise intended to take out the hearing of all within range. Despite it reaching the highest octave she wasn't pushing the button down.

"Why isn't Mom getting up?" Lola asked, coming into my room.

"She had trouble sleeping last night."

"I had trouble sleeping last night. I better stay home."

"School as usual today. Mom will be up soon."

After I punched Mom's snooze button I checked the kitchen cabinets. We were out of Lola's favorite cereal. She didn't like these disruptions to her routine.

"I'm going to wear the same exact clothes I wore yesterday to school," Lola said with that brand of defiance I had come to love in her. It drove me nuts when it surfaced, of course, but I couldn't imagine how she would make it in this world without it. That's what I wished for Mom—that she had more of that fierceness.

When Lola was dropping bits of egg down her throat with her head tilted back, which had something to do with her affection for seals, I went into the bathroom. I quickly buried her undies from yesterday in the bottom of the hamper and told her I couldn't find them, so she'd have to wear fresh ones. As soon as she was dressed, Mom came around the corner of her folding screen and said, "I can't believe I slept that long. What's this?" she said, looking at Lola's outfit. "Is this from yesterday? Did I sleep … backward?"

This got a quizzical look and finally a good laugh out of Lola.

And there it was—my mother's brave face—an image I also needed to capture on film.

Mom was going to meet her new boss that morning to get detailed instructions and keys to the first three homes on her list of trashouts. She was evasive when I asked where the first batch was located, saying that she would have her phone, as if automatic dial would keep her from being attacked or that no one would ever steal her phone. I thought she might cave under the pressure. Geary had said that sometimes the ones who consistently manage are the ones who crack the hardest. He was talking about Diane Arbus and her strange and remarkable images. She had two daughters and kept everything going until she couldn't.

I got into Geary's early. He was still upstairs with his wife, Lettie, having a long breakfast. His studio in that old brick firehouse had a roll-up door that had gone off its track years ago, lodging it permanently shut. There was a smaller door along the side. He had worked on that place little by little with the help of friends, hoping the fire inspectors wouldn't bring it down. It had few windows at street level, and the ones that were there were painted over with black paint on the inside. The main bank of windows was higher up and provided plenty of natural light.

Geary was a genius when it came to black-and-white photography. He had worked with Gordon Parks and done prints for Avedon, but he never bragged about stuff like that. Geary didn't have many notable shows to his name. Always too busy supporting his family, and then the extra hurdles of being black in a mostly white game. But a lot of photographers knew his work, and several fashion photographers used him for print work. He did a lot of C-prints. They knew him as a master printer, and they sought him out in that old building in Evanston. Work came from as far away as New York and Los Angeles.

If you were a former student of his—back when he was at the high school—and you had stayed with photography and shown any kind of passion for it, he would help with your portfolio and never send a bill. If you lost one of your parents, he would stand at the graveside with you. His kids were grown, the two who had survived.

I had interned at his studio until he hired me. When he learned I couldn't go to college for a while, he said over time I would learn what I needed working with him. Sometimes, especially when he sensed I was going through a particularly rough patch, he put on a jazz LP from his giant collection and gave me technical assignments to work out. To the sound of Nina Simone or Miles Davis everything became light source and aperture. We worked on a platinum palladium print together for one client.

After I printed another shot of Lily's I went through half a box of photo paper trying to print one particular image from my childhood. I had found some unmarked negatives that might have been Mom's but might have been someone else's, maybe a friend's or a relative's. In the print I was eight years old and stood in the middle of our old street in Evanston on a busy Halloween night. There were trick-or-treaters on porches and up and down the sidewalk. My father stood a few feet away. He looked so young, his face without a line. I stood in a horse costume under a streetlight as if I was the star of something.

Geary got out his glasses and bent over the table. "There's a kind of tragedy to your horse. I like the way the nose has gotten pushed in a little. And how your father is breathing out a cloud of steam but you aren't. Burn this area more," he said, pointing to a spot I should have considered. "Maybe all of a second's worth."

"I remember stopping in the middle of the street, feeling tired and ready to go home. It was a really cold Halloween. But I forgot how my father looked in this picture."

Geary took the print out of my hands and said, "The funny thing about his expression is that he looks devoted to you, yet he isn't rushing to get you out of the street. You can see the lights of a car coming. And the person taking the shot…Makes me think of war photography, recording but not intervening."

I didn't know what to say when Geary saw the things I missed in my own life. But I was used to the fact that he rarely paid direct compliments. The flattery was the time he spent dropping his own work to help you arrive at yours.

Richard

Alma sent us off with a bag full of foil-wrapped burritos. I slipped them under the bench seat in the cab of the pickup and put the fishing and camp gear in the truck bed, following Sor's directions. Alma clearly didn't want him to go, but Sor said he was taking his nephew fishing.

When he wasn't looking she pulled me aside and handed me a list of hospitals around the southern half of the state circled on a highway map just in case. I assured her I would keep an eye out. Sor tossed me the keys, and Alma stood on the porch watching us go. I double-checked to make sure my wallet was in my pocket before I pulled away.

I didn't question the old guy when he directed me to head east along the southern tip of Lake Okeechobee. Handing me a thermos of iced coffee, he said it would come in handy with the AC broken. He pointed out the window-washer fluid behind the seat in case I had to pull over to fill the reservoir. We went past the thirty-foot-tall concrete dike that surrounded most of the lake, and he told me something about the floods that had prompted it. I didn't know—if I lived around there—whether I'd rather be protected from the lake or have a chance to see it. Sor said you could get to it from a place called Fisheating Creek, though mostly the lake was enclosed. You could drive along the top of the dike for a while, but there was no walking up to the edge to taste it, no throwing yourself in to shake off the heat in a normal way. Somehow a big, shallow lake behind a wall seemed like a useless piece of business.

After a while Sor grew quiet and looked out at the landscape.

"I always hoped you'd come down this way at some point. I could have shown you some real fishing. You do much camping?"

"Liz likes the state parks—you know, anyplace with a shower. One time we were at Yellowstone. I think Mona was eight. While her mother stayed at the campsite reading a book, Mona and I went to see Old Faithful for a second time. When we got there we found a group of people watching a car in the parking lot with binoculars and cameras. A man was trying to coax a bear into the front seat of his car on the driver's side. His wife was sitting on the passenger side. He wanted to get a photo of the two of them together."

"No end to crazy," Sor said.

"I meant to ask a ranger what happened, but we left early the next day, so I never found out. I think that was our last camping trip. You know, life just takes over."

When we got to the town of South Bay Sor directed me to a road that sent us due north through the heart of Belle Glade. Shuttered homes, closed gas stations, and small nameless markets came into view. Sugarcane filled the plains and grew up ten feet tall along the road, the smell of the plants and smoke and a dark molasses scent wafted through the open windows of the truck. Migrant workers busted their backs in the heat.

"So I was thinking about what you told me yesterday, about how you and Mona got in an accident once." He uncapped the thermos, filled the cup halfway, and passed it to me. Keeping one hand on the wheel, I took a long draw.

I had already worked up quite a sweat in that heat. "You aren't worried about my driving, are you?"

"No, but it got me thinking. It must have been a bad one."

I nodded and handed him the drained cup. Then I got the wipers and fluid going. He was right about the insects. I began to hear a loud buzzing. A wasp started dancing along the dash. I glanced over at Sor, who was making quite a study of me.

"It's funny how we're born with so many parts," he said. "The one that prepares for the best and the one that prepares for the worst; the one that tries to get things right, the one that's our own undoing; the one that wants to fit in and have everyone look up to us, the one that's ready to run free and do whatever it damn well pleases."

I remembered the way he used to go off on these rambles. I knew what he was doing.

"I have a feeling there's one part of you that would be relieved to say what happened that day. The part you can't explain away."

Until that moment I hadn't understood that the radio in the truck was on. The volume was so low it made me think of the way Liz went to sleep to the radio or the television. I came in late some nights and watched her in the dim light from the bathroom, curled on her side, the radio glowing. I should never have left her.

"It was a hit-and-run," I said.

"And Mona was sitting up front with you."

"That's right."

"Did she get hurt?"

"Mona was just a bean sprout then. I should have had her in the back. I stuck my arm out and her head hit my arm and my arm hit the dash and after that I kept thinking if I hadn't had that reflex ...
... It scared the hell out of me."

"I can see why a nine-year-old would struggle with something like that. Not just the impact but the idea of someone driving off that way." Sor kind of laughed. "If only we could protect them from everything by sticking out an arm."

"I went off," I said, "thinking this new job was going to make everything right, and all I end up doing is abandoning them and tanking financially. Mona's not in college; Lola barely knows who I am; Liz keeps trying to patch together anything she can to make ends meet; the house is gone."

"I understand. I've known my share of hard times. The best thing is to start fresh when you get back. And remember, Mona is older now. She's had to shoulder real responsibility. Treat her with respect, and she'll come round. Turn at the next stop and head east until we hit the town of Loxahatchee. Road's a straight shot from here. They ever catch the driver ... of that hit-and-run?"

I felt the heat overtake me. "No, they never did," I said and asked Sor to pour me another cup of iced coffee.

Handing it my way, he said, "Some people get away with murder." And then he was tired, like a child excited by a trip for the first stretch but quick to nod off from the motion of the car, the humidity.

"Wake me up when we get there," he said and leaned back. He put the brim of his hat down and dropped off.

Loxahatchee is the rural, westernmost portion of West Palm Beach County. I kept an eye out for a sign to a fishing hole. After a while Sor woke up again, as if he had heard an alarm go off.

We traveled down a long private road that ran through a vast citrus orchard and pulled up to a home with a porch that wrapped three-quarters of the way around it. The driveway spit gravel as we came to a stop. We parked under the shade of a live oak. There were various outbuildings on a property that stretched for miles into the distance, and it felt good to be firmly in the shade.

Sor was alert now, but he looked tired, more than he had the day before. When he told me to grab my gear he said, "Whatever you do, don't act surprised."

"About what?" I asked, but he hushed me and knocked at the door.

When it opened I was introduced to a woman in a white button-down shirt with a silver-and-turquoise necklace, jeans, and hand-tooled boots. She could have been an older fashion or cosmetics model. Her name was Honey. This was my first time in that part of the state, in this house, but I paused for a moment to let a strong feeling of déjà vu drift through. Squinting hard at me, she finally broke into a smile and grabbed me tight. In a ringing Florida accent she said, "Let's break out the Jack Daniels."

Sor was already lining up glasses on a rolling drink cart, fishing cubes out of the silver ice bucket. I sat down on a leather sofa and put my feet up on one of the cushy ottomans. Whoever Honey was, she clearly lived a comfortable life. I was reminded of a home in the architectural magazine where Liz's sculpture had appeared, with the addition of a couple of snakeskins stretched on the walls.

Sor and Honey nestled in close on the couch opposite mine. She gave him a kiss on the mouth, straightened his collar, then sat back. "So tell me how my nephew's getting on," she said, gazing directly at me.

I had one of those classic moments of turning and looking around to see if someone had entered the room. Sor winked at me and said, "Don't be shy."

I was trying to puzzle out the family tree, but maybe my brain had soaked up too much heat on the drive over. Soon Honey had us up and walking around the house with our drinks, stopping in the library to see the wall of family photos. The children, three girls, all blondes like Honey, were grown and settled elsewhere. I saw that Sor figured prominently in many of the groupings. The house and the property had been in her family for generations, she said, and she was proud that her yields were almost as big in blood oranges now as they were in navels.

We went down a wide hallway. Here she had a row of framed black-and-white photographs that I found a little off-putting for all of my uncle's stories. Honey told me the titles as I stopped at each one. "*Albino Sword Swallower; Circus Fat Lady with her Dog, Troubles; Tattooed Man at Carnival; Hermaphrodite with Dog ...* You know Arbus's work?" she said.

"I'm sure my daughter Mona does."

"We'll expect you to come down and pay us a real visit with the whole family, then. Married to the man thirty years and this is the first time we're meeting." She laughed.

And then I had to laugh too ... and not look surprised.

"Love of my life," Sor said, squeezing her around the middle.

I wanted to grab the old man and pull him aside, but Honey was a constant presence. None of us fished that day, but we talked about citrus, and how carnivals were changing, and some of the travels Honey had made over the years. We had a light luncheon, then a key lime pie and good strong espresso. We watched the windows lighten and darken as the workers out in the orchards quit work for the day. Sor seemed as comfortable in this state of abundance as he did in Alma's modest habitat.

When evening came and another meal was finished, Sor showed me a bedroom on the second floor that looked out over the groves. I had my own bathroom, and there was a tub with jets that could do just about anything but pound away my confusion now that I understood that my uncle was a bigamist.

"Have a good long soak."

"Hold on. Help me understand," I said.

Sor and I sat down across from each other on the twin beds. "Not much to explain, really. Alma came up from Mexico years ago. We'd act like a couple when we came off the road—you know. She was doing craft fairs, and of course I was a carny by then. When I heard the INS was out for her, I stepped up. We didn't plan our first girl, but somehow we settled in. Alma is salt of the earth, and I love her dearly."

"And ..."

"And then I was going through a particularly rough time—maybe not too different from what you're going through now—and she did everything she could to get me to go see this palm reader named Honey over in Loxahatchee."

"But you've said Alma has a way of reading people. ..."

"You know, it's like doctors, they like to consult one another. And Alma can be pretty assertive when she wants to be. Before I knew it I was looking into Honey's eyes, and what do you do when you know, without a doubt, that you've met the one? Honey was willing to take me whole cloth. She knew about Alma, so we never could get married, but we lived our own kind of common-law marriage."

"So they both know?"

He shook his head. "Alma's too possessive, and I'm afraid she has a devotion to the pope. Divorce would have been too hard for her. There were times I came close to telling her. I might have breathed easier if I had. You know, you read about these men who have two families and how it's just second nature to them. They have it all worked out in their minds. But it's never been that way for me. I guess all I can say is that some secrets keep our families safe and some cause too much sorrow."

I didn't realize I had my mouth open until a small bug flew in, maybe a mosquito, and I began to cough and couldn't stop coughing. Sor went into the bathroom and ran the tap.

I sat dumbly there after draining the glass, not knowing what to say.

"Join us downstairs when you're ready for a nightcap," he said. "I'll show you around the property tomorrow and we'll talk some more."

It was pitch black out when I came down to the living room. I had written a letter to Liz after a long soak. Sor and Honey were sitting at the dining table. The surface had been stripped bare except for a bottle of cognac and three glasses.

"You've joined the world of the living," Sor said.

I dropped into a chair across from Honey and rested my hands on the table. They were rubbery and wrinkled from the bath. She poured the drinks. We talked about her grove manager, who had a son with cancer. They were thinking about the best way to help the family. When I expressed my sympathies, Honey reached over and held my hands, as if to say she appreciated my good thoughts. I was surprised when she asked to look at my palms.

I laughed and said, "I think I soaked too long."

"She wants to read your lines," Sor said.

I don't know if I had ever said this outright to Sor, but just about anything related to divining the future, well, that stuff spooks me. It's not that I necessarily believe any of it, but it's possible for a prediction to sit in the back of your brain and work on you over time. I've seen that happen to people. I had one client who tripled her life insurance policy after talking with an astrologer.

"Your immediate dilemma is family and home," Honey said.

I wasn't going to spoil her moment, but if you know a man has been away from his family and his city for a long time, it didn't take a lot.

"As much as you want to be with the people who matter the most, you're strongly attracted to travel, exploration—maybe the idea of running off, running away. There's a woman who'd be happy to help you do just that if you decide to. But your biggest fear in life is about doors shutting and locking. She can't help you with that. You're worried that your wife will drift."

Sor must have realized what this was doing to me because he started to interrupt her.

Then I jumped up and said, "I'm going to get some air."

Outside a motion sensor clicked on and lights flooded the drive.

I began to walk, and the lights shut off after a while. I followed the line of the drive. It would be easy to keep going, and I began to understand how worn I was. The things that had fascinated me as a young man were too much for me now. The world of carnies and soothsayers, Alma's truth-telling apples, Honey's palm reading tricks. The light from the barn cast elongated shadows that looked like people lined up. My head was swimming.

Maybe it was the waves of heat coming off the drive, the cognac, or the night thick and oppressive with cicadas. I was pissed at Sor for getting me into this jam. What the hell would he say to his wives and children and grandchildren when all of them gathered at the hospital? Had I been invited down to speak on his behalf or worse, to referee? I considered Alma's survival hinging on the sale of dollhouse furniture. I didn't know why the old man was binding me up this way. I had my own troubles. My intestines began to twist.

I wasn't paying attention to how far I had gone when I was aware of the lights flaring up behind me. Turning and peering in the direction of the house, I saw Sor's figure in the entryway, waving for me to come back. I took my time at first, listening to the sound of my shoes and the low wind. It's possible I heard something like a snarl, though I didn't know what types of cats prowl in the Everglades, if any, and if they bother with citrus orchards. Peering into the dark, I wondered if it was only a wind machine starting up. I straightened and tried to formulate the conversation Sor and I might have to help him understand my limitations.

He left the spot of light and started to move toward me, and then he was running. I could see something was wrong, and I broke into a run too. I realized in that moment that there was no hat. Sor didn't exist without his hat. More sounds I didn't recognize echoed through the orange groves and up under the live oak. I couldn't run fast enough. It was Honey, not Sor, trying to reach me.

"I called an ambulance. Hurry."

Sor was slumped over the table, his hat knocked from his head. I checked his pulse, his breath. Nothing. I managed to shift him around so he was on the floor, on his back. I performed CPR.

The ambulance seemed to take forever, and when it finally arrived the siren came in long, slow stretches toward the house. Honey put her hand on my back, but I wouldn't stop until the EMT guys made me stop. I looked at his face drained of color, the thin wisps of white hair. I picked his hat off the floor and dropped it in the center of the table.

I grieved for him and for all the other losses. I missed my family too much, and I was deeply aware that everything can go in a second.

They transported his body to the nearest hospital, a small building marked clearly on the map Alma had supplied.

I talked Honey through the process of signing papers at the hospital. And in the long vigil I kept with her that night, while her daughters were flying in to be with her, she talked on and off and sometimes wept quietly or got up to look out the living room windows as if Sor was about to appear in the drive. I made coffee and rubbed her hands and listened.

I worried that in the next few days there would be not only a body to bury but also a man to somehow lay out and divide.

The next morning I made plans to break the news to Alma. I called my employer. I called the airlines to postpone my flight until after the funeral.

"I should tell you that my girls don't know about Alma," Honey said as she handed me a thermos of iced coffee the way Sor liked it. I nodded to say I understood.

When I got to the truck I realized Sor and I had forgotten the lunch Alma had packed. The cab was filled with flies and the stench of sour food. I was surprised some animal or other hadn't crawled up inside it. I found the trash barrels and then I got on the road, the hot air and bad smell running riot over me.

It was on the way back to Clewiston, in the smoke and raw sweetness of Belle Glade, past the boarded-up stores and homes, that I began to hear the roughness of Sor's voice in my head.

Alma was torn apart by his death. When she couldn't stop crying I convinced her to try one of his sleeping pills so she could lie down and get some rest. The house felt smaller than it had on my first visit, the air closer, and once again I was looking at their daughters' high school trophies from years back, their ruffled bedspreads.

I turned out the lights and spoke softly over the phone so Alma wouldn't arrest out of sleep in the other room. The walls were thin, and sounds carried easily through the open windows.

"Liz?" I said. "Sorry to call so late."

"What's wrong?" she said.

"Sor didn't make it. I'm going to stay for the funeral."

"You poor thing. Where are you?"

"With his wife, Alma, in Clewiston. Yesterday morning we were riding around in his truck, and now ..."

"I feel so awful saying this, and I do want to hear everything, but can I call you tomorrow? They've been working on the rails all day with heavy pneumatic equipment. I just haven't gotten any sleep, and I have to make a parent-teacher conference with Lola before school starts. It takes longer coming from Chicago, and ..."

"Yes, tomorrow, of course. I'll be eager to hear about Lola's report. You get some rest."

"I'm really sorry about Uncle Sor."

Slipping the phone into my pants pocket, I went as quietly as I could down the hall and through the living room. Smacking a leg on the coffee table, I stood there hunched over for a moment. I listened intently, but Alma didn't stir, and I was out the door, out under the stars, watching a car go by on the far road.

Edie had told me to call at any hour, but I must have woken her. "Richard," she said in a dreamy way.

"I should probably call tomorrow."

"Talk to me," she said.

"I want to hear what's going on with you," I said.

Edie told me about some minor trouble her son had gotten into at school and how her ex was only making things worse. She was taking a gardening class, and there was some thought about Europe next year, touring the grand gardens. Her sister had had a bad mammogram and was going in for a biopsy. Finally she said, "There are days when I wish I had become an astronaut."

"I don't—"

"So I could look at the Earth and gain some distance on things."

I told her about losing Sor and the discovery of the legal and common-law wives.

"I don't envy you telling Alma there's more than one of her," Edie said.

Eventually I got to the palm reading fiasco and the concept I'm afraid of: doors locking me out. "Or maybe it was *locking me in*," I said.

"Was she right?" Edie said.

"Probably. I don't know."

Edie said I sounded awfully tired and suggested I go back in and stretch out on the bed, where I could whisper to her.

I crept through the house again and up to the room where I was staying.

"Don't even bother to undress. Prop the pillows and put your ear against the phone so you don't have to hold it. I'll be here until you think you can fall asleep. Tell me anything. Or rest. Whatever you feel like. Imagine I'm curled around you. Imagine I'm holding you."

"I don't—"

"Shhh," she said. "I know."

I should have thought about the phone, burning up time, but I had lived for so long now as a careful man. I was bereft. And so I stopped and listened to Edie's voice and felt the air, maybe one degree under hot, push through the window, and I couldn't say anything. But I kept going over Sor's divided life. And what scared me was thinking maybe I knew what that's like.

I was torn down the middle and couldn't fit the parts together anymore. The boy who'd learned how to guess in a carnival midway was somehow supposed to be connected to the man about to bury his teacher. The good earner and the seller of cheap trinkets were one and the same. I was once a man who knew how to walk with a golf bag slung over one shoulder, joking about the good life. And now I would gladly take a job carrying anyone else's clubs. I would spend all day washing golf balls or hunt them in the rough to sell for pennies apiece.

It was still dark out when I heard a faint pulsing signal and realized Edie had hung up. I picked the phone up, and the light from the screen filled the room. I was startled to see Mona there in jeans and a T-shirt, a camera around her neck. She was looking through the desk drawers, searching the bookshelf, pulling books out and letting them drop to the floor. Finally she turned and saw me there. She came over and sat down next to me. I froze up.

"Mom is ..." she began in a clear, ringing voice. I lay still so I wouldn't miss a word.

"Mom is what, Mona?"

Her expression was unbroken.

"Mom is what?"

When Mona began to fade, I saw that the books were still on the shelves, the desk drawers shut. But I felt as if I had been gone through, rifled with. All that day my mind would return to the dream and the need to get home. It had been two full years.

Alma woke with a terrible headache. Her eyes were swollen and downcast when she came into the kitchen. She insisted on making the breakfast. She said she would call her daughters, arrange for a funeral home, and so forth. "I guess I should call the hospital first," she said.

Before she could ask which one, I said, "Everything happened so fast. I gave him CPR until the EMTs arrived. I had your list of hospitals."

"Where were you when it happened?"

I hesitated, and she saw I was wrestling. I knew she would find out soon enough. If some hospital worker didn't tell her, the medical records would. Honey had signed all the paperwork as his wife. I guess we hadn't thought that through very well. Alma squinted like the room had flooded with light when I told her there was someone else, another woman, another family.

"That's impossible," she said.

She asked *the woman's* name, and when I told her I believe Alma stopped breathing for a full minute.

Finally she spoke in a measured way. She told me she had been troubled by her father's death for many years. Her family had been *guest farmers*, itinerant workers, in the cane fields of Belle Glade. He had died of heatstroke when he wasn't allowed to have a drink of water all one day because of some minor infraction. He was working out in the summer sun until he dropped. She drove over to Loxahatchee to get some advice from this palm reader named Honey she had heard about. Alma said she wasn't expecting a rich woman to do her reading, but Honey seemed nice, offering her lemonade and little sandwiches when she arrived.

"She wouldn't accept any money, and she looked me directly in the eyes and told me my father had finished his time on earth and was on his way to heaven. It put my mind at ease, you know? I no longer saw him coming down the hallway at night or sitting out by the tree swing. The next week I sent Sorohan off with a homemade cake to return the kindness she had shown me and hoped she might be able to help him as well."

I didn't say anything, just listened.

"I don't know what kind of nephew you are," she said, as if she were finally able to steel herself for what was ahead, "taking my Sorohan away and coming back like this. But I want his body returned to me for a proper Catholic burial in Clewiston, and I want you to make all the arrangements with *the other person*. And then I will be happy never to see or hear from you again."

Mona

I had just pinned up some prints to dry—the drying machine was acting up again—when Geary asked me into his office, crowded with boxes of photo paper and chemicals and cameras. I looked at the winterscapes newly tacked on the bulletin board. The snow had been thoroughly represented again that year by his Saturday-afternoon students. Snow with a cluster of red berries on a twig, snow piled at the end of a drive with a shovel stuck in it, snow and the impressions left by sled runners, snow falling into Lake Michigan, snow landing on a boy's tongue.

"You look tired," he said.

"I'm tired of looking at snow," I said.

"There's a competition I'll be on you about. It carries cash awards for the winner and two runners-up. You need to be doing this kind of thing."

I don't know why I resisted.

And then he told me, as he often did, how great it was that I was investing the time to really learn print photography from film. Geary was always pushing against the digital tide despite being thick with digital equipment and computers, with two large-format printers. He wanted me to embrace the work of Weston and Cartier-Bresson, Parks and Avedon, Bourke-White. ... He said over and over that it was essential that I think *archival*. I believe *archival* was his favorite word.

As much as I loved the man, I wanted to say that the world is no longer archival. *We're apocalyptic now, Geary.*

Tipping back in his wooden swivel chair, he put his hands on his extended belly—a condition he enjoyed blaming on Lettie's rich cooking.

"Adjusting any better to the new neighborhood?" he asked.

"A guy was shot and killed in the park last week."

He pushed to the edge of his seat. "I hope you know you can always call us for anything. Is your father sending money?"

"I don't think so. I've got an interview at the comic book store on Howard soon. A friend works there, so she's pretty sure I'll get it," I said. "It would only be part time, so I can keep on top of things here."

He placed his Hasselblad in front of me on the desk and dumped a handful of black-and-white film into a bag. He referred to cameras like this as *honest machinery*. He knew I had wanted to try a Hasselblad for a while now "You have this on loan for three weeks. Think about making a visual statement of an obsession."

I laughed. "I guess the assumption is that we all have one."

"One of mine is this camera. But it takes getting used to." Demonstrating the release, he popped it open and handed it back to me. The viewfinder sits on the top of the camera, so it's necessary to look straight down to see the image. Everything appeared upside down, the image split in two.

Before I could express my gratitude he said, "We have someone coming in for a shoot. Why don't you look the part of the busy assistant?"

My phone rang just then. I apologized but looked at the number, saying, "It's my mom."

She wasn't a frivolous caller anymore, so I knew to answer.

"I have to get something upstairs. Come up and get me when you're ready," he said, tipping out of his chair. "Simple, clean background today. Let's try gray, nothing fancy." Around the studio Geary had several rolls of background sheets strung up along the ceiling and various pieces of furniture and props for most occasions.

"I'm having trouble finding someone to help me move a couch and a washing machine," Mom said. "I tried doing it myself when the other worker didn't show, and I ended up wedging the couch in the front doorframe, where it's stuck. I can't leave until I get it in or out and the lock-box back in place."

She had to repeat bits of this several times because of the phone reception.

"What are you going to do?" I asked.

"Saw … off," I heard. "… have to find a hardware …"

"Saw what off?"

"Legs. The couch legs," she yelled.

"You're kidding."

"You'll have to walk over … Lola up and take … dance cl—"
By the time I heard her say, *"Sorry,"* her voice was the sound of a firecracker that hadn't yet exploded.

I unrolled a couple of backdrops, moved the lighting around with Geary, did some cleanup in the darkroom, and was on my way. I wrapped the leather case of the Hasselblad in my wool scarf and nestled it in my pack. Two or three inches of new snow covered the ground. The way it was coming down, I wondered if we were going to have a blizzard.

I took off along Church Street. My running shoes quickly soaked through, the cold stinging my feet. Turning on the iPod Cynthia had loaned me, I dug my wool hat out of my pocket and put it on as I watched cars swerve and stall in the streets. Everyone seemed in a hurry to make it to schools for pickups and stores for provisions before things got worse. I rushed to Lola's school, hoping to make it a little early so she wouldn't worry if she didn't see Mom out front.

The walk to the dance class was a little far. When we arrived, Lola discovered that no one had helped her remember her leotard and footless tights. She was devastated. The dance teacher said, "Go ahead and join in, Lola. It's all right. Just take your socks off."

"I'll be watching," I said.

The look Lola gave me as she reached the dance floor. The instructor turned to me and said, "Are things okay at home, sweetheart?"

I began to stuff things back into Lola's bag as I tried to figure out why I was this woman's sweetheart.

"Your mother usually comes in."

"She had to work late," I said.

"Be *lions*, girls! Be lions!" the teacher called to them.

The girls moved and stretched toward the long sets of mirrors. I saw Lola turn to a small girl in a shiny green leotard and roar into her face. The girl yelled, *"Stop it!"* and the teacher went over and moved Lola to the other side of the room, then whispered something in my sister's ear. I thought it best if I didn't interfere.

Returning to our conversation, the teacher balanced on one foot now, the sole of her other foot flat against her inner thigh. "Your mother has always paid us on time, and she promised she'd bring a check today. We do give Lola a sizable scholarship. It seems important to your sister to keep her lessons up."

Lola shot me another look. It wasn't as if she could overhear, but maybe she sensed that I was ruining things for her. Matters were always different when it was about Lola. I felt helpless.

"I'll go ahead and watch from the observation window," I told her teacher. "I'm sure our mom will mail in a check right away."

Each new humiliation was about the debt our father had accrued.

When we got home I suggested to Mom that we do something
special for Lola.

"The drive-through has dip cones now," Lola said knowingly.
She loved the idea that you could just drive up to a window and
someone would hand you a meal with a dessert, a toy, a crown,
a special decorated box with games printed on the bottom and
punch-out game pieces, and maybe a top to spin and spin until you
lost yourself.

Once we were lined up outside, I checked to see if we needed
additive. Lola took the backseat, where we'd had a new seatbelt
mechanism installed. I sat shotgun. Mom turned the engine over.
I waited to see what would happen when she eased the clutch out
and gave it a little gas because this often didn't work out well for
her. But she managed to engage, and we were about to pull away
from the curb when Ajay appeared in my side mirror.

This was the first time I had seen him since the night on the
rails. As he approached my door, Mom got startled and let her foot
off too soon, and we jerked forward. She slammed on the brake; I
let out a muffled scream; the van died, barely tapping the car in
front of us. Lola's bobble-headed snowman on the dash went into
furious motion.

"Mom." Lola laughed in that way that can turn to tears.

"Hold on," Mom said. "Everything's okay."

I rolled down my window, and Ajay looked to see if there was
any damage. "You're fine," he said and gripped my window well.
"Mrs. Hunter. *Lo-la.*" When he said my sister's name musically, I
looked back and saw she enjoyed this. Lola was big on boy flattery.

Mom tried to start the van again, grinding the ignition too
hard.

"I don't think that's the way you're supposed to do it," Lola said.

"Why don't I save a parking spot for you, Mrs. Hunter?" Ajay said after her attempt failed. "I can use my grandfather's sawhorses with a sign."

"That's okay. We're just running a couple of errands. Have a good night."

"You know,, this street gets pretty bad," he pressed.

"It's Ms. Hunter, actually," she said, not with a mean spirit, but it was awkward that she corrected him. "We'll be fine. Thanks for the offer."

"If you change your mind, Ms. Hunter," he said with a thoughtful look, "just give a call."

In a low voice he told me his number and that he was always up late.

Mom was struggling to get the van into reverse. Otherwise I know she would have looked for a way to short-circuit our exchange, as if I were still in high school. Finally she maneuvered us into the street, which meant Ajay had to back up suddenly, though he managed to keep one hand on my door the whole time, even as he tripped a little walking into a pothole. Mom pulled forward, and he let go.

"You're not taking his number?" Mom said.

"No worries," I said. I had already punched it in.

T he first thing you see when you enter Evanston from Chicago, after curving around the lake and the cemetery on Sheridan heading north, is the other life. The lakeside apartments, the houses, the bigger houses, abundant trees, the estates where only certain people deserve to see the water up close, the beaches requiring tokens we couldn't afford even if we used a fake address. There were, however, plenty of dogs that would be tagged and let loose on the shore the next summer.

I was aware of these things and the fact that our world had become a constant adjustment to temperature extremes. The heat in the van cranked until we couldn't take it, but turning it down meant turning it off, essentially. Opening the windows brought freezing drafts that hit Lola in the backseat, so we kept them shut.

By the time we pulled into the drive-through, Lola was asleep, her head resting against the window. I noticed they had raised their prices but called the tiny ice-cream dish they threw in *free*.

"You better get her a kids' meal in case she wakes up," I said.

We pulled up to the speaker and Mom rolled down her window. She ignored the voice as she counted the small mountain of change she dug out of the glove compartment to see how much we could buy. She was on a new jag about not using the credit card, but I didn't understand why she had waited until we were at the speaker to count change.

"Thirteen, thirteen twenty-five, thirteen fifty …"

"The guy's waiting," I said.

"Damn it." She looked in the rearview. There was one car behind us and another just pulling in.

"Mom?"

"Do you really think she's going to eat anything tonight?" she asked. "Make that sweater in the back into a pillow for her head. What was that, fourteen something?"

"Thirteen fifty," I said as I unfastened my seatbelt and climbed into the back. I lifted Lola's head away from the window to nestle the sweater in place. "I don't want to be around if she doesn't get her Big Kids' Meal," I said, returning to my seat.

"I wasn't suggesting we not get *anything*."

"She can take it for lunch tomorrow if she doesn't eat it tonight."

"Cold chicken fingers? Cold fries?" Mom said loud enough to be heard over the sound of the engine.

"Is that the six-piece or the ten-piece meal?" the voice answered from the scratchy speaker.

We had both seen too many movies with this kind of gag moment, but we cracked up anyway.

"I'll get extra ketchup packets," Mom said.

"Make sure she gets the boy Avatar glass, *not* the girl."

Lola wasn't able to fall back to sleep when we got home, so Mom warmed her meal up and washed and filled the new glass with fruit punch. As Lola turned the glass to study the pictures, I wondered about the world she was piecing together. She hadn't seen the movie, probably wouldn't for a long time. She gave us a dreamy look.

It's possible Mom was struck with the same helpless feeling I had in that moment, wondering how we would see that things turned out well for Lola.

"Your sister said we had to get the one with the boy avatar," Mom said and smiled at me.

I went down to Cynthia's a short while later to tell her I had seen Ajay and had no plans to call him.

"You came downstairs to tell me you're not going to call him?"

That's when she told me about this article she was reading. She had stop-sign-red hair that week, so everything she said had an emphasis, as if she were talking in high alert. "It says that some of us, no, most of us, have a story about one particular event in life that explains the things that happened before it and most of the things that happen after it."

When I quizzed her on this theory, she said this event is typically something terrible that happens in childhood.

"People make this shit up all the time because it sells magazines," I said.

"So you have one of those stories," she said.

"The Brothers Grimm made things up, things that were terrible and sold some books. But I'm not sure ..."

"You're afraid to say."

"I am not," I said.

"I'll just listen, I promise," she said.

I waited as a train passed.

"It's a stupid idea," I said.

"No shortage of those," she said, lighting one of those foul herbal things and blowing the smoke toward the hanging lamp over the table.

"It makes me think of those surprise balls where the thing in the center is some junky little prize."

"Do you feel like you might unravel if you say? I have some vodka."

"Pass," I said. She poured me a coffee and nudged the cup my way. I took a sip, burned my tongue, put the cup down, and said goodnight, going back upstairs.

Outside our apartment I paused for a minute and studied Anna Lily's door. I didn't know if she had secured the lock on her door again or if I could simply grab the doorknob and enter. There was no peephole, but I didn't know if she was inside—counting her cameras, labeling her boxes.

I dropped off to the sound of water running in Nitro's darkroom sink the next day and found myself at Niagara Falls with Ajay. We watched whole lakes fall over the edge of the earth, the last of the tour boats docked for the night, people shedding their blue rain ponchos.

Slipping into a passage cut into the rock, we stood behind the falls by an opening where the pounding water sprayed us. Pressing his back against one of the blue walls, he drew me close, and we kissed in a lit-up state.

"Hey, hey, you fell asleep," Nitro said, shaking me.

"No, I didn't," I said, unwilling to open my eyes. I wanted to be back in the dream.

"You looked content."

"Then I don't know why you woke me."

"You asked me to if you fell asleep."

I brought the loft into focus, his face. I was curled up on his couch.

"Are you keeping something from me?" he said, as if I should get the context.

I laughed. "You don't? Keep things from me?"

"Not anymore. So what film do you want to watch? *Manhattan?*"

"You put that on last month, and I'm not sweet like Mariel."

"You hooking up with that guy in your building?"

I didn't say anything.

"I think about you more than you realize. I ... I'll load a bowl while you think about a movie," he said.

Coughing and letting the smoke billow out, I said, "I do have a story to tell you."

"Ah, better than a movie. Don't leave anything out."

Trying to gather my thoughts was like trying to take a photograph with a homemade box camera. There was only the one pinhole in the cardboard and the effort to keep my hands steady. "I'm sure I will, even if I don't mean to," I said.

"I won't be looking for the things you leave out," he said.

"I thought you were dating that photographer," I said, looping back.

"I told you, you're ruining me from seeing anyone else." He looked contrite, and I began.

"On Sunday mornings my dad used to polish our convertible, and sometimes he drove out to Arlington Racetrack to play the horses. You like that start?"

"That's a good start," he said.

"My mother, who didn't want to spend her Sundays betting on things to work out, never came along. Instead she built *objects* in our garage, sometimes with scrap metal and sometimes with clay and molds that became sculptures that filled our yard. And when we ran out of room they were crated up and driven over to friends' yards. Each one a metal work with surfaces that mirrored the things around them."

"The good and the bad?" he asked, fiddling with the hookah.

"I guess you could say that. I know she hoped he would never gamble too much or drink too much, and she believed if I were with him it would be a safe family outing, little more. She was pregnant at the time and eager to get as much work done as she could before the baby arrived. The thing was, I loved being with my father in those days, riding in his car, listening to his stories. I used to lean back and feel like the road was sailing right through me."

"I know the way that feels," Nitro said.

"I was nine when he asked me to come along and whispered that he had reserved a table in the Clubhouse. He said this would be a lucky day. "We won't tell Mom," he said and he cupped my chin in his hand the way he did sometimes and I heard his watch tick against my ear. Having a table in the Clubhouse was … what do they call it now, the Million Room?"

"Not sure."

"Anyway, that table was an extravagance he said he had saved up for, just for us."

"Do you want another hit?"

I shook my head. "'We'll take the back roads,' he said and beamed at me in the rearview. Once we had gone a few blocks from the house, I asked if I could sit up front this time, and he pulled along the curb and I climbed over the seat. I was small for my age then, so the seatbelt was a little loose. But he folded his coat up and tucked it behind me until the belt was taut. That way I could keep my eyes on everything and we could talk."

"You always seem to know what you want."

"I asked how he and Mom had met. And he told me about working for his uncle who was a professional guesser, a carny."

"You're wonderful," Nitro said.

"But you see I asked him this question a lot. I think my hope was that the story itself would make him fall in love with her in that same way again. For a while it had seemed that when we got home from wherever we were going all they did was fight. It almost didn't matter over what. Grocery bills, *needless* art supplies or lawn equipment purchases. They met when they were so young. I hoped if things improved she wouldn't bring up his shortcomings and he wouldn't get on her about sculpting *while Rome burns*.

"We parked in the big lot on the racetrack grounds, and when we were inside we stopped for a while to watch the horses walk around the paddock. That was my favorite part. I would be tall like my mother and father, but that year I wanted to remain my exact height and weight and become a jockey who wears red silks."

"You have to bring me a picture of you at that age," Nitro said.

"I don't think so. Anyway, at the entrance to the Clubhouse my father slipped the hostess a folded bill, and she seated us by one of the giant windows. There we had a linen tablecloth and linen napkins and goblets of ice water and heavy knives and forks. 'I guess your dad knows how to treat his girl,' he said and leaned over and kissed my forehead. I wanted to say I was sorry Mom couldn't come. But I had learned that there were certain conversations you could have before a race and others that were better left alone. I wasn't always sure which was which, and I didn't want to be the one who had jinxed him if he lost. So I sat quietly while he considered the *Daily Racing Form* and the other tip sheets. My father was a handsome man with a solid jaw, and his lips moved slightly when he read something significant. He liked to follow lineages,

jockeys, and so on, and sometimes he shared some of this with
me, but it never stuck."

"Sounds like he was successful."

"No, he always lost. I mean, if he had a formula, I'm not sure
what it was—if he even knew. With each loss he ripped up his tickets and let the pieces drop to the carpet, and on this particular day
he called the waiter over to our table and ordered another drink.
That day he lost by straight bourbon.

"'And bring my girl a fresh Coke,' he said as he loosened his
tie. He didn't want me to feel slighted in any way. Three Cokes
had been delivered to me already. I could barely start on one before
the next arrived. Soon the man with the carpet sweeper came along
to nudge the last round of ripped tickets into his machine. The
horses thundered past those giant windows, the boards lit up, the
tickets were torn in two, and the drinks continued to arrive. By the
seventh race my father looked red-eyed and confused. He put the
last of his money on a serious long shot with a misshapen white star
in her forelock. She was so jumpy it took three men to get her into
the gate. The announcer said, as he always did—"

"'And they're off,'" Nitro said.

"We watched as our horse gradually broke out from behind
all the other horses, the jockey whipping her hard. She won by a
nose. And so with one pale-orange ticket my father had suddenly
earned $7,688. But instead of jumping up and down he sat back
and smiled to himself, as if to say, *It was only a matter of time.* And
I floated along with him, thinking everything in our world had
changed.

"We collected the money in hundred-dollar bills at a window
where the cashier chewed mint gum that she snapped when she
reached each thousand. Her supervisor looked on like an umpire
as the cashier fanned the bills out for our inspection. My father
glowed and I glowed. When the bills were tucked safely in his

jacket, we went downstairs and through the turnstile. To find our car out in the lot we had to walk a long time, and I hoped the extra walking would clear his head. He was weaving quite a bit."

"You must have been scared."

"I was sure he wouldn't drive if he was drunk, and he said we'd stop for more coffee as soon as we got to the place where we always stopped along the way. It wasn't far. Dad and I joked and laughed while I looked for our silver sedan. Silver, it seemed, was a popular color that year, but he said, 'You'll find it. You're clever like your mother. God, is she going to be happy.' There were tickets strewn everywhere along the ground, and in a sudden gust of wind I saw a dust devil carry some of them upward, but just as quick it stopped, and I marveled as the tickets rained down on an old station wagon."

"That would be beautiful to film."

"It was. Like a movie. When I finally found our car I looked at his reflection curved around the fender, and I thought that the high gloss mirrored something sort of underneath that moment. A sense that our happy life wasn't all that happy, or that he wasn't. I knew that some shift had occurred that let me see a little deeper into my father.

"We drove back through the flatlands and stopped at this place that served thick malteds out of one of those metal cylinders that hold the spillover. He had a cup or two of coffee and left a huge tip and told me to always remember how hard people work and treat everyone with dignity. And then, against the cheerful red-and-white interior with framed drawings of cows and sloping hills, we turned fat with possibilities."

"*Fat with possibilities*," Nitro said.

"'I might buy one of those leaf sweepers for the lawn,' he said."

"That's what he wanted?" Nitro asked.

"'And I just might get you an aboveground swimming pool with a ladder and deck to go around the edge. What would you think about that?' he asked. Pressing his hair down with his palms, he said, 'Everything's looking up. You get that, don't you? Really looking up.'

"So once we got in the car again I leaned my head against the back of the seat and I … looked up. Driving by the hedges and fences and empty swimming pools and empty toboggan runs, I began to feel the car slide back and forth over the two sides of the road. I sat up and nudged his arm so he'd stay alert. A horn now and then let us know he had gone too far. His eyelids sometimes lowered. I wanted to call my mother, but neither of us had cell phones then. I was glad to see the water tower, the halfway mark before we got home. I loved that large metal bulb at the top painted brightly, standing out in the landscape like a color television. 'Look, there it is!' I called.

"'I climbed that thing once with some of my high school buddies,' he said, his fatigue lifting. I turned away from him for a moment and thought about what it would be like to climb up the ladder to the top of the tower. And then what it would be like to let go and drop, arms out. The tower was even more beautiful now that the sun had finished setting, and the clouds stretched out the way they do—in one long, flat view. A woman's voice was on the radio, and the balding tires raced on the asphalt. The traffic was just a trickle as everything for miles turned blue.

"It took me a moment to realize that the car had begun to swerve again. I turned and saw a station wagon on the other side of the road, almost the color of the sky. We hurtled straight toward it. Then the screech of tires, the sound of metal hitting metal. My head hit something, maybe the dash, maybe my father's arm."

Nitro sat back and squinted at me, waiting.

"I guess some people would say we were the fortunate ones. When we stopped and I felt brave enough to open my eyes I saw that we were on the shoulder, on the opposite side of the road from where we had started. We had hit the back of the blue station wagon with our fender, and the station wagon had careened off the road and plowed into a giant advertising pole, the kind with a sign that turns at the top. Their hood was folded into the shape of a tent, and smoke rose from it. My father was already starting our car again, and I heard metal being wrenched apart as if the noise of the accident was playing backward.

"As we drove in reverse, I saw two people in the car, a woman in front and a little girl in the back strapped into a car seat. The woman was trying to open her door, and the girl looked stunned at first and then started to cry. I was so scared for them I couldn't breathe. The woman kept pounding on the glass.

"Dad backed up and quickly drove a few hundred feet ahead to the end of the shoulder. Our car made a terrible noise. All that time I didn't say anything because I knew we were about to turn around and help the people in that car. I just wanted him to hurry because everything felt like it was in slow motion. He got out of the car and told me to stay put. There was a lot of smoke coming from the other car, and he tried all the doors. He popped our trunk and rummaged around, and I guess he didn't find what he was looking for and slammed it shut. He shouted something to the woman in the car, then came back and quickly tied up our fender. Once he was done we did a quick U-turn right across the double yellow line and headed back toward home."

"Didn't he try to flag anyone down?"

"No, he didn't do that. There weren't a ton of cars, though."

"So he just drove away?"

"He drove a short way and turned until our car was heading east. I yanked on his arm as if it were a lever to move the wheels and said, 'Are they going to be all right?' He said, 'Quiet down, Mona.' I wanted to say, *You have to save them!* Instead, in my panic, I said, 'You have to save me!' I did what I could to correct myself, urgently, but he said, 'Police cars patrol that strip all the time. They'll be along any second now. We're looking for a pay phone to make sure they know, just in case.' When I couldn't settle down, when I started to hyperventilate, he put his hand on my knee and said, 'The sooner you get quiet, the sooner I'll be talking to the police.' I was nine, and maybe I stopped because I thought it was the only way to save anyone at all.

"He pulled into a 7-Eleven and used a pay phone while I sat in the car looking at the window advertisements that made me feel dizzy. I had a terrible headache. When he got back in the car, he told me he had talked with the police and they had already arrived on the scene and the mother and daughter were just fine. I felt as if I could finally take a full breath.

"We drove to a long commercial strip next, where we pulled in by a couple of Quonset huts. One of the huts had a sign over the door, *Dave's Body Shop*. A man came out of the door, and he talked with my father for a while, and I saw my dad peel off some of the winnings from the track, or all of them, and hand this bundle to the man, who gave my dad some keys. I took my purse, and we got in another car and went home. But before we got there he talked to me about Mom, reminding me that the baby was due in a couple of months and that it would be best not to get Mom upset. If she heard we were in an accident, it would be hard for her. 'Best not to tell anyone, Kitten,' he said. 'Because someone might tell her, and with your new little brother or sister on the way … I gave the man who's fixing our car enough to fix the other car and help the people. Everything will be all right now.'

"Before I went to bed that night I took off the dress my mother had laid out for me that morning as if I had been on my way to church. And then I wasn't sure why, but I wrote down the date and the name of the garage on a slip of paper, and the color of the car we hit. I tucked this inside a locket that had been my grandmother's, and that went into the jewelry box I kept on my dresser, with the key taped to the bottom of my bed frame. And this act with the jewelry box became a ritual I performed whenever I wanted to keep things hidden."

"Leaving the scene without providing information, the payoff at the body shop, babe, that's a classic hit-and-run."

"He had to get to a phone to call the police."

"But he didn't say he gave them his name."

"It was a long time ago."

"There's no statute of limitations on hit-and-runs, Mona."

"What?"

"Your father could still be nailed on a felony."

I got up from the couch. I began to unlock his complicated industrial door with its many latches and pins. "I don't need you," I said and ran down the stairs and out into the street.

He called out to me from the fire escape, but I kept going.

Lola was playing with a wooden dollhouse when I got in. It had hand-carved cupolas, balconies, porticoes. I knew Mom had hauled it out of one of those houses and cleaned it up for my sister. It was seven thirty, and they had eaten dinner. Mom was lying on top of her covers, asleep. I watched as she sat straight up and said, "God, I must have dozed off."

When she was certain both Lola and I were all right, she watched for a while as I cleared the table, wrapped up the left-overs, wiped the kitchen counters down, and loaded the sink. Mom always thanked me for doing my share as if she didn't quite trust that I'd do it again. Before long she went off to fall asleep in the small tub. When I was done with the kitchen I helped Lola look for furniture and a mix of different-sized people from her toy box. Not a family, exactly. More of a mash-up, the baby the biggest one of all, the father quite small with patched jeans and a sullen look, the mother's hair white. We couldn't find me yet.

Before long Lola's growing pains took over. She got in her PJs and brushed her teeth without my asking. I rubbed her legs.

She said, "Dad's going to like the little house."

"You've been thinking about him again," I said.

"He's going to come home soon," she said matter-of-factly.

"What makes you say that?"

"I feel it in my bones," she said.

Our grandmother on our mother's side often said she felt things in her bones, so I tried not to make too much of this. Soon I tucked Lola in and kissed her and told her to get right to sleep. Mom pulled herself together enough to drain the tub, dry off, and get into her nightgown, and she too came over for Lola's affection.

Richard

"I'm going to ask you a favor," Honey said when she picked me up at the bus station. "Go to see my second cousin, Jimmy Starr, the funeral director—I'll loan you a car—and arrange to have Sor's body sent to Alma. He can find out the funeral home she plans to use. Tell Jimmy to fill another casket with anything he's got lying around that will seem like the weight of a body. When the girls get here we'll sit and pray over a closed casket and get it buried on the property."

A minister would come out to the house on Monday, and the eulogy would be as quick as the sudden downpours that happened each afternoon.

My three female cousins and their spouses, who had flown in in succession like cranes landing on a spit of land, sat around the living room, mostly silent except to ask me an occasional question about my family. I got overheated even in the chilled air conditioning. When we received a call that the minister would be an hour late I removed my jacket, unbuttoned the top button of my shirt, and rolled up my sleeves. Honey tied up her hair with a scarf and asked me to take a walk with her. Cousin Sarah volunteered to rustle up something in the kitchen for after the service, though we had all just eaten lunch.

We headed out in the bright sun. Honey began to talk about her growing concern with *greening*, a disease spreading through the citrus belt. "I've been lucky so far," she said. I could see how she grieved, that it was important to distract herself.

When a car started down the long drive we moved to the far right side of the road. In the sun's glare we couldn't see who it was, but she said the minister must have broken away from his other obligations earlier than expected. The passenger had to be her cousin Jimmy Starr. "Now we can get this charade over with," Honey said.

But without warning the car picked up speed. It began to pull from one side of the road to the other. I grabbed Honey around the waist and pulled her to the shoulder behind an orange tree. Dust kicked into the air as the car came to an abrupt stop a few feet from us.

Alma emerged from the passenger seat in a shirtwaist black dress. She glared at Honey, who had righted herself. I recognized Alma's daughter Tina from a photograph as she got out of the driver's side and stood timidly by her door. She looked as if she had been warned not to interfere. I could only imagine how they had fought for control of the wheel.

"Can we help you?" Honey asked in a guarded way.

"So this is the whore?" Alma said, coming right up to my face.

"Hold on," Honey said. "You're on my property."

"And this one," she said, "he's just here for your money ... the way Sorohan was."

"Don't you have someone to bury now?" Honey said.

What happened next came so fast there was no time to think. Alma was suddenly holding her paring knife. Maybe it dropped from her sleeve into her hand. She rushed Honey, and I stepped in front of her. Alma cut me across my left palm.

Everyone stopped. The blood pooled and began to spatter on the gravel.

"Now she can read your miserable fate instead of mine," Alma said. I could see she was shaking from her own boldness.

A muffled sound flew from my throat. Tina said, "Oh, God," as if she hadn't known her mother would let things go this far.

"Get back in the car," Alma said to her daughter. Tina did as she was told and fired up the engine. Alma joined her on the passenger side.

Honey removed her scarf and wrapped it around my hand, telling me to keep pressure on it. Tina angled and turned the car as if she were doing this maneuver for the first time. After they drove off Honey said, "Don't move." She fell into a light jog in the direction of the house.

At the hospital I said I'd had an accident slicing a bagel. The doctor who created the nineteen stitches across my palm commented on the precision of the cut, and I said nothing.

If a hand is a map of your life, mine was now divided from the base of my palm right up my middle finger. It was what I had become, a man split from himself, the present unhinged from the past. But it was when I was driving back to the house with Honey that she offered her own interpretation. "You're probably wondering what this does to your future."

"I hadn't thought about it, to tell you the truth." I hoped she'd realize I didn't want to hear any more forecasts.

"Given the direction of the line," she said, pausing as we came to a stop at an intersection of two rural roads, "I think it's the big *fuck you* to everything."

It felt good to break down and laugh.

"Seriously, though. There's something to be said about having the sins cut right out of you. Sor showed me something about that. He had a sense of freedom I did everything I could to emulate. *If there's something holding you down, you might just start living your life*, he'd say. And that's whether you head home or run off somewhere."

"But he came and went as he pleased, leaving you with the child rearing, the household, the ranch to manage. ..."

"I signed up for that, and he worked awfully hard around here when he *was* home. You spent a summer with him, so you know. Up early in the orchards so he could keep up with things. He knew every ranch hand on the property, their wives' names, their kids' names, their medical conditions. ... He rebuilt the cabinets in the kitchen, started restoring the outbuildings ... took the girls to their athletic events, their plays. And, you know, I kind of liked having things my own way—calling the shots—making the big decisions on the business, the family. He had a heart larger than his circumstances. That's what I think. I'm going to miss the hell out of that guy till the day I'm gone."

The cousins stalled the minister at the house until we returned from the hospital, and a false casket filled with blankets and phone books was lowered into the ground on ropes. It did occur to me that the funeral director, who drove out with the minister, might have switched things around and that we were actually burying Sor. But I didn't ask.

Honey made up some injury for me. By the end of Thursday everyone had flown off to their respective homes in various states of mourning and reluctance. I knew there wouldn't be another reason to delay pushing on. I just didn't know where I was going yet or how.

For months I had checked the online job sites daily, and I had continued to do so while I was at Honey's. The Sunday after my cousins left, she and I lingered over lunch and took a long walk late in the day, going in the opposite direction from the gravesite. We stopped near one of the outlying buildings. Pushing the door open, she said Sor had been remodeling this one. There were no outside steps yet, just a couple of crates. I gave her a hand up, not thinking she was used to getting in the door on her own steam.

"It's a usable studio if you want to stick around," she said and showed me that the shower and toilet worked. Only the interior framing was in place and some of the countertops but no drywall. There was running water in the kitchen sink as well but no appliances. A plywood floor was in with Saltillo tiles in stacks and a couple of tubs of grout. She marked where she could supply a bed and chest of drawers. "Come to think of it, I have a refrigerator down in my cellar."

I went over and stood by the door, looking out, and watched crates of oranges being loaded onto a flatbed. Maybe she would offer me a chance to pick oranges if my hand healed right. Or make me a watchman or teach me the business of selling oranges. Maybe she'd stock the place with bedding and towels and even line me up with something to drive so I could get into town. I was not unaware of how remarkable it was that not one but two people had offered me shelter in the last few months. I could make something of this dwelling, get some insulation in, throw up some drywall. But I was also aware that in doing this I would be no closer to home.

When I took stock, I had a little over sixty dollars, a coupon for a free donut and coffee in Atlantic City, and an hour of phone time left on a prepaid card. I sat at her computer to check employment sites yet again. I was used to moving through the endless screens, but then I realized I might have seen something and clicked back to the last page, and there it was: *Experienced Insurance Salesman.* Of all things the contact number was in Chicago. I wondered if the contact, Matt Finnegan, was the same Matt Finnegan I had met at a Toastmasters luncheon a few years back.

There was his picture on the company site.

I called my former boss in New Jersey, pretending to be a new client so I could reach him. Before he could hang up on me I told him I would no longer pursue my commissions if he would send one hell of a recommendation letter to Matt Finnegan before ten a.m. the next day, stating that I had filled in until his brother returned to work. He agreed to give my true sales figures if Matt called, but he wouldn't put them in writing. I just had to keep my fingers crossed he'd do one decent thing here.

By eleven a.m. I had attached an updated résumé and sent it off to the firm in Chicago. I made a good accounting of what I had done in the time between the two companies, noting my heavy involvement at the senior center in Evanston. I had put in three days a week for months when I lost my first job, at Liz's prompting, and I said in my cover letter that this had given me an understanding and appreciation for seniors' needs and wants, something essential in working with baby boomers—the primary group Matt Finnegan was after. Rather than list the dollar store, I stated that I had been helping a close aunt and uncle on their ranch until they got on their feet in difficult times. It's all a matter of how you tell the story.

I got a call back the next day from Matt's personal secretary, who wanted to set up a Skype meeting. Phil had come through. I put on my suit, knotted my tie, and set my talking points down on the blotter next to me. I kept my injured hand out of the camera's reach and pulled my hair back into a ponytail, hoping I wouldn't need to turn my head. I should have gone to the barber. When the signal came through, I gave away some of the best ideas for capturing this market, reserving enough to deliver in a second meeting if I got one.

Matt told me frankly that he was very impressed but warned me that since he was in a start-up phase, the pay would disappoint.

I did not say, *Compared to the dollar store?*

We scheduled a lunch in Chicago in four days to discuss terms. Honey loaned me plane fare and a little extra and drove me to the airport the next day. She told me to come back anytime. Once I reached O'Hare I planned to take the Kiss-n-Fly bus and surprise Liz and the girls. It was time to get my house in order.

When the steward came by I purchased a Johnny Walker to toast Uncle Sor from the clouds. I don't know what it was exactly. Even before I had a sip I noticed that colors appeared more intense. The sky brighter, the lakes and farmlands more vivid, even the boy next to me who watched a movie while his mother flipped through a glossy magazine—the way the light touched his hair from the uncovered window—he seemed to glow.

His mother placed an arm around his shoulders. I sat back and took a sip, and everything Honey said to me about Sor the day I was injured hit my mind like saturated light. I had been a foolish man. I would never let this happen again.

"How old?" I asked the mother.

"Five."

"I have a five-year-old," I said. I was aware that my eyes were starting to fill. Looking away, I studied my ticket.

By the time I got to Evanston Lola would still be in aftercare. They wouldn't know me at her school—it had been a lifetime since Mona had gone there, and people move around, administrators change. I doubted Liz would have filled out a form saying I could sign Lola out. Why would she?

Liz would still be at work. My thoughts moved from court to court, wondering which side she'd land on when I appeared.

It's possible I could catch Mona at her job, where I might begin to make some repairs. The bus ride was long, but it gave me time to think. Snow began to fall in large flakes.

Once I got to Davis I walked the ten blocks or so over to Church. By then the snow was coming down steadily. I had second thoughts about showing up at Geary's. The worst thing I could do to Mona was crowd her.

I was close enough to the L, and that would practically take me to their door. I stood for a minute by the alleyway next to the bakery, where we used to get fresh bread and cookies and often a coffee cake on Sundays. The bright neon sign and fogged-up windows. I watched the steam roll out of the kitchen vents, pumping out the smells of baked goods, and decided to get everyone a treat. That's when I spotted Mona. She was right there, about to walk past me.

I called out. She had her earbuds in, and I meant only to touch her arm as I called to her again, but I misgauged her reaction, the slick surfaces. I began to lose my footing. Mona was jerked backward along with me.

"What the fuck!" she shouted as she swung round like a door flying off its hinges. Wet snow clumped on her cap, forcing it down over her eyes. Her earbuds came loose, and the sound of tinny music hit the air.

We regained balance, and I gently let her go. She yanked the cap from her eyes, snow easing down her face and neck, and I thought for a moment she was prepared to shove someone's nose up into his skull before she realized it was me.

"Are you all right?"

"Am I all right?" she said, shaking and pulling snow from her collar.

"I'm sorry, dear. I slipped. I was calling your name."

She straightened out her jacket. "What are you doing here?" she asked.

Both of us realigned our packs. "Let's get out of the cold," I said. "Deli all right? I was thinking of catching you at Geary's, and suddenly you were there."

"Okay," she said sternly.

I wanted to put an arm around her, but I waited.

We waded through the slush, and once we were inside the deli I hung my coat up on a hook. It was the same wool coat I had when I left, but it had frayed at the cuffs and was in bad need of cleaning.

I chose the booth we used to sit in on Saturdays. "You used to love this one," I said.

She shrugged and sat down.

I placed my pack so that it blocked my side of the booth and I could grab it easily, as if someone might steal my stuff if I set it down for more than a second. Brushing the snow off the top, I dug my phone out of my pocket and placed it on the table.

Nothing had changed in the deli, and I found that comforting. On the back ledge and along the wall a number of items were glued into place: a cluster of plastic calla lilies; a wooden decoy duck that had once been a working phone; a ceramic ballerina with a scratchy pink skirt and two green rhinestone eyes, one gouged out with a pen or knife; a photo of Einstein speckled with a coating of resin; two broken 45s. When Mona was little, these were fascinating objects. I wondered if they now looked to her like junk the owner had hauled down from his attic.

Where some fathers play Hanged Man or Tic-Tac-Toe with their children to get them through restaurant waits, I used to tell stories. Liz liked to say that some of them were odd, even a little sinister, but when I'd tone them down, Mona said they were dull. Sometimes I made up a quick tale about each person in the restaurant, and it was her job to match the tale with a face. I remember her being disappointed at times when the food arrived. She loved to win at this game.

I was a little stunned when she took her wool cap off and blue hair tumbled out, as I kept trying to adjust my thinking about the daughter I had left two years earlier and the one I had returned to. Even her eyes scared me a little with the piercing through one brow. I don't mean she looked scary but that I was scared for her, not sure what these things meant yet not wanting to grill her.

She opened her pack, and I watched her unwrap an old camera

case she had buried in a winter scarf. Pulling the camera out, she placed it on the table and popped it open.

"That's a beauty," I said.

"Geary's Hasselblad."

"I'm sorry you had to put college on hold. I hope I'll be able to fix that soon."

She sputtered, almost laughing, and said, "It's a waste of time to go to art school to be a photographer."

I think that was a show, that she was sparing me a conversation over rudimentary economics. When I looked away for a moment to grab the attention of the waitress, Mona took a shot of me, and then another when I turned around. I didn't say anything, though I might have looked troubled. She cranked the film into position again. I recalled Liz telling me a story about Geary, that he had taken photos of his father in his final illness and then moments after his death and at the burial. Liz said this was how Geary got through it. His sister and brother wouldn't speak to him for a couple of years after he shot the open casket.

"I can't believe I'm sitting across from you. I've missed you so much."

As a large extended family came through the door Mona turned to watch them. There were the ones who seemed to belong together by features and body type, and the ones who didn't. Neither of my girls had my features, though we did share good dental health and hearing. And all three of us had cowlicks at the hairline. Everything else was Liz.

When the waitress looked over I raised an empty cup. Mona cocked her head to one side as if she understood me better at a tilt. She took two more shots as our coffees were poured.

"I like it," I said. "Your hair."

"You stand alone," she said. "How long are you here for?"

The waitress was tall and stooped at the shoulders with a round belly half covered by an apron. She poured the coffee and pulled her pad from one of its pockets. "What can I get you folks?"

I poured cream and sugar almost to the brim, as if I were trying to make a meal out of it, a habit I had picked up in New Jersey.

"We'd be grateful if you'd keep the coffee flowing. We're chilled to the bone," I said. Then I brushed at something on the front of my shirt as if a stain would fly off at my insistence.

"You need a few minutes to decide?"

I asked Mona if she'd like something, but she said she'd eaten a late lunch.

"I think," I said, looking to Mona for agreement, "that coffee should do it today."

"We have a minimum at the booths," the waitress said and pointed to a small sign taped to the register.

I felt myself flush, used to this business of being kicked out of places whenever I was trying to catch a little rest and get warm. "There are quite a few empty tables," I said.

"I'll bring you a menu," she said, turning away. "Or you can sit at the counter if you'd like. I don't make the rules."

While the waitress was still in earshot I said, "She just enforces them."

But I realized right away that I had made Mona uncomfortable.

I looked for conversation. "So I imagine you have a boyfriend by now," I said, but again I was instantly aware that this was a stupid thing to bring up.

"The postcards ..." she said, changing subjects. "Lola collects all of them in a scrapbook. The picture of a boat moving through the Everglades. Sun out, water shimmering, cranes in motion. She loved that one. We loved knowing how comfortable your life had become."

I didn't bring up the postcards she had sent me, as much as they continued to trouble me. "There hasn't been a day when I didn't miss all of you," I said.

She took two more shots.

"Maybe we could give the camera a rest for a while?"

She left the Hasselblad open, sitting on the table, and sipped her coffee.

"If you really want a picture of me I should freshen up, comb my hair at least."

"I'm just taking a test roll. I'll junk it when I'm done."

But I knew there was no such thing as a junk roll with Mona.

"How's our little girl?" I asked.

"My sister loves school."

"I can't wait to see her."

The waitress came by again, but Mona really didn't want anything, so I ordered eggs. Then, given a choice of fresh fruit or potatoes, I said to the waitress, "You decide."

She eyed me as she topped off our cups. Mona picked up her camera and recorded this exchange as well. I watched the waitress walk over to the grill and talk with the other waitress and the short-order cook on duty. All of them looked our way.

"I should clean up a little anyway before we head over to the house. Maybe we'll get the eggs to go."

"Apartment," she said. "Head over to the apartment."

"Of course. I guess you're pretty close to the lake."

She didn't reply.

"I'd like to surprise your mom. I have some good news to share. With all of you." I put my pack on the seat next to me and dug around, getting out a comb and a toothbrush and toothpaste. I should have spruced up at the airport.

Mona

There were times, after he left, when I would see my father go by on the street or look at me from a car window—in fleeting seconds. Then I would realize the trick my mind had played. When I was younger and my cat died, for weeks afterward, out of the corner of one eye, I saw him run through the kitchen or dart under a table, making ghost images.

I hadn't expected him to return, and certainly not in an alley in the middle of a snowstorm to give me a fucking heart attack. Then to see him standing there like a scarecrow. He was so thin, his hair scraggly and almost bald on top, his coat stained. He had this serious bandage on one hand. I thought he was sick or had gotten into a brawl or both. But then he said he had good news, and that didn't sound like cancer or a bar fight to me.

I saw how sorry he was about things. He even told me he liked my hair. I recorded that lie with the Hasselblad and the way he flinched—he could be pretty straight-laced. The minute he wanted to go over to the deli I knew that if I sat down and heard the whole miserable story of the last two years, I'd feel sorry for him. I'd feel so sorry I'd do whatever I could to drop the hard days he had handed us like a collection of broken tools we could neither fix nor throw out until he got home. But then, as we were sitting in that booth, I thought about it again. And I imagined as soon as he'd walk through the door Mom and Lola would flutter with nerves while I looked on, wondering what he was up to. I didn't want to see them get hurt a second time.

"I brought everyone a little present," he said. "Just something from the airport. I didn't have time to plan ahead."

It occurred to me that his pack contained everything he owned now. He had left the furniture when he went to New Jersey. He had left his share of the wedding china and the silver set, the linen and rugs, the framed art and the lamps, the appliances—all the items we had to sell. He went away light of possessions. He came back thin and empty. We didn't need empty. We had enough of our own.

When Dad got up from the table and went off to the bathroom to make himself presentable, I knew this was about Mom. And in that moment I honestly didn't care who he was if he was going to show up out of the blue and make things harder for her. I felt jumpy and picked up his phone.

He didn't have any pictures or music or much in the way of apps. He always said he was all thumbs, that it was easier to sit down and write a letter or talk by phone. He didn't have a password, and the number code was the one he always used: 5050. I started to scroll through, saw the name Edie, and had no idea who that was. I heard the door to the men's bathroom open. I saw him pay the check at the register and make arrangements with the waitress to wrap the food. Sliding back into the booth, he placed his things in his pack, held it up, and then seemed to realize how damp it was on the bottom. He wiped the seat and rested the pack on the floor again.

As he stirred his coffee, I had this picture in my mind of cutting the ropes to the bottom of his feet and watching him drift off, getting smaller and smaller.

"I assume Mom and Lola won't be home for a while," he said.

"Do you want to go by the house on the way? Just to look at the old place again? I'm curious to see if the new owners made any changes."

"I'm not ... I'm sorry you didn't call first. Mom's just ..."

"What's wrong?"

"She told you she has a boyfriend, right?"

He shifted his head like there might be a spot where he had better hearing.

"They took off with Lola and his kids to Michigan to get some skiing in. I would have joined them, but I'm drowning in work."

He began to clear his throat as if something was lodged there. "You're not serious," he said, waiting for me to let him up.

"He's nice enough, I don't know, maybe a little dull. He's a lawyer and his father is a federal judge, so David is thinking he might take that route in time. His kids are okay. We get along."

"David," he said and sat back in the booth, his face drained of color.

I took a photograph of his sorrow and then one of his effort to recalibrate. I set the camera down when the waitress brought the food wrapped to go. She topped off our coffees once more and told us to have a good day the way someone wishes you a little poison with your sweet. I watched my father stir his coffee again and throw the spoon down. I don't think he meant for it to skid across the table. He tried to grab it back while I pulled the camera out of its path.

"Sorry," he said, shaking his head as if he was coming out of a fog. "Sorry. How long?"

"I thought you knew. Six months or seven. Mom said something about you being in Florida. Maybe you could send tickets so I could bring Lola down this summer when we have some time. Are you north or south of Universal Studios?" I asked.

"I don't live in Florida, Mona. I've come home," he said.

When I first started driving my mother went over a list of things that could go wrong so I would know how to handle those situations. The engine might overheat or a tire could pick up a nail or a hunk of glass and someone with sinister intent might pull over and offer to help. But we never discussed the idea of arriving at an unmarked split in the road, out in the middle of nowhere, without a guidance system or map.

He pressed his fingertips to his eyelids and I saw the edge of the cut, the rest covered by a bandage. This looked like the beginning of a line of stitches.

Maybe he hoped when he opened his eyes again he'd be in another world where I would be dark-haired, small like a jockey, and openhearted. I put the camera strap around my neck and tucked it into my jacket to give it the best chance of staying dry. I zipped up and put on my gloves, trying to picture how things might have gone differently. I couldn't come up with anything.

When I looked up I saw my father as if he were sitting in the middle of a frozen lake, the ice starting to crack beneath him. I began to wonder about the prints I would get from the camera that turned everything upside down when it opened up.

Pushing my way out of the booth, I hurried to get away. As I opened the door to the restaurant I heard him call my name and then a loud commotion. A chair hit the ground, dishes clattered. I turned back and saw that he had tripped over his pack and was splayed on the floor.

I ran for blocks, sometimes skidding in the snow. Avoiding the L, where I thought he might appear, I stuck to side streets. The difficult part was keeping the camera steady under my coat. When I came to an abrupt stop to avoid an ice puddle, I felt the Hasselblad hit my ribs as if it might knock one out.

I knew I had reached the lake in the sheeting snow when I

found the summer snack bar. Behind me a waste of giant homes I couldn't see but recognized. I got under the eaves and took my phone out. I tried to get in touch with Cynthia, but she didn't answer, then Briana, who had been a good friend in high school and intermittently streamed things to my phone. But she was going to school in Canada and had her own snow to deal with. I tried a couple of other friends, but no one was anywhere near my part of town.

More than a mile from the L, from a bus, three or four miles from the apartment, and my feet and hands were ice and bone. Everything was soaked through or half frozen except my jacket, that large all-weather endurance jacket I now thanked my mother for buying for me three winters earlier, though I hadn't much liked it at the time.

It occurred to me that Ajay seemed like a guy who could locate a car in a pinch. He picked up, and his voice dipped in and out of reception, but when he got what I was saying he told me he'd hurry. I paced by the snack bar, up and back along the walk covered by an overhang. I could almost make out the lake through the flurries and thought about the times I had come here with my family in the summers. Everyone suited up, the towels and lotion, umbrellas and cold drinks, weight distributed so that my father would carry the heaviest load.

The snow had eased by the time Ajay arrived, the world thick with plows and salt trucks. He drove under the speed limit, babying an old Impala.

"It's possible the vacuum pump might go," he said, locking on to me as he drove.

"What?"

"That noise," he said over the noise, his eyes still fixed on me.

"Don't do that," I said as I put my boots up, moving them near the heating vents.

"Don't do what?" he asked.

"You know in movies where the driver looks away to have a conversation, and five minutes later you wonder if he's ever going to look at the road again."

"Someone should do a montage of that." He laughed. "Starting to warm up?"

"Ask me in a week. Where are we going?"

We had just passed the turn to our street.

"The Sears Tower." He reached over, pulled my visor down, and popped open the mirror. I had mascara streaked to my chin. Using the snow caked on my scarf, I cleaned my face.

"No, seriously," I said.

"A guy I work with gave me passes." He pulled them from a jacket pocket and handed them to me.

I thought about insisting we go home, but I knew my mother would occupy herself with trying to read my face. "Why not?" I said.

I sent a message to her that I was taking the L downtown to do snow pictures so she wouldn't stress. I rarely checked in, but I could imagine her watching the sidewalk, fearful about the storm. Turning off my phone, I sank into the front seat, and before long we were passing the Lincoln Park Zoo on one side of the Drive, the lake on the other. Pointing out a stand of trees by a breakwater, I said, "I hung out with a friend in late August when the waves were insane. She stretched out under the trees, and I used a waterproof camera."

"You'll have to show me," he said. I didn't know if he meant the place or the pictures. Even though he drove with care we did some sliding. Shortly after the Mies van der Rohe buildings—he seemed pleased that I knew about them—we turned inland to see the winter lights on Michigan Avenue. We drove past the Tribune Tower and across the river.

"I never see you with friends," he said.

"And you have so many," I said.

"You've been watching me." He looked pleased.

"Cynthia fills me in on all the neighbors."

"Ah, Cynthia from the second floor."

We listened to the sound of the vacuum pump.

"A lot of my friends have taken off," I said. "Cynthia keeps inviting me to her friends' parties, but they smoke like mad and talk about ... well, one time this girl cornered me and talked about light-bulb wattage and compact fluorescent bulbs, and finally she hit on grow lights. Someone else picked up on this and said he was going to start a communal beet farm and did I know anything about manure. And I don't know how many people handed me mai tais, and I don't drink mai tais, and after the first one I kept dumping them over the balcony. I mean, I love Cynthia, but you know."

I was pretty wound up. He just let me talk.

We found a parking spot and walked over to the tower. With no one else waiting in line, we ducked under ropes and got on the elevator with a couple of vacationers, probably in their fifties.

Although my ears began to seal over from the quick altitude shift, I heard a recorded voice blast from the speakers: *Upon completion in 1974, the Willis Tower, first known as the Sears Tower, was the tallest building in the world.*

"Ha. Taller than the World Trade Center towers." The man laughed.

"Did he just say that?" I asked, maybe on the loud side. But who could tell with the pressure on the eardrums and the grating, cheerful music leaking around the voice? The man pointed his guidebook at me and said, "That's not necessary."

"You don't think making a joke about the World Trade Center is in bad taste?" Ajay said.

"The world's in bad taste," the man said. "Get used to it."

Ajay, who was on the other side of me, began to push toward him, and I pushed back, saying, "The guy's a jerk."

Now the woman looked worried and yanked on her husband's sleeve.

He said, "I told you we should have gone to Atlanta."

Ajay and I laughed and blew them off, the doors opened, and we walked out into the large open space surrounded by windows on all sides. We went past the informational displays and the photo booth, straight to the east-facing windows, where we stood for a long time, looking out at the ice ripples.

We became transfixed. I remembered a story I once read, "The Falling Girl." I felt, in that moment, that I could be her, or my version of her. So that when Cynthia would knock at the door looking for me, my mother would say, *I think she's out falling.* Or if a census worker came by, Lola would say, *I'll tell her you stopped by when she reaches our floor.* And when my father would appear in another alley, I would look down at him and see that I still had some altitude left and call out, *I've heard the collision over and over in my sleep. Sometimes the car explodes. I see hands and teeth and eyes and bits of bone fall through the air. If I can catch all of those pieces, I'll ship them to you. Be sure to send your address.*

"You okay?" Ajay said, pulling me back in.

"Sure. Great views."

As we moved along the windows he pointed out some of the sites. I heard him mention Al Capone's headquarters and something about the Field Museum. "Sorry. Architecture school," he said. "Stop me if I get carried away."

I kept wondering what Richard would do now that he was back. What I would do.

Ajay took me lightly by the shoulders and coaxed me to turn until I faced him. "I'm a good listener."

Cynthia once told me that it's fairly common for people to tell strangers things they won't tell their family or friends. And maybe that's why I told this guy who lived on the first floor of my apartment building that I was probably the only one who witnessed something my father had done, something for which he could go to prison.

"So what are you going to do?" Ajay asked.

"Exactly," I said.

We slogged through the snow and got back in the car, but it wouldn't start. Hot-wiring didn't work. We went into a store, where he made a couple of calls, and eventually a tow service came and pulled the Impala away through the slush. Ajay said he and his friend might get it to run for another month before the next repair. It was that kind of car.

Soon enough we were standing in an L car heading home. Holding on to a pole together, we watched the woman seated by us, the way she tucked into herself. We made a great effort to avoid knocking against her thin legs or pressing against her birdlike feet despite the people pushing against us. She folded and refolded her newspaper as well as herself in an effort to be undisturbed, and when she got absorbed in her paper I glanced at an article about a woman in Ohio. I had heard about her on the news. She had been arrested for falsifying documents about where she and her kids lived so she could get them into a decent school district. This woman was about to graduate from the University of Akron with a degree in education. She was working with special needs kids when they hauled her off to jail. I turned away, feeling my ribs ache.

So I could baby the camera, Ajay had insisted on taking my pack.

I asked about his parents.

"My father was a rather brilliant structural engineer, living in India, when he was offered a job with one of the best firms in Chicago. My mother was a translator, and she planned to look for work here too, though she didn't share his enthusiasm for America. My father wanted her to stay home at least part time and hoped for a large family. They brought my grandfather along because he was a widower and my father was his only child. I was to go to Harvard one day or MIT. This was determined when I was six months old."

"No expectations."

"Right? My mother was serious about most things and quite elegant. My father was a generally happy man, into all things Western. He loved Western suits and shoes and hamburgers and fries."

"I had a dream about your parents."

"Tell me."

"I can't remember most of it," I said.

He laughed. "Go on."

"I was in your apartment. There was a picture of a man and woman in a small frame—at least I thought they were your parents—she was tall and beautiful and wore a dark-green sari with silver edging, and he was short but stood very straight. He wore a cream-colored linen suit. There was more to the dream, but that's all I remember."

"That's them. That's how my parents are dressed in a small photo in the dining room."

"Now I'm spooked," I said.

"That makes two of us," Ajay said.

One time Geary and I were looking at images by Ralph Meatyard—the photographer known for putting children in scary dime-store masks for some of his shots—and Geary had talked about the line between the mystical and madness. And that's how it felt, this strange kind of knowing I had with Ajay. But since I didn't believe in mystical things, I wondered where this left me.

I had an aunt who went mad. My father told me she wanted to save all the dogs in the world, believing that her two-bedroom home in Michigan was the center of a dog universe that she was responsible for. She kept more than seventy dogs, a number that she stole outside grocery stores and restaurants where their owners had tied them up. She fed them, bathed them, and outfitted them in suits and skirts and bonnets. Each dog had a bed frame and mattress with a full set of linen and towels. She had a village of dogs, a town full of her own madness.

A sudden movement of the train wedged me against Ajay. I righted myself when the woman next to us squeaked loudly. The train completed the turn.

"Keep going—about your parents."

"My father loved American television. I mean the absolute worst that sitcoms had to offer. And he was a great punster. My mother was a wonderful cook. When we first got here from India they were eager to move out of the hotel so my mother would have a kitchen again. They set out to look for a new home in the burbs. I was four, and they decided to leave me at the hotel with my grandfather so they could move quickly through a string of open houses. My grandfather had to hold me back to keep me from running after them, just on that day, he said, no other. I cried and cried when they left, and he had no idea why. I don't know if my father was the best driver, but he was still learning the American rules of the road and it was raining out. A truck hit them head-on. My family came from India. Too many of the roads, especially the ones in the villages, have no signs at all."

I moved my hands so they covered one of his as if to anchor him and the train we traveled in.

"I barely remember them now. I don't even remember getting the bad news. My grandfather talks about them regularly, though, and he likes to remind me that we lived in a beautiful, large home in India with a big staff. But between two governments, four attorneys, and five banks we lost everything. My grandfather was a retired mathematics professor. After my parents died he needed to go back to work to support us. He couldn't find any work in his field here and thought about returning to India. But his father had been a welder, and my grandfather had helped his father out when he was young, so he knew how to weld. Hoping he might get enough work to keep us going, he bought some basic equipment to start out and let some of the people in the Indian community here know he was available. They all knew about the accident. Someone hired him right away for a project. Pretty soon he was busy and managed in time to get a work permit. He got dual citizenship, set up his own business with a partner and made a go of it. I owe the old man a great deal, you see."

The train rocked into Edgewater station, slowly clicking past moneylenders, donut places, locksmiths. People shuffled in and out of doors.

"Go out with me," he said. "There's a restaurant I want to take you to."

"Not the best timing," I said.

"Then let me kiss you so I can work on my timing."

The woman next to us gave me this look as if to say, *Please get it over with.*

"Why were you on the tracks the other night?" I asked.

"I was waiting for a train, and then I saw you at your window. I used to go out on the rails all the time with a friend when I was younger. Thankfully my grandfather never found out. I just kept inching over that way. And then you waved, and I heard the train and jumped."

"I'm seeing someone," I said.

"I guess I *do* need to work on my timing."

I took hold of his jacket then. "Sorry. Mixed signals," I said and pulled him toward me, just a little, and kissed him a great deal.

"I don't mind," he said finally and kissed me back.

Mom dropped in at work as I was cleaning up to go. We picked Lola up from aftercare, and she showed us the new painting she had done of Dad. He was standing under an orange tree. The oranges were the size of small planets, and they didn't seem to be attached to branches, as if they were all about to drop on his head.

He hadn't shown at our apartment yet, and I began to think he was on his way back to Florida.

We drove to the A&P, where they were promoting a chance to win a vacation in the tropics. Cardboard pineapples strung across the ceiling danced in the breeze from the overhead vents.

Lining up a cart, Mom said, "I have two hundred dollars, and my goal is to buy enough for three weeks. I have a list."

Our groceries averaged a hundred twenty-five dollars a week or more, and we always ended up going back to the store for milk and bread and eggs.

"Huh," I said.

"Huh," Lola mimicked. She didn't have a clear sense of time despite drawing hands on analog clocks on her school worksheets. Now her face expressed too much concern for a five-year-old.

"Let's start with household items, paper products, and so on," Mom said. She opened the calculator on her phone. "We're looking for generic products."

"Generic toilet paper?" I said.

Lola's jaw dropped, and she took a few steps back, drawing too close to a stack of cracker boxes.

"Your sister is fooling around," Mom said and pulled her away.

By the time we got to the deli section at the far end of the store, we had $224.23 in items before our frequent-shopper discount, coupons, and sales tax.

"I get a cupcake," Lola said firmly.

"I'll put the bleach back, the shampoo ..." Mom said, starting to reach into the cart.

"We're out of shampoo." I said this lightly so she wouldn't get too concerned.

"Okay, the pocket pizzas and the hamburger buns."

"We can't have hamburgers without hamburger buns," Lola said, her lower lip starting to quiver.

"Okay," Mom said. "Help Lola pick out cupcakes. Two."

Under those spinning palm trees and beach-umbrella cutouts, we watched her load her arms with food products we would have gladly argued to keep. As she walked away, she dropped the heavy jug of orange juice—I almost called after her, and then other items began to cascade from her arms. I moved to help, but she put up a flat palm so I'd halt.

"Lola," I said, turning round. "Oh, wow, bunny-rabbit cupcakes, balloon cupcakes ... this is going to be hard."

We got in the checkout line a short while later and were half unloaded when our old neighbors Beth and her father, Art, got in line one register over. We used to live down the street from them in Evanston, and Beth and I had been in the same graduating class at the high school. There were moments of artifice whenever we ran into them. "Hi, Art," Mom said. "Beth sure has gotten tall."

"I keep telling her she should go out for the NBA." He lined several six-packs of soda onto the belt.

"Okay," Beth said, rolling her eyes.

"She warned me when she got into Northwestern that I'd need to keep the mini fridge stocked at all times."

"Such a great school. Mona's working in a photographer's studio."

Lola and I went ahead and stacked items onto our conveyor belt. This was something she loved to do, slowly, meticulously.

Our cashier said, "That will be one ninety-eight sixty-four with your rewards card."

"Excuse me, Art," Mom said, going over to where the checker waited. She pulled a new card from her wallet. It was a food-stamp card. She dropped her voice and handed this to the cashier. "This is my first time."

The checker said, "You *slide* a SNAP card, just like a debit card, in our keypad and—"

Mom looked intimidated, so I pulled the card out of her hand and swiped it in the machine before the woman could finish.

"*Only* the assignee is allowed to make purchases. And you can't get household items on a SNAP card," the cashier said, staring my mother down. "You'll have to pay for those separately."

"Are you sure?" Mom said. "No one told me that."

"They didn't give you the list of restricted items?" the woman said loudly, as if my mother was trying to run a Ponzi scheme in the A&P.

Mom took an audible breath. "What's on the list?"

"Household items, cosmetics, paper goods, things from the *deli* … You really have to go to the website." The checker looked at the line that had formed behind us.

"No, *they* didn't tell me anything. May I talk with the manager?"

"Don't, Mom," I said touching her arm, as if I were trying to keep my mother from walking into oncoming traffic.

"I have to get these things," she said turning to me. "I only have fifteen dollars until I get paid."

"Jesus," I said. "I have five dollars with me." When I looked up I saw Beth, who appeared to be making a video of our transaction with her phone. I had no idea how long she had been recording us.

I'll get paid on Wednesday," Mom said on the way home.
"You didn't tell me we're on food stamps," I said. With the engine noise and the pleasure of a special dessert, I hoped Lola wasn't
paying attention.

"The manager came over and sent everyone else to another line.
Thank God he recognized me. And I did buy the shampoo and the
toilet paper."

"This is his fault," I said.

"No, no, he really was nice. He even finished ringing things up
himself."

"You know who I mean."

We drove in silence for a while, my mother lost in thought, her
brows drawn together. I wanted to see this as just another of the
downward shifts, but I knew this was different. There was nothing
of the rallying, the quick effort to mend. She had found a million
ways to normalize for us, furniture sold but always making the
environment inviting; a shift in the play-date routine but making
sure Lola saw her friends; the effort to find that stable job that
would bring in enough cash. I never heard her complain about not
being able to sculpt, not once. But this was the first time she had
been pilloried.

I turned around. Lola, who was approaching her baked good
slowly, with great care, said, "I love this cupcake."

"I'm glad, sweetheart," Mom said without breaking her gaze.
Lola drifted, peering out her window, content.

Richard

When Mona was young, maybe eight or so, we used to take our bikes to Lincoln Park and ride the paths. One time we went over to Wells Street for lunch, not far from Second City, and I told her about the *Ripley's Believe It or Not!* that used to be across the street. She badgered me until I described Fish Woman. I'd seen her years ago, bright scales up and down her back. "She could breathe under water," I said, "and swim across the ocean."

"Who else?" Mona asked.

I told her about the man who could pass spears through his body without bleeding or feeling any pain. "This made it difficult to dress, you understand, when he would forget to pull them out." She asked me to keep going and I did, at least until our hamburgers arrived, though the truth is I had never been inside the exhibition.

Sometime after that we went miniature golfing with Liz. Mona said Alice lived beneath the golf course. Her mother was reading *Alice in Wonderland* with her at the time. "She fell down one of the holes," Mona said, "when they were large enough for a girl to fall through."

This is what Mona and I did, competed with tall tales, when she was still her father's daughter.

She would show me her report card first. She dragged me to the beach when she wanted to swim. I was the one to tuck her in at night. Insisting I sit next to her at the movies, she curled into my side while Liz patiently held the popcorn. We had our home and Liz worked away at her sculptures and we had big potlucks with our friends and my daughter adored me as I did her. I was in so many ways a joyous man.

Then Mona spent increasing amounts of time looking at art books or helping in the garden Liz was planting. She would have a sudden need to understand something about welding. A ten-year old girl who had nothing better to do in this world than to learn how to weld.

There was one day when I offered to take Mona to the ice-cream parlor and she said she had to go down to the basement and clean out the lint trap in the dryer. She has her mother's dry sense of humor, so I laughed and said, "Okay, after you do that we can go out and treat ourselves to hot fudge sundaes." Liz, who was standing nearby, said she could see my thoughts travel across my face as I attempted to look upbeat, or at least accepting, when Mona turned me down.

Liz assured me many times that this was a phase some girls go through where they gravitate more toward the mother's side of the planet. She had read her share of books on childhood and adolescent development and told me not to worry.

I happened to walk into the kitchen one day when she and Mona were sitting at the table outside under the umbrella, their backs to the house. They didn't seem to realize I was standing there near an open window. I believe Mona was twelve at the time. Just that morning I had stuck my neck out again. I had offered to take her bowling with a couple of her friends that weekend.

Liz said to Mona, "You know, it's not unusual for girls to spend more time with their mothers when they get to a certain age, and

I know you're busy with your friends, but is everything okay with you and Daddy?"

"Everything's fine," Mona said and guzzled her iced tea.

I watched Liz watch Mona. "You used to be pretty close with your father."

"I'm just busy with school and stuff."

"I know," Liz said.

Then Mona took her old Nikon out of its case and changed the lens to a 50 mm to get a nice, straight image, I guess, and she started taking pictures of Liz. And Liz didn't change her expression or shift about to alter the moment. Where I would have tensed up or at least felt I should button a shirt button or smooth my hair down, Liz was comfortable with this kind of intrusion, even encouraged it.

"I know he misses your company," Liz said. "Maybe you'd like to give him another try."

"You're making too much out of the bowling thing," Mona said. "I don't like bowling."

"Suggest something else," Liz said. "I'm sure he'd be flexible."

"Why are you pushing this?"

"I guess I just want you two to be close."

They gave their conversation a break for a while, nursing their beverages. Then Liz gave things another stab. "I'm going to go ahead and say this. And I'm not suggesting I think this is happening because if I did, I would take swift action, but if you ever get in a situation where anyone, *anyone* at all is ever doing anything inappropriate to you ..."

I was horrified. I didn't know what to do. I really didn't.

Mona lowered her camera and said, "Jesus, Mom."

"You're the sun and the moon to me, sweetheart. That's all."

"You really need to chill, Mom. I'm just ... Dad and I are different. You're in the arts. He's ...we don't have a lot to talk about, and I'm too old to do the daddy-daughter crap like miniature golf and go-carts. Now, can we change the subject?"

Why wasn't Liz defending me? She wasn't speaking up at all. And why in God's name was she letting Mona get away with that kind of language? I wanted to run out there and say, *Hey, this nice house, this nice neighborhood, the camera around your neck and the four others in your bedroom, they're all paid for by my ability to sell insurance.* But I didn't.

"Yes. Yes, of course," Liz said. "I'm sorry. That was a completely idiotic way of saying you can come talk with me about anything, anytime."

"What I *want* to talk with you about is my new shots. I did a triptych. ..."

Twelve and she was talking about triptychs. Honestly, sometimes I think that's the day I lost her. Right there.

"I really want to take a photo class with Mr. Geary, Mom. I'm under the age limit, so he wants to see what I've been doing before he'll admit me. Can you take a look?"

"I think we can arrange that," Liz said, scraping her chair back. I moved slowly, noiselessly, back to the living room so they wouldn't know I had ever been there.

Mona came through the door first, grocery bags in hand. I was on the phone, checking in with Honey, pausing long enough for the elevated train to pass, when I heard the keys in the locks. I had waited two days to show my face again. Honey was convinced that giving things another try was the right thing.

When Mona saw me she dropped one of the bags, and something shattered inside.

Standing there with a deep scowl, she noted the coffee maker with its red, glowing light and the box of sugar where I had left a spoon stuck in the top—her look saying I had no right to use their coffee, their water, their granules. I told Honey I'd call her back and scrambled to stand and turn off the phone.

Liz came through the opening to the kitchen next with Lola in tow. My arms dropped to my sides, my hands open, but everyone was frozen on the spot, and I felt this well of confusion.

"It's really good to see you," I said, looking first to Liz and then to Lola.

Liz looked as if she weren't able to release her grocery bags from her hands, and Lola got right up behind Mona, hiding. I couldn't believe how big she'd gotten, how much she resembled her sister. I had photos, but those were a few months old, and it's different in person. I understood she didn't recognize me.

"Let me help you with those," I said. But in that quick moment Liz let me know she had it covered.

She hoisted the bags onto the counter and said, "I'm just a little breathless from the stairs."

I went over and touched her arm and said, "One of your neighbors took pity on me and found the super down in the laundry room. He let me in. I'm glad you weren't away."

"The super let you in?" Liz said, clearly trying to keep up.

"I showed him my license, explained everything."

"What's *everything*?" Mona asked.

The room got still and Liz gave Mona a harsh look and maybe I hoped my expression said something about forgiveness—the kind that might move between Mona and me with a little effort.

"Mona, put the rest of the groceries away," Liz said, "and then play a game of Chutes and Ladders or something with Lola. I'll be back in a while."

"You sure you don't want me to call someone?" Mona said.

Maybe she meant the police, the Halyards, Liz's brother. Who knew? I felt criminalized by my own daughter, and to make matters worse no one was cueing Lola in to the fact that her father was standing right there at arm's length.

"Do as I ask, love," Liz said.

I got on my coat and followed in Liz's wake.

"Are you coming back?" Lola called.

Liz circled around and hugged her and kissed her the way I wanted to. "Of course I'm coming back, goose. No more than an hour or two. Mona's in charge."

As we walked through the neighborhood over to Howard, Liz warned me about the park and showed me the mace she kept in her purse. She assured me Mona also carried a can.

"You should have told me how bad things were," I said, shaking my head.

"And you've lost too much weight," she said. "What happened to your hand?"

"I'll explain later. Right now I want to hear about you and the girls. I don't think Lola even recognized me."

"She'll take a while."

"She's getting so tall."

"Her pediatrician thinks she'll tower over Mona and me."

"I almost didn't come after I talked with Mona. She explained about your having a boyfriend."

"What? When did you talk to her?"

"Two days ago, when I got in. She said there's a lawyer on his way to becoming a federal judge, with a vacation home in Michigan?"

Liz stopped and said, "Wow. No, there's no one like that."

"I came by to drop off a letter to say I understand. Your neighbor Mr. Kapur, he was so insistent I get out of the cold entryway. I didn't want to start into the whole business about why I've been away. I thought I'd just go ahead, make some coffee and gather my wits before taking off again. I thought you were away."

"It's all right. Tell me about this talk with Mona."

After I filled her in Liz said, "You'll have to be patient, Richard."

"Maybe she's involved with someone?" I thought that might explain the attitude.

"I suspect a photographer, but she's not ready to talk about that yet. Look, just tell me if you're ill."

"I haven't been eating right. That's all."

Liz brought up Sor, and I told her about his two families.

She told me about the trashouts. "Someone pulled the copper pipe out of the last one, but that's for the repair crew to worry about." She talked about the homeless men up in Detroit and other cities who spent their days hunting for any metal they could pull out of anything that wasn't moving. Whole houses stripped clean. One of the top U.S. imports to China scrap metal. "Scavengers spend their winter nights trying to keep warm around fires built in metal drums, just making enough to get a decent meal here and there."

I didn't know if I would ever be able to tell her where I had been. "I have some good news," I said, and talked about the lunch interview coming up.

Liz was the organized one. I remember going up to the attic one day to look for an old putting mat and finding an endless number of plastic bins she had purchased and filled, each clearly labeled with its contents.

She said she had a few of my better shirts and ties still, and the two best suits were hanging in the closet. There was a tailor she liked. Maybe if we explained how important this was, he'd be able to make the alterations in time—at least on one of the suits—and see if he could do anything with the coat. Otherwise she had a consignment shop in mind that sold men's office attire.

"I'm going to get us out of this neighborhood, Liz, and see that Mona makes it to college." I wanted her to know I meant business.

"That's what I've been attempting to do all along," she said.

"I know. I didn't mean …" I put my hand on her back and noticed her hair. She had told me about the stove incident.

"I'm trying to talk my boss into moving into North Shore foreclosures and putting me in charge. If he won't, well, we'll see. I might find a way to branch out on my own. There's something ghoulish about it, but there it is."

As we trudged upstairs, she must have sensed I would do anything in the world to make love with her that night, like a man let out of prison

"Why don't you head into the kitchen and make us some coffee," she said, "while I talk to Mona. I'll let you know when we're done."

"Sure, sure."

I began to wonder, as she snapped the locks open with her vast set of keys, if I was being welcomed in or locked out. I thought of the times when she had leaned her head against my shoulder after our date nights, right when we got to the door, signaling to me as if to say, *Tonight. The things I'll do to you tonight.*

"Lola," she said as she stepped into the living room, "I've decided to let you use my extra-special, Moms-only bubble bath for being the world's best grocery shopper today."

"Yay!" Lola said.

I ducked into the kitchen. There was no door between this room and the rest of the apartment, just a large arched doorway, but I moved out of view, tucking myself into a back corner, wishing I could disappear into the walls. I told myself things would change. I just needed to hang on. I got busy filling the coffee pot.

"*However,*" Liz continued, "the *only* way I can get the cap off that bottle is for you to get undressed and in the tub in one minute flat." The water started, and I heard Lola kick off her boots.

"You aren't allowed to move the pieces while I'm gone,"

Lola told her sister. Mona had always been good, at Lola's age, at memorizing the coordinates of Candy Land if she had to leave the board. Perhaps Lola had started to display the same tendency.

Once she had settled in the tub—the door open so they could listen to her humming to her sinkable action figures—I stuck my head around the doorframe to ask if anyone was ready for coffee. Liz and Mona sat on the big bed in the dining room, and Liz said, "In a while, thanks."

I poured a cup for myself and went back to my spot. I was surprised to hear their conversation so clearly until I saw the open vent in the baseboard.

"It must have been hard not letting me know he was in town," Liz said. She was good at empathy with a solid scold.

"He's completely broke, isn't he?" Mona asked.

"He has a meeting for a job downtown next week," Liz said. "With a good firm. The CEO said he was impressed with Dad after they talked by Skype."

"So where's he living?"

"Mona …"

"Great. The family that SNAPs together stays together, right?"

Liz didn't make a sound at first, but I could imagine her mouth as she counted to ten. "Forty million people are on food stamps, Mona."

"Right now he doesn't have a job. And where the hell is he going to sleep? Lola said he looks scary. *Here's your dad, Lola, this scary guy who abandoned you,*" Mona whispered.

"What?" Lola called. She must have heard her name ping against the bathroom tiles. I hoped that was all she heard.

"We were just wondering how that tub is," Mom said.

"I have a new hairdo," Lola said.

"I'll come see in a minute," Liz said with the uplifted voice she reserved for such moments.

"Okay, but I'm ready to get out," Lola said.

I heard the tub start to drain and Liz helping Lola rinse her hair just as the front door closed roughly.

I'll admit there were times when pressures stacked up pretty hard before New Jersey. Liz wouldn't understand why I was working late again; she needed me to *talk* to her—*to open up* more; she needed more time in the studio, wondering aloud how she was ever going to make it at this pace. *I should have gone to New York,* she'd say, *when I had the chance.* Around that time Mona unlatched and walked out the back door and went over to our neighbor's dry fountain. After I lost my job it was worse. It seemed like every small thing began to wear on us. Lola was still not using the potty, though she was too old for diapers. Mona was staying out too late. The refrigerator needed more Freon.

My father had been moved to hospice care while all of this was going on, and I made trips over there to keep my mother company, though I had sworn never to see him again.

There was a night back in Atlantic City when too many thoughts had built up, and I was walking around carrying them like a sack of old clothes and bedding all in need of a good wash, and I went down this particular street near the boardwalk. There was a long string of streetlights, and when the power went out they didn't all shut down at once but went out one by one. It occurred to me that I might be able to shut my thoughts off that way, one by one, until everything was quiet and peaceful.

As I sat at the kitchen table, stirring my coffee, that's what I attempted to do. I listened to the elevated train go by, and there was no other place I needed to be, nothing else I needed to do except quiet my mind so I'd be ready for that first day of work.

Assuming all went well, soon enough I would be writing out rent checks, lining up a debit card, and looking for a decent car. I would be milling around Liz's art openings even if I wasn't always sure how to make conversation at those things ... but for now, I reminded myself, all I needed to do was not overthink tomorrow's lunch.

Mona had already stopped in from work. She had changed her top and shoes, put on makeup, and switched cameras without speaking to me. She didn't answer when I asked her directly if she'd be back for dinner.

I got out my notes and was thinking about a good icebreaker for meeting my coworkers when the downstairs bell rang.

I reached out to hit the buzzer, thinking Mona must have forgotten something, but I stopped at the last second, remembering the flood of cautions Liz had given me at the start of the week. There were so many things she was worried over now. I had watched the way her neck tensed as she recalled additional items I needed to be aware of if I was going to be with Lola by myself. She had talked to me as if I were a newly hired babysitter. It was hard to see her that way.

I leaned on the intercom and heard a man's voice. "I'm looking for Mona."

"Who's looking for Mona?" I sounded back.

"Photographer friend. She there?"

I realized this might be the guy. If I grilled him a little, without being too obvious about it, I might be able to put Liz at ease. If he turned out to be a lowlife, we could figure out how to protect Mona together.

I buzzed him up, opened our apartment door, and stood at the top of the stairs, catching glimpses of his head. He had a ponytail. As he climbed, I saw the shoulders of his leather jacket, the shearling collar. When he got to the top of the stairs I backed up and stationed myself in front of our door.

He looked me over in a deliberate manner and got his cigarettes out of his jacket, tapping one my way. When I waved it off he lit one for himself. All this time I hadn't invited him in, and he seemed in no hurry. If he was seeing Mona this was worse than I imagined. Even when I considered that smoking might have aged him—there was gray in the hair bundled in the back—the guy had to be at least forty.

"I don't think I caught your name," I said.

"Nitro," he said. "You can't be the guy from the first floor."

"I'm Mona's father."

"Interesting. Is she home?"

"I don't know that I'm all that interesting, but she'll be home in a minute. Come in and wait." He started to follow me inside, and I turned and said, "You probably want to put that out," looking at his cigarette.

"That's all right," Nitro said.

I got him a saucer so he wouldn't knock the ash on the floor and said, "We have a young daughter. Smoke's a bad idea."

He dawdled stubbing it out. I told him to have a seat at the kitchen table. I would open the doors and air the place out as soon as I had what I needed.

"How did you meet Mona?" I asked.

"She didn't tell you?" He said this with a slight smile—at least I think that look was a smile.

"We've been a little busy lately. Can I get you a cup of coffee?"

"Black. I'm sure she'll tell you when she's ready," he said and stretched his legs out so that if I needed to get up I'd have to step over them. "You said she'll be right back?"

"Any minute. What type of photography do you do?" I asked, stretching to pull one of the cups off the hooks rather than go around him. There was just enough in the pot for one cup. I poured this out, though I'd been saving it for after dinner.

"Fashion. Fine art. You know."

"Mona's doing some work for you?"

"We're enjoying each other's company."

"What would she enjoy about being with a forty-year old man?" I said, and maybe that question didn't come out right, but his response was worse.

He laughed and said, "I'll let her break that down for you."

"You're talking to her father," I reminded him.

"You asked me an honest question." He shrugged.

"That's offensive," I said.

"Maybe the harder it is to be honest with yourself, the more offensive it seems."

"We're done here. Don't count on seeing my daughter again anytime soon."

"Aren't you just passing through?"

I was about to grab his arm and shove him out the door. But he was going on his own accord.

"I'll let her know you stopped by," he said, "on your way to nowhere."

Mona

Someone stole my wallet a few months earlier. I was in a coffee shop in the neighborhood, and I had slung my pack over the back of my chair. For some reason I thought leaning against it, feeling the strap along the muscles of my back, kept it safe. But the thief was soundless and weightless as he slid inside the zipper, reached to the bottom, fished it up, and disappeared through the main door. Within minutes he was down the street, charging things on my debit card.

With that same kind of speed my father was ready to tap us for room and board, rides around town, dry cleaning deliveries, meaningless conversation, anything that would make him feel safe and close, even if it was a false closeness, a phony safety. I would have said something after I dropped the groceries and the peanut butter jar shattered, but Mom was suddenly asking me to play Chutes and Ladders. I would have raged if not for the fact that Lola was standing there. I don't know if she understood the way she anchored us while we worked to anchor her.

Almost before our parents were out the door Lola asked me who that man was, and I shrugged and lined up the bags, trying to breathe. I should have said, *An old friend.* I couldn't think.

"He looked scary," she said.

"Mom's fine. I want to be the red player today. You don't mind, do you?"

As I expected, she said, "Red's my favorite color."

"All right … I just said that to get the yellow."

"Yellow is my other favorite," she clarified with a modest smile.

"How about I hand you things from the grocery bags and you figure out where they go?" I said. "And then I'll let you pick out the color you want the most." I took a seat at the table and pulled a box of generic crackers from the first bag, careful to avoid the mess at the bottom.

"How about I give *you* the things in the bags." She took a seat on the package of twenty-four rolls of toilet paper and handed me a jar of pickles.

"Okay, deal, as long as I can do the messy bag. Have I told you I love your assertiveness, Lola?"

"My what?"

"The way you do the things you do. Hand me anything."

I just had to keep Lola busy until Mom came back and I could get out of there and have some time to think about statutes of limitations.

When I found Constantina in the entryway the next day I ran upstairs and got a camera. I asked her to stand in front of the mailboxes. I don't know why I wanted to capture her ordinariness.

She measured me with those dilated eyes. "I asked him if he got my note, and he said, 'What note?'"

"I lost it somehow, but I thought if I made a print of you, you could give it to him." I explained that I worked at a photographer's studio.

"You better be straight with me," she said, eyeing my camera. She got out her phone, looked at the screen, scrolled, sent a message, waited for a reply, sent another message, adjusted her hair and removed flecks of mascara from below her eyes using a large mirror she had tucked in her purse. Then she moved a few inches so that she was next to Ajay's mailbox and said she was ready.

As she sharpened and came to rest in the lens, it's possible I saw something of myself there, the heartbroken one, but I quickly pushed this away so I could take a few head shots and full-length frames. I told her I would make a print of the best one that day.

Later, when Geary looked through the images, he said I could have made better use of the graffiti in the background, but at least we agreed that one of the shots made sense. He also remarked that I should do a series of people standing by their mailboxes. "They'll be obsolete one day," he said.

"Mailboxes or people?" I asked.

"Both. Look, I know we'll all be glad when you get out of that neighborhood, but you would have lost some decent work if you hadn't moved there."

He had seen any number of prints come out of that world. *Decent work* was high praise. I leaned against his arm for a moment and thanked him for everything. Then I got to work cleaning up. I placed the best print of Constantina in an empty photo box that I slid into my pack.

She was hanging out on the sidewalk late that afternoon. It was bitter cold, and I felt the sting on my face and hands, so I knew she had to be frozen to the bone. Patches of melted snow had frozen over the walk. The super hadn't been around yet to throw out salt. Her boots had heels like needles.

I put the box in her hands and opened it for her. She picked the print up and stared at it for a long time. I watched her eyes move in the exact way I had intended. Cropping was everything on this one. "Did you give him a copy?" she asked.

"I wouldn't do that without your permission." I said, "You're the first to see it."

"I didn't know it would be black-and-white. My eyes are like really dramatic."

I had done some tricks when I printed it to make sure she wouldn't look like a raccoon.

"Ajay thinks I'm too emotional," she said and gripped my arm. I guess she was worried about slipping. "Me and Ajay, we're meant to, you know ..." Her voice began to quaver. She let go of me and felt around her head now, as if she had lost several of her hairclips.

"... to be together?" I said.

"Everyone can see it. My aunt told me I could come back here— you know, to Chicago—and live with her. She's practically around the corner. People you're tight with, that's everything. You live with both your parents?" she asked.

I thought if I answered, things might move faster. I was eager to catch the light. "My mom and my little sister," I said.

"*And* your little sister. I have lots of little nieces and nephews. They're so cute. How old is she?"

"Just turned five."

"Super smart, I bet. And beautiful. Like you."

I couldn't tell if she was jealous of Lola or me, but either way, why?

"Listen, I should go."

She looked at the print again. "Do me one more thing," she said.

"I really—"

"This will only take a second. I promise."

She handed the print back, fished around in her bag, pulled out a lipstick, and added a deep red color to her mouth. Then she took the print back, pouted slightly, and placed a kiss next to her face, right over my family's mailbox.

That print took a good hour of my time to make.

"Give this to Ajay. He'll understand."

"I don't know, I—"

"You won't *lose* it, will you?"

"Wouldn't you rather just give it to him yourself? I hardly know him."

"I think he's watching me. Take it."

"Ajay is watching you?" Their blinds were drawn, and I couldn't see any lights on inside.

"His pissy old grandfather," she said, looking at the apartment. "He's looking."

"I don't see Ajay much, but when I do ..."

"I'll never forget this," she said.

Some of the moms in the neighborhood had gotten to know me a little and understood I would make free prints of their children. They also knew I had a little sister who got heavily photographed. So they would let me circle their kids on stoops and benches and sidewalks, change lenses, and wait until I got shots I hoped Geary would want to talk about. He kept on me about paying more attention to fill light and tone when photographing people.

I was taking shots of three boys pushing each other up and down the street in a grocery cart when I decided to stop back at the apartment. Just as I got to the third floor Lily opened her door and came halfway through the doorjamb and stopped. She had a Duaflex IV around her neck. I had the Hasselblad around mine.

"Hello," I said.

Lily narrowed her eyes and studied my camera as if I were a camera stand or part of a display. Finally she looked at my face with an almost angry expression, as if she knew what I had done.

"I'm Mona," I said.

She looked at my camera again for a moment and then she pulled the door behind her so it snapped shut. Drawing her collar in, she went downstairs. I heard both doors open and shut. I went down to the landing, and from the window I saw her trudge off, trying to get that last light. She began to take pictures of the kids I had just shot, almost as if to show me up. I tiptoed back to her door.

My heart was sick with pounding as I took the handle and felt it turn.

The apartment was dark. I set my backpack down right inside the front door and, using my phone light, got her negatives out. I turned the light on in the walk-in closet. Where before I had been aware of boxes, now I knew I was looking at a remarkable archive. I fixed the negatives into the right sleeves, sealed those boxes again, and was about to leave when a label caught my eye.

The date was just a couple of months ago. The subject: *Rogers Park, Mothers and Children.* I knew what I was doing probably as much as she did. You can't steal people's lives like that and not know. There weren't any prints, but I took a sheet of negatives from the box and resealed it. I turned out the light and went back into the main room. I wanted to look at those cameras again but heard someone on the stairs. My hands were shaking badly when I slipped the negatives into the box in my pack. I left, again without changing her lock, so that I could return what I had taken.

Richard was in the kitchen when I got in. The whole place smelled like cigarette smoke. I went straight into my bedroom and shut the door.

From my window I saw Lola in the yard. With her small plastic shovel she scooped bits of snow into a pile our mother must have helped her start in one corner. Just then Mom came up from the basement into the yard with an armload of metal pieces, including long and short pipes. I wasn't sure if this was Mr. Kapur's stuff or gleanings from her trashouts.

She dumped this load, and I heard the metal ring and clang

against the ground. Taking Lola by the shoulders, Mom leaned down and kissed her cheek, and Lola hugged her. Then Mom put the tiny shovel against one wall of the yard. Together they dragged some kind of disk into the spot that Lola had started to clear. It wasn't as big as a manhole cover, but I could see Lola's breath working in hard clouds. Once this piece was in place my sister brushed her hands together, proud of her work.

A few feet away Mom placed a flat square of black metal meant to hold an outdoor umbrella in place. Picking up a few wide pieces of pipe, she set them vertically on top of the disk, then stood back several feet to consider her plan. Lola did the same with her own pieces of smaller pipe, placing them on the square. I don't know if she understood what Mom was up to since she was so young when our mother stopped sculpting, though she seemed eager to join in. Either way, I doubt Lola realized how her own well-being was bound up in Mom's first new work.

When they came upstairs a short while later Lola barged into my room and shut the door behind her, the way she did when she really needed to talk or just be around me and not have to talk. I sensed this was the former, so I didn't remind her that she needed to knock first. I took her winter gear as she squirmed out of it, setting the boots and jacket and snow pants over a chair near the radiator to dry. Maybe I looked a little flushed from the heat because Lola crawled into bed with me and asked, "Do you have a temperature?" She got me to lean forward. She touched my cheeks and forehead and pronounced, "Nope. Cool as a cucumber." That was Mom's expression.

"Thank you, Doctor," I said.

"I might be a doctor someday."

"I would bring all of my children to see you," I said.

After a long silence she furrowed her brow and asked, "Did Mom tell you who he is? She told me."

"Yes," I said. "And then I recognized him. Not at first, though." I didn't want her to feel cheated, thinking all of us knew and she didn't.

"But you're sure now?" she asked.

"Yes, I'm sure."

"Am I supposed to love him?" she asked.

In that moment she looked prepared to believe anything I would tell her. I kissed the top of her head, then looked her in the eyes, our foreheads practically touching. "I think things have to feel right to you, Lola. Like with Mom. I never have to tell you how to feel about Mom."

"So I get to decide?"

"I'd say that's what you should do. Take your time, and when you're ready, you decide."

"He doesn't smell like my father."

"Ah. I love you, Lola."

"I love you."

And this seemed to satisfy her, at least for the moment. Lola curled into me and fell into a quiet state while the trains rocked by. I did some reading, and eventually I drew her hair into a long ponytail and whispered close to her ear, waking her when Mom knocked to say dinner was ready. I said I had eaten late and needed to take a bath, though the apartment was filled with the smell of stir-fry, something she knew I liked.

That's when a friend sent me a text: *Did you see this?*

While I sat by the window, L trains going by, I watched an Auto-Tuned video. There was the face I made as I tugged Lola from the store, the clown cupcake crushed in my other hand; the manager coming over to the register; every last item removed from the bags as Mom stood there in her shame; Art stopping to see if he could help.

It was called *SNAP.*

Checker: You can't get household items on a SNAP card.

Mother: No one told me. No one told.

Checker: They didn't give you the list? The list?

Mother: What's on the list? No one told me. What's on the list?

Checker: Cosmetics, paper goods, things from the deli.

Mother: May I talk with the manager?

Mona: Don't, Mom.

Mother: I have to get these things.

Mona: Don't, Mom.

Mother: I only have fifteen dollars.

Mona: Don't Mom.

Mother: May I talk with the manager?

Mona: Jesus.

Mother: No one told me.

Mona: Jesus. Jesus. Jesus.

There were 3,247 hits already. It's not that I was dumb about this kind of stuff, but the reminder of how things can travel away from you hit hard. I felt as if I should brace for anything now: floods, plague, famine. I was ready for an invasion of locusts. I thought of the time Geary had me go through Depression-era photos from Parks and Lange, Wolcott and Rothstein, Lee and Welty.

I filled the tub, and as I soaked I was reminded that in the morning four people would be fighting to use the leaky faucet that had made a patch of rust by the drain and a toilet with a seat that threatened to come unhinged. I thought of my father's thick facial hair clinging to the white foam of his shaving cream and slowly settling in the sink's catch until Mom would fish it out.

When I was in my robe I recognized her cleanup sounds in the kitchen and heard my father's storytelling voice. Cracking the bathroom door open, I angled a hand mirror around until I saw

Lola standing at a careful distance from him. He was sitting on her bed. And though she wasn't curled into him the way she would have been with Mom or me, I was worried that she was becoming mesmerized.

"And so he lost his sheep and his cows, his ducks and his pigs …"

"*Everything*," Lola said in her knowing way.

"Yes, exactly. *Everything*. He was a man who had nothing left but the clothes on his back and a small rucksack. And so he began his journey."

"Is this story about you?" Lola asked.

Lola was a smart girl, but she had never been weirdly smart like one of those kids who reads *Remembrance of Things Past* or *Harry Potter* by themselves in kindergarten. I couldn't imagine that she knew the word *rucksack*, yet somehow Lola had used one of her mental drill bits to peer into Dad.

"Maybe in some way," he said.

I wiped the fog off the mirror to see how Lola took this information.

"Why did he lose everything?" she asked.

"Well, this particular man, the man in the story, had done something he couldn't forgive himself for."

There it was. He was finally able to say it. The ills visited upon our family came from that moment. He would always be driving away from that mother and child trapped in their car pleading with him to save them.

My mother stopped what she was doing and leaned into the doorframe that separated the kitchen from the living room, a dish towel thrown over her shoulder. I don't think she wanted to hear what the man had done, but even more she didn't want Lola to hear because she interrupted to say, "Let me know when you're ready to have me trim your hair, Richard. The kitchen would work."

"We're almost done," he said.

"Lola can wait to hear the rest later."

"So he was a bad man," Lola concluded.

"Or a good man who did something he regretted, something he was very sorry about."

Then he reached out, as if he was about to put his arm around Lola's waist. But Lola moved away and said, "I have to see what Mona is doing."

"Don't you want to hear how the story ends?" he asked, defying our mother. "I think I want to."

"I have things to do," Lola said.

My father had always unwrapped his stories slowly, sometimes in serialized form. They were the presents he crafted for days, the way some fathers toil at a lathe and band saw to produce toys for their children. They were the trick stories: the ones that suggested that stories, like people, are no more reliable than a bet. And sometimes, when he'd had a drink or two, they were the stories he lodged in your heart or taped under your rib cage, where they might eventually detonate. Until I understood this I used to lean in too close, listen too hard, trust too much. But not Lola. Lola wasn't buying any of it.

His favorite story, or at least the one he seemed to like to tell the most, was about the day the sky opened up and money fell in a hard rain. It fell right on top of a man going off to work. The money poured down, and he removed his hat and filled it to the brim. He filled his pockets, his hands, even his mouth. I remember asking once if the money in the man's mouth was in bills or coins because I knew from my mother that if you swallowed a coin, you'd choke. My father laughed and told me I took things too literally, like my mother, and then I had to go ask her what *literally* meant.

I sometimes wondered what it was to have enough money, what mysterious amount that might be. And then I found myself wishing for a sudden windfall that would be the right amount. I hoped a distant relative would leave us a fortune in rare coins or that I would trip on a bag full of thousand-dollar bills on my way to school. As soon as I understood what my father did for a living I hoped our house would burn to the ground while we were out at the store so a truckload of insurance money would be shipped to us the next day. And when that money finally appeared, I would give it all to my father so he would have enough.

Of course now we were in a different kind of game.

Lola knocked on the bathroom door and asked if I would read to her before bed. "I'll be there in a minute," I said, finishing my makeup. I heard Mom and Dad moving chairs around in the kitchen, sheets of newspaper being unfolded. She did a decent job of haircutting, even if it ended up a little sculptural at times. Either way I imagined he was grateful to lose the long, straggly stuff. He couldn't look like the man who had lost everything for his business luncheon.

When Lola fell asleep and I was done with my own reading, I carried her into the dining room, where Mom pulled back the covers. I held all of Lola's weight in my arms for a moment and then gently slid her next to Mom.

The TV had been moved around, and I figured it was about making sure Dad wouldn't have to strain his eyes from where he rested on Lola's bed. It made me realize we'd had few moments of TV or radio quiet since he'd come to stay. He was in the middle of a crime show, and some woman's corpse, stabbed twenty-three times, was being prodded and poked by the forensic team discussing the case. As I went into my room and shut the door, I wondered if he identified more with the team of experts or the corpse, and I wondered when my fury would hit the open air.

My father was like a street renamed by a city that always manages to get you lost. And I didn't want to be lost anymore.

I heard Mom call softly to him from the other side of her barricade, "You'll have to turn it down, Richard."

"No problem," he said in a kind of wonder, his voice straining above the work of the detectives. Perhaps he had become a little hard of hearing. It's possible he lowered the volume a notch or even two, I wasn't sure, but I bet she was chafing. I imagined her rubbing her forehead the way she did sometimes when she was looking for answers. I didn't understand her long patience, and I hoped she was starting to doubt her decision about taking him in or back or whatever she was doing.

I heard her go into the bathroom and eventually get back into bed. I turned out my lights, and that's when I heard his voice drift from the living room and seep around the edges of my door like a house fire.

"Maybe Lola would like her bed back," he said to Mom in a beguiling tone. "I could rub your shoulders, help you relax a little."

"Securing that job tomorrow will help all of us relax," she said. "But if you aren't ready to sleep, you can take a walk or something. I hung your coat up in the front closet."

As an afterthought she said, "You can use the can of mace in my purse."

When my phone thrummed against my pillow a short while later, it was Ajay. We talked for a while, and our conversation quickly became sleepy and random until he asked about my father.

"It's like watching a bad remake of a bad remake. He's breaking everyone's heart."

"I'm sorry," he said.

"My mother has this generosity she can't shut off. When we lived in Evanston, I was looking for a pan to heat up some soup one day, and she told me the Veterans' Association had called, and they had run down a list of household items people need the most. Pans with lids were big on the list. So she took all but one of ours, boxed them up, and left them out by the curb for pickup."

"Are you thinking about leaving?"

"Right now I have to look out for Lola."

"I have this vague memory of my mother saying something like that to me about my grandfather the day they were killed, that I should look out for him."

"And that seemed right to you?"

"At the time it seemed funny to me, I was so little. Now he's having his share of difficulties. He really should stop driving. At least I think I've finally made him realize he can't use a welding torch anymore. His business partner, an old friend, said my grandfather can be useful in other ways in the office, so he'll continue to go to work for a while. But some days he's angry one minute and tender and emotional the next."

"I think he gave all of his metal stash to my mother."

"He said she's making something *quite unique* in the backyard. I guess they talked for a long time. I think he respects your mother very much now."

When I grew quiet again he changed course. "You asked about Constantina."

"And you didn't want to talk about her," I said. "That's all right."

"We were together for a year. We had a group of friends in common, and it was easy to be together at first. We weren't in love. At least I wasn't. I did the tat on a kind of dare. When we fell apart I found out she was huffing spray paint."

"I can't imagine." Though I could when I thought about her eyes.

"She told me she likes the gold and silver colors the best. And glue. She loves glue. She started showing up unannounced. For a long time I'd say okay because I worry about her and I thought I could help. But I call her aunt now as soon as Connie shows up, and her aunt takes her to a clinic."

I wasn't expecting her to be *Connie*.

When I heard the shower going the next morning Mom and Lola were still sound asleep.

Dad had left Lola's small bedside lamp on. He'd laid out an outfit in the shape of a man. Suit pressed and ready to go, shirt fresh from the cleaners. Belt, cufflinks, and two ties to pick from, handkerchief, boxers, undershirt, and socks. Alongside this the leather briefcase Mom used when she showed her sketches to clients. Key chain with a lone apartment key, wallet, and phone. Shoes on the floor paired up. Every last thing ready for the interview.

I opened his wallet to find a picture of Mom in the top window where someone else might have kept a credit card. I was sliding my fingers into the sections of his billfold when the shower shut off. I placed the wallet back on the bed and went downstairs.

I used Cynthia's bathroom and crawled into bed with her. She had blue silk sheets shredded at the bottom from her boyfriend Luke's toenails or rough heels. There was a big white comforter.

"Poor baby," she said once she realized I was there and she had a chance to see the clock. She told me, in this drifty way, how Luke used to ride his motorcycle out near Ravinia while he was on Ambien. "You want some of that?"

"That stuff will knock you on your butt," I said.

"Some people have a little give in their systems."

Sex, basketball, riding elevators up and down waiting for the cables to snap, head shaving. She told me about life in a trance state. "I knew this girl," she said, "who could cook six-course meals while she was on the stuff. Somebody posted a video where she's asleep, roasting chickens."

"No, thanks. I just came down to avoid my father for a while."

"I was terrified of everything thanks to mine," Cynthia said. "Until I met Luke. He says you either get with love or you treat it like a weed. Most people dig it out by the roots or scald it with boiling water—but he isn't like that."

"I'm sorry he had to go away."

"He needs to be alone for a while. It's killing me."

"There was a boy I liked in high school named George," I said. "One night we parked near the lighthouse in Evanston and started to make out. Each time a car streamed by its headlights washed over us in the backseat. A sharp flash and a trail of red. Then all of a sudden this shipping truck passed so close I screamed into George's mouth. Driving home that night, we got stuck behind this street sweeper. We sat there, completely awkward, waiting. All I could think was that the driver of the street sweeper would be out there all night cleaning up after a bunch of accidents like us."

"Your dad's getting you all worked up," Cynthia said.

"And all Mom's doing is trying to hold the world together. Each time it drops through her fingers and shatters she runs around telling us not to step on the pieces, not to get our feet shredded on the fucking pieces."

"I don't think your mom has mean bones, though, do you?" Cynthia asked.

"No. I think she's a giant, actually."

"We're lucky if we get one of those. Hey, I have to show you this site where there are people photographed flying and ..."

"That's trick photography."

"I know, but it looks real. Here's my question: When you're having those flying dreams, do you run into phone lines and shit?" Cynthia asked.

"I just fly. It's like walking without gravity. Or swimming without water. I had one dream where I went to flying school and someone taught me how to do loop de loops."

"I'm sick with envy," Cynthia said.

"But I had one where Ajay set himself on fire."

"There are videos where people start tiny fires in their palms with that hand-cleaner gel. They're supposed to put them out immediately, only some people get taken to the ER with second-degree burns up to their chins."

"It wasn't like that."

"I think the only way you can stop that kind of dream from happening again is to have sex with him."

"Right," I said and climbed out of her bed.

"God, I wish Luke would set himself on fire in my dreams."

"No. You don't. At all."

"We could change your hair color before you go to work," she said. "I bought some new neons."

"No, thanks," I said. "Just coffee." I gave her a kiss on the cheek and stumbled out to the kitchen.

Lola covered her ears when Dad opened the bottle of cheap champagne. Roasted drumsticks with baby potatoes and sautéed carrots sat in the middle of the table on a platter. I stood at the opening to the kitchen, watching this scene. Mom made a point of telling him to pour a glass for me, and I made a point of saying I'd pass.

"Sit down anyway," Mom said.

Lola pulled out the chair next to her, and I took a seat for her sake.

"Go ahead. Tell them," Mom said.

He could barely contain himself. "I have some news, girls."

"What?" Lola said, looking worried.

"Don't make them wait," Mom said.

"I've been hired by a new insurance agency in downtown Chicago. I'll be working full time starting Monday. It will take me a while to earn my commissions, but I ... This is a very solid company with excellent backing. Your mother and I want to get us back to Evanston as soon as we can. And once we move," he looked at me, "our big goal will be to get Mona settled in college."

"Stop," I said.

Dad ran his thumb over his upper teeth, studying me.

"I understand, Mona," Mom said, but she rested a hand on one of his hands instead of mine. I wasn't sure if this was about getting him to slow down or if this was about affection. "Richard, why don't you pass the chicken?"

The tension in my father's neck was evident.

"I have a story," Lola said. As Mom served the potatoes and Lola carefully dished up carrots, I noticed how long my sister's hands had become, how graceful her fingers were, as she remained poised to tell her tale.

"Yes?" I said.

Lola made a sneaky face.

"Go ahead, dear," Mom said once the last plate was filled.

Lola took a long time pushing her fork into her potatoes, watching us.

"I wouldn't be surprised if you have a natural gift for storytelling, Lola," Dad ventured.

Lola took a drink of lemonade and put her glass down. I nudged her with my elbow. "We're waiting, goose."

"What?" she said with that amused expression.

"Tell us your story," I said.

Forks and knives came to a rest. My mother winked at me. Dad smiled to himself as he sipped his champagne.

"This is it," Lola said. "*This* is the story."

"You're so postmodern, Lola," I said.

"What the heck?" she said.

"Exactly." Mom laughed. "What the heck."

"Did you get it?" Lola said. "We're all in a story. Do I get to stay up and watch *Beauty and the Beast*? It's on tonight."

"I checked the schedule," Dad said. "It doesn't start until eight."

Lola was always in bed by eight. We didn't have a recording device on our TV and only five, sometimes six stations, and all of them knew how to fail.

"Oh, I think just this once, since it's not a school night. If we can turn the TV around so you can watch from my bed," Mom said.

"I love this table," Lola said.

For the last year or so she had had moments at meals where she would stop and look at Mom and me and say, *I love everyone at this table.* I think Mom understood as I did that her new arrangement of words was meant to somehow include our father, but not entirely. Then we all grew quiet and uncomfortable and even more uncomfortable in our own ways and ate the meal before us.

Geary taught me there are times to slow down and wait for a shot. He said that all the rapid-fire cameras in the world couldn't get that one image where truly seeing something and being ready, being available to the moment, could. When I considered my father's face I knew I needed to wait.

After dinner I took off for Nitro's. He had just gotten a call from his ex and was upset because she had scheduled a ski trip when he was supposed to be in France to see their child. We killed a great many people on screen that night, and he gave me a T-shirt he knew I would like and a bag of chocolates from our favorite movie theater.

I told him I couldn't when he asked me to spend the weekend. I said he could use me, but that was about it. He said he had never used me and paced a lot after we had sex and smoked a cloud of cigarettes.

The large uncovered windows woke me at first light, and I took off while he was still asleep. I left no note, only a print from the new batch of Lily's negatives. My printing technique had improved, he'd comment on that next time, but I left it for the sadness in her work, the isolation, an intention that came out of her honesty—without chasing after it.

I went home and got into my own bed, shifting into the sweet spot. Soon I fell into a state where I didn't feel awake, but I didn't feel asleep either. I found myself watching for Ajay.

I guess that was the way. When things began to crack I took flight. Night after night I glided over Lake Michigan and followed a line of buoys and lighthouses. I tore between the tall buildings downtown as if I were a figure in a single-player game. I dreamed over the Mississippi, and I went out across the plains. There were lucid moments that started with a slow tug, an easy pull in the direction of flight, but other dreams yanked me upward as if a rope were tied around my waist. Sometimes I felt as if I were being hauled from drowning at the bottom of the world. Some people describe flight as a drunkenness, but I feel sharpness, like the view through a good lens.

I entered a house. There was a woman, and she was pulling her favorite green sweater over her head. She fastened the button in the back and zipped her straight black skirt as I watched. She checked her hair and makeup in her dressing-table mirror before getting her heels on.

Her husband called up the stairs to say he was moving the cars around so the station wagon would be at the end of the drive. "All gassed up and ready to go!" he said. The woman straightened her stockings and slipped into her heels. "Are the guys still coming over for the game?" the wife called.

"Five out of six. Mac's got to help his sister with something. He might be over later," her husband said.

"Can you put some apple juice in a sippy cup for our girl?" she asked.

"You got it," he said.

A little girl ran into the big bedroom and flopped against the bed, throwing her hands over her head, facedown, waiting for her mother's affection. Her mother kissed the back of her neck and checked to see if she'd used the potty. When they descended the stairs, one slow step at a time, the husband beamed up at his girls. "How can one man be so lucky?" he said.

The woman stopped at the bottom landing and tilted her head slightly as if she were trying to remember something. She got to the bottom of the staircase and touched his face. While their little girl ran and got her small blanket for the ride, the wife said, "If anything goes wrong, if the car blows up, make sure to look for my wedding ring. It should be somewhere between the road and the woods. You'll find a fragment of bone from my ring finger there. It's always good to have something to bury, something to remember. The rest of me will be holding on to our little girl."

I guess my mother heard me scream and came running into my room.

"I'm okay, I'm okay," I said, gasping for air. "I'm okay."

"Poor love," she said, rubbing my arms. "Do you know what you were dreaming?"

"No, no. Did Lola ... ?"

"She's fine. She didn't wake up. Do you want a glass of water?"

"Yes," I said.

When I heard her out in the kitchen, I became aware of the many times she had tried to lessen a pain she didn't understand. I forget how many times we'd been at this place where she and I knew entirely different things.

I heard them out in the living room. It was ten in the morning, and I had managed to fall back to sleep for a while. Mom said she was going to take Lola to her Saturday dance class. Dad volunteered to haul a particularly heavy piece of ironwork up from the basement out to the backyard. Mom directed him on some of the other pieces she wanted out there. She would decide where they would go as soon as she returned with Lola.

"You don't have to tiptoe when you come back upstairs, but do let Mona sleep in. She really needs to catch up," Mom said. "And don't forget to take your keys. I have the latches set to lock automatically."

"Next time I'll come see you dance," Dad said.

"Only Mom and Mona get to see me dance," Lola said.

I could imagine his expression, the restrained acceptance, the effort not to look beaten down.

"We're going to be late. Let's hustle," Mom said.

I waited until I heard them leave and my father go down the back stairs. I gave Mom extra time in case she and Lola had to rush back up for something they'd forgotten. Then I got up.

I laughed aloud to find a copy of *Siddhartha* in my father's pack. This wasn't the kind of book he read, but it was completely dogeared with underlined passages. Maybe he was studying to become the Buddha.

There was a framed picture of Mom, Lola, and me that I didn't remember. A box with his father's cufflinks, one of them broken, was down toward the bottom. I had no idea why he dragged these things around. His kit bag had a few toiletries, the rest wedged into the bathroom. The receipt from his plane ticket to town was in a side pocket. I found the world's most beat-up pair of shoes. A rain poncho in a separate compartment must have been forgotten from the way the polyurethane smelled. His world had become so emptied out I almost didn't bother with the wallet again. It tumbled out as I was stuffing the rest of the things back in.

I remember him letting me look in all the compartments of

his wallet once. I had become curious about what a man hides in his back pocket. I felt the weight of this one in my hands. He never changed his wallet, even when Mom bought him a new one for Christmas one year. He said it was his lucky wallet. Inside, the picture of Mom was still there. I found six dollars, an almost expired Illinois license, and defunct AAA and medical insurance cards. The CPR card listed his blood type as A+. A tide chart and coupon for a bagel and coffee were from Atlantic City. He had a one-dollar raffle ticket. Though it was pretty frayed around the edges, he had wedged a photo of Lola as a newborn into a sleeve along with a picture of me from middle school on the other side. I made a point of returning each item to its exact location after examining it.

Once I was done I remembered that some wallets have hidden money compartments. When I lifted the leather flap it was like pulling a bandage up from raw skin. Inside was a folded piece of newspaper. It broke in two and two again as I unfolded it. I decided to put the wallet back and take the article into my room in case he should finish what he was doing quickly and return upstairs.

Closing my door, I braced my desk chair against the handle. I pulled my top sheet taut, making a smooth surface to reassemble the article. There was no headline, and it was only a portion of a story. Something about a hospital expansion.

I felt ridiculous when I realized I was reading the wrong side.

As I moved the bits around, I saw the headline:

Northbrook Mother and Daughter in Fatal Hit-and-Run

Their names, I finally learned, were Dorothy and Nan Kaminski. There was a picture of them with Mr. Kaminski, standing in a doorway to their house in Northbrook. They had been married six years, Nan their only child. Their picture formed a bright display in my mind as if electrical current came off the fragile paper.

Dorothy and Nan looked like the people in my dreams. But then I had seen them once, struggling in their car.

My hands shook as I read. *Dorothy Kaminski, a part-time nurse active in her community, was a 26-year-old wife and mother. Her daughter, Nan, had just turned three. They were both killed in a hit-and-run late Sunday evening. Their car was struck at approximately 6:15 p.m. as they returned toward home from a shopping trip. Police estimate the driver of the other car was going 35 to 40 miles per hour when the perpetrator swerved and crossed over into the other lane. The victims' car exploded within minutes. The Kaminskis were unable to get out of the car in time. Police are looking for any witnesses who might have seen this car by the side of the road or the vehicle that struck it. Detectives are combing the area for evidence. Anyone with information is asked to call the police.*

I think I had always known.

When I had calmed down enough I looked at the date on the article. I teased out the small box I kept inside the toe of one boot in my closet, unfolding the papers inside. Even before I looked I knew I would find the same date printed out along with the time and the name of the garage in the Quonset hut. On another slip of paper were the make and model of our old car with the license-plate number. All in a nine-year-old's handwriting. I used to keep them in a locket, but I had emptied the locket out when I gave it to Lola.

I was trembling when I went out to the living room and stuffed the pieces of the article back into his wallet. I washed my face and brushed my hair. My mind began to flood.

Cynthia once told me about a man in China who went on the weekends to save suicide jumpers at the Nanjing Bridge. People propelled to take flight when the ground beneath them burned away. It's the longest bridge in the world, so sometimes he couldn't get to them fast enough, though he ran hard. Or he found himself barely holding on to one of them by an ankle or an arm. He was a strong man, but he wasn't always strong enough. She told me he'd saved over 150 people, and he knew they would continue to drop. He had a regular job too, far away from the bridge, so there was nothing he could do on the weekdays.

I wished I could have saved them all.

Richard

There was a night when I was sixteen and Sor drove us through Gary, Indiana, on the way to the next carnival. I held my nose, the stench coming off the factory smokestacks. The sky was yellow, my throat burned, and there was a bitter taste in my mouth. When I asked Sor again to roll up his window he straightened his arms, sitting as far back from the steering wheel as possible, and said, "A sheet of glass won't do you any good in this stink, but you can have a drop of whiskey if you sit up like a man and stop fussing."

A half case of Wild Turkey was settled into the back footwell from our stopover in Kentucky. I pulled back the blanket that covered the box and helped myself to a bottle. Sor took the first draw. Before long I felt the rotten sky pass through me like a breeze, and Uncle Sor began to sermonize about what it is to be a man under those smokestacks that he referred to as the Gods of Industry. His spouting didn't always add up, at least it didn't at the time, but I listened intently.

"We're always in the middle of one kind of destruction or another," he said. "Life is never at rest. That's a fact. So if you find the kind of work you love and the right woman, well, I hope someone has taught you the word *transcendence* by now—so you can appreciate it when it comes your way."

I don't know what it was exactly, maybe the bourbon, maybe the freedom of being away from home, but I put my head out the window and hollered into the wind. He laughed and took another drink and said that mostly I shouldn't listen to anything he had to say but that on this particular score he knew what he was talking about, and I should probably keep my head in the car.

When I came home from burying that guy, and Liz helped me get my suit altered, I rode the elevated train down to the lunch meeting in a sweat and sat at a table with six people, some eager to see if I was the right fit but at least one trying to trip me up. I landed the job despite that and after everything that had come before it, every last bitter thing. Then I knew exactly what Sor had meant. I was that kid again, passing through the stench of things not working right, and suddenly I could put my head out the window and gulp air and holler my lungs out and drive without stopping.

Liz was working on her first sculpture in two years, and few things could have made me happier. When she asked me to help her haul some of the heavier metal pieces up from the basement before taking Lola to her Saturday dance class, I felt like a man finally sitting down to the table again. I had a job that could, with any luck, see us through to retirement. And even though we weren't thirty anymore and there was Mona's schooling to take care of and we had to work our way back into Evanston, I planned to keep my head down and put in those long hours on a steady basis. Liz was tired of telling Lola that she should walk softly because of the people below, and that would change too. I thought, little by little, Lola was starting to warm up to me. And even with Mona, I don't know that you can forget all the good things a parent has worked to put in place. At least I hoped she wouldn't.

I kept the radio and television off so Mona could catch up on her sleep. I know how a lack of sleep builds and builds, and I told

Liz this had to be affecting Mona's spirits. Liz just looked at me and said, "I'm sure you can imagine a world of things that affect Mona's spirits." These were the places where we strained. But the more I thought about it, I was certain Mona couldn't be herself or even know how to address things if she wasn't getting a good night's sleep.

I heard her bedroom door click open and the shower go on. Mona liked a good long shower and never skimped on time in front of the mirror, so I put on a television talk show in the living room to keep me company. A woman in Toledo had, in all likelihood, killed her husband fifteen years ago but wouldn't admit it. The host was trying to get her to take a lie-detector test on air. I always wondered how they convinced these people to bludgeon themselves on television.

I opened a package of Oreos and poured a cup of coffee and settled in. Mona came into the living room.

"I was wondering when you'd be up," I said.

Without looking my way she began to rummage in the hall closet.

"You shooting pictures today?"

She turned around but instead of facing me went over to the windows and looked down to the street.

"Mom said she planned to watch Lola dance for a while and then run some errands. I'd give them about forty-five minutes," I said.

Just then the woman from Toledo laughed. "Why the hell should I subject myself to your *bleep* scrutiny?"

I walked over and turned off the set. Mona stood there, locked down, watching me. I put my arms straight down by my sides, holding my hands out as if to say, *I'm doing everything I can here.*

Liz had said not to run the water in the sink, especially the hot water, when one of us was taking a shower, or the temperature would drop. Maybe this was about filling the coffee pot. But I thought I had used cold water like I always do. Maybe it was nothing.

I waited for Mona to correct me, to bring up some infraction. But she said, "You left the book of national monuments out on the kitchen table, open to one of the pictures. Why that book, that particular picture?" She asked this in a prosecutorial tone I didn't understand, though I was relieved that she was talking with me at all. I wanted to be extra careful to get the answer right. Maybe she meant something I did years ago. I searched my brain but had no memory of this. "Which picture?" I asked.

"The bison in Yellowstone, in the National Monuments book."

"The bison. I've always been crazy about that one. But I don't remember—"

"When you left for New Jersey. You left it open on the kitchen table, weighted down by the green carnival-glass salt and pepper shakers from the stove."

I would have done anything to retrieve this memory. It was clearly significant to her. But I couldn't. So I reached for anything I could. "It must have made me think of your photography. You do unusual things like that."

"Unusual?" She laughed.

"The bison look like they're running off the page."

"It's called cropping," she said, her voice elevating, the anger brimming.

"You'd know better than me," I said. I felt the muscles in my jaw working, tension collecting around my temples.

"That's good to hear. Because I'm contributing to the expenses here, and I told Mom I should have *a say* on whether you stay or go."

I took a shaky breath, thinking of Liz's cautions to go slow with her, that I could lose her if I didn't. "Look, I ... I'll be paying back every cent you put in. With interest. And I'm serious about seeing you through college. Without debt. Whether I understand photography or not, I recognize talent when I—"

"I don't get why you think we need you," she said, displaying that mix of horrible and triumphant emotion she had become so good at.

I felt that sorry headache move across my skull. "I know making up a boyfriend your mother doesn't have was a way of getting me to go away. I know you're angry that I left, that things have been tough. I really do know. This job should—"

"She goes on dates," Mona said. "There are better men."

I looked at the worn linoleum. "Who wouldn't want to ask your mother on a date? She's beautiful. But we have a lot of years in, Mona. There's no one else I can talk to the way I can talk with your mother. I think she feels the same way about me. I'm as in love with her now as the day we met. More."

I thought I saw a tear run from the edge of one eye. Maybe it was the angle of the light, the sun clearing the buildings. I wanted to comfort her. But when I pushed away from the bed, my sleeve snagged the package of cookies on the table and knocked it off the edge. I watched it drop. Oreos rolled out across the floor. I startled her as I came close in order to chase them. We both looked at the last one as it came to rest near one of her shoes. I pushed my hands into my pockets.

"We save the Oreos for Lola," she said. "And the lion's share of fruit and most of the milk."

"I'll get more Oreos and fruit and milk when I go out later. Please sit down so we can talk," I said.

"You sit down," she said, like she was ordering a dog around.

I cleared my throat and began again, out on that ledge where she thought I belonged.

"Maybe you think I can read you the way I used to, but I can't.

I'm sorry. I'm doing everything I can to stay even-tempered here and get through this with you. Tell me what I can do to make things right," I said.

"You can tell me about the day you slammed into another car when we were on our way home from the racetrack."

My temples felt as if she had lit a match to them.

"I thought you'd forgotten," I said. "You've never brought it up."

"I was supposed to bring it up?"

"No, I don't mean—"

"I was in the front seat. I was nine. How would I forget that?"

"I had to get to a phone," I said.

It's possible I told her that day, or some other Sunday like it, that when a horse is a strong competitor weights are sometimes added to the saddle to make the race a closer one, to push for a photo finish. The faster the horse, the heavier the weights. As I dropped into one of the kitchen chairs I saw how much weight she had taken on, what she had seen, what she knew. But she wanted me to say it.

"Go on," she said.

"There's not a lot to tell. We were returning from the races, and I was tired and I must have nodded off for a moment. The car drifted over the yellow line. We hit ... I hit a car on the other side of the road. The other car hit a pole. I stopped to help."

"Stopped to help *who?*" she said.

"A woman and her daughter. Their door locks were jammed, and I didn't have my crowbar in my trunk, so I couldn't smash their windows. I ... we hurried to a pay phone, where I called the police right away."

"You could have found a branch in the woods."

"I didn't think."

"And the woman and her daughter?"

She knew, I knew, everything said and unsaid, but I seized up.

"We drove to a body shop," she said as if she were trying to pry a pit from a rotten piece of fruit. I wished she would ask, just ask what she wanted to know.

"That was probably our mechanic," I said. "I'm not entirely sure, but I think we were due for service. There was a body shop next door."

"It was a Quonset hut with a sign over the door that read, 'Dave's Body Shop.' You handed the man who met you at the door your winnings from the track. Seven thousand six hundred and eighty-eight dollars. Maybe you don't remember anything that small," she said.

She glared so hard at me it was almost as if she were smiling. I tried to think if I had seen any Tylenol in the medicine cabinet. It always got worse if I didn't treat it immediately. We both had that kind of headache. I would be better prepared if I could think straight.

"We got into another car, a loaner, and drove home, and you said if I told Mom what had happened, it would be very bad for her since she was pregnant. And when she lost that baby, Richard, can you imagine what I thought?"

"Oh, no," I said, never having made that connection, never having that thought.

"I wondered if I had said something in my sleep. Or if I had given Mom some hint without realizing it when I was awake. Did she pick up something in my body language, some clue? You start to wonder, you know? Especially when you're *nine*."

"Mona, I ..." It felt as if she were standing on my head, the weight of her life ready to snap my neck in two. I didn't know how a man could break any further. If she could just wait until things settled, until I was able to show her a better life, get her the help she needed.

Tears ran down her face. "It must have been awful for the mother and her little girl when the smoke started to fill their car and we pulled away. You didn't even go out on the road and try and flag anyone down. I can't tell you how many times I wondered who they were and why they had to hit the pole and why we didn't. You ever wonder that?"

"Sure. Sure, I've thought about that, Mona. But I always tell myself at least you were all right."

"And *they* were all right, isn't that what you said? We were all all right, weren't we?" She began to hyperventilate.

"Take deep breaths," I said.

"And what did Mom say … when you finally told her? Because once she lost the baby … I mean, there was no reason … not to tell her, right? You must have … said something then. But I … can't remember you telling me … I could finally let that secret go."

"It's been so long I can barely …"

The room got quiet, her breathing worse, and a rolling, drumming sound started up in my head. If the elevated train went by, I didn't hear it. If the ice down by the lake broke apart or someone was firing a high-powered rifle in the neighborhood, I couldn't hear that either. I saw Mona move her mouth, a slash of fury, but I didn't hear anything she said after that. Maybe it was a trick of light, but she seemed to disappear. All at once the kitchen and living room, everything was soaked, flooded in light, that's all I knew, that light. And then I heard her shoes running down the stairs, running down the block, running out of herself, out of me, as far from everything as she could possibly go.

I heard the sound of a train as if my ears had popped. It roared in my brain, and I wept for the first time in a very long time.

When I realized, when I looked over at the clock on the stove, I knew Liz and Lola could be home any minute. I went over to the sink and washed my face and smoothed my hair back and found the bottle of Tylenol, thinking I should buy another bottle to replace the tablets I used. It was possible they were Mona's or she was counting each one even before it was swallowed. *I'm not here to rob you,* I wanted to shout. *I'm here to take care of you. Let me take care of you.* But I guess that's what she'd been feeling all along, that I was robbing her of something she couldn't get back, couldn't put back in the bottle.

As I shut the medicine cabinet. I heard Liz buzz to get in, and I went over and leaned on the button to the downstairs door. My senses cleared, and I bent down to gather up the Oreos, trying to force them back into the package.

"Richard, my hands are full!" Liz called through the door.

"Just a minute!" I pushed the crumpled package of cookies to the back of a cabinet.

"Richard! Can you get the door?"

I ran back to the door.

"Let me take those," I said, grabbing her bags.

"I should have had my keys out," she said.

"I was just throwing some clothes on. Where's Lola?"

"She got invited to an overnight with a sweet little girl named Tina in her dance class. Her mom said they'd loan her a nightie and things, so I'm going straight down to the yard and get to work."

"All the metal's out, stacked and ready to go."

"That's great. You all right?" she asked and touched my neck. Her hand felt so cool on my hot skin I didn't want her to pull it away. But she did, and I said, "Headache. Took something for it, but I'm still in a fair amount of pain."

She looked over at Mona's open bedroom door. "She's out early for a Saturday. Did she say where she was going?"

"Gone before I knew it."

"She does that sometimes."

Icruised the neighborhood, driving down around the lake, looking for Mona. Finally I had to head over to the gas station. After that I took a couple more passes up and down the blocks where I imagined she'd be, though how could I know? I kept thinking I could make things right with her despite everything.

I knew Liz might need the van soon, so I drove over to the A&P to get those grocery items, only once I was there I realized I had been in a daze. I had spent most of the money I had on gas for the van and would probably have to borrow from Liz to take the L on Monday, so the groceries would have to wait. I pulled into a parking spot just to stop for a moment to catch my breath, and a woman came up to the car and signaled so I'd roll my window down.

When I did she said, "Where's your handicap permit?"

"My what?"

She pointed to the blue sign I hadn't seen.

I looked in the side mirrors and began to back up.

"My mother is a paraplegic, and it's assholes like you that make her life more difficult."

Stopping the van, I said, "I'm sorry. I just—"

"Who gives a shit if you're sorry," she said.

A car waiting for the spot began to honk.

"No one. Not a fucking soul," I said and rolled up my window and maneuvered my way out.

I pulled down a side street under the tracks, turned the engine off, and tried to clear my mind. It was important not to get ahead of things. That's what I told myself when I was wandering around at night in New Jersey. There was little I could do if Mona talked to Liz. And maybe the only way Mona could get through this was to talk to her mother. Maybe I should just go to Liz and tell her. But I worried with everything she'd been through the last couple of years she wouldn't hold up under the stress. I rammed my forehead into the steering wheel and felt the pain splinter and multiply.

I sat up, locked my jaw. In two weeks I would receive my first paycheck. I would endorse this to Liz and tell her all I needed was enough to ride into work and back and to have the other suit taken in. I knew they had coffee at work and a refrigerator, so I could bring my lunch. I didn't need anything else. I was, after all, someone who knew how to clean his teeth with a supply of baking soda carried around in a pack. I had made meals out of free creamers and crackers I'd gotten with a cup of soup the day before.

My forehead felt bruised, and I tried to remember this myth I had read about once. A daughter is born out of a god's head or forehead. I wondered if it hurt this much. And then I told myself that falling apart was a form of indulgence. The important thing, no matter what, was to be strong for the family. That's what Sor had said.

I turned the key in the ignition, checked the mirrors, and was about to pull out into the lane when I saw a runner. He was a tall, lean man, and he approached from a few hundred feet. The closer he got, the more familiar he seemed. I didn't want to be reminded of the image of Mr. Kaminski, but someone like him was running toward me. I felt the way his slim weight moved down the block. He kicked his heels up and kept his shoulders back. I felt as if I had crawled inside someone else, just for a moment. And then he was gone.

Liz worked most of the day down in the yard. After a long walk around the neighborhood looking for Mona again, I had to start reading the company manual. It was already downloaded to the laptop the new firm provided. I worked for a while on the demographic I was covering and started to expand on some of the

ideas I had pitched at my interview. My headache loosened a little
but stayed around.

When I took a break I reminded myself I never intended to
hurt anyone and that this should make a difference. Once we got to
the restaurant, driving back from the racetrack that day, I was sure
I hadn't gotten up from that table until I was sober. I had my share
of coffee. I tried all of the doors on Mrs. Kaminski's car. I looked
for a crowbar. I sped to a phone.

What if I had stood out on that dark road with my young
daughter waiting in our car? What if I had tried flagging someone
down on the road? Maybe no one, not a soul, would have been brave
enough to pull over for some strange man and I would have wasted
time. Or worse, maybe no one would have seen me in my dark
clothes around the turn at night and taken me out while Mona sat
there and watched. And then, when the other car blew up, Mona
would have been sitting right there. Our car might have gone up
too. ... I had to stop. Stop.

All these years I had never thought of finding a heavy branch.
How was that possible?

I wanted to go down and take another look at the sculpture. It
was unlike anything Liz had done. This was not a piece that would
be poured or polished. This was something she was making out
of scraps she cut and fitted together until it grew skyward. But I
knew better than to disturb her. I waited until eight at night, when
she was working entirely by the one floodlight she had brought out
to the yard, and took her a coffee.

That's the way she liked to work, hours on end, without concern
for the cold, for her body. She wore fingerless gloves and an old
jacket that was torn and spattered and fit snugly under her welding
apron. She often wore the same heavy shop apron whether she made
eggs or burnished metal. Maybe she liked the weight of it.

She pulled her mask up long enough to set the mug down.

"I got a text from Mona. She's staying with a friend tonight," she said.

Maybe Mona was finding a way to calm down. I could try to explain things to her in a way I hadn't yet if given another chance.

"Do you want to get the dinner started?" Liz said. "I'm close to wrapping."

"Sure," I said, though I was no good in the kitchen.

"There's one chicken breast left from last night. If you pull the meat off that and cut it into pieces and sauté some onion and carrots in a little oil, not too much, and at the very last add the chicken, that should work. Keep the flame low. There should be plenty of pasta leftover to go with that. We'll save the Parmesan for the girls. I corked the rest of the champagne, and we can finish that."

I got dinner started, though I kind of burned the carrots and onions, and after a while she came upstairs, hung her work clothes on a couple of pegs in the kitchen, and jumped into the shower. I was surprised to see her put on something nice. The air was overly hot and then chilly, but she seemed unfazed in a light spring dress with yellow flowers and a cardigan. She had combed her hair, leaving it wet, and as we sat down at the table I watched the occasional drop of water soak into the fabric, dotting her shoulders and breasts while we ate. She was as beautiful as the girl I had met at the carnival grounds.

She talked in an animated way about the conversation she'd had with her boss. It looked like she would be moving into suburban foreclosures in the next month or so. I was still worried about this kind of work. Some of the companies were getting more aggressive, trying to boot the owners out while they occupied their homes.

The champagne was flat, but we made a toast or two, and soon the bottle was done.

"Don't go away," she said, putting her knife and fork down. As if I would go somewhere. She got up from the table and searched around in a cabinet over the stove and brought down a quarter of a bottle of gin, probably left over from before I'd left. We didn't have lime or much in the way of ice cubes, but there was a small bottle of tonic in a side pocket of the fridge, also probably left over from a couple of years ago. Liz had never been much of a drinker.

I thought again of that word Sor had used once: *transcendent*. It was like being back in our early years, when resources were scarce but we saved as much as we could for each other.

She proposed a toast to my new job, and I made one to her sculpture and her new territory. She leaned forward. I could see all the way down her dress to her belly. I had forgotten that bra or hadn't seen it before, and I hoped no one else had. She laughed lightly and kissed me on the mouth.

The good hard work of her day glowed from her skin. Pulling back a little, she took my hand and led me over to her bed, which used to be our bed. We made love with generosity, and I stopped being lost. I stopped entirely.

Mona

There used to be a sword swallower in Millennium Park, and she did something called The Drop. This is a move where she let the sword free-fall through the pharynx and esophagus, straight into the cardiac opening. She explained this at the start of the performance, making sure we understood that the tip of the sword would pass within millimeters of the aorta and the heart. I tried to imagine I had the discipline of that sword swallower after I read about the Kaminskis. I walked around knowing I was millimeters from a pain that could take me out. I tried to hold it together until I could pull the sword out or be brave enough to let someone draw it out of me.

I was in that kind of shock where someone is talking right into your face, someone you've known for years, but you have no idea who they are.

As soon as I saw Richard after my shower, it hit me that he'd be standing there next week, and next month, and the month after that, doing everything he could to make the world appear normal, but he would be the constant reminder that it wasn't. He would become more of a sign than a man. He would point to the sudden drift, the impact, the explosion.

I had opened the conversation. I knew he was hoping I'd talk with him about anything irrelevant, any nonsense. When I turned and saw him open his mouth I gave him a chance to break it all down for me. He was the storyteller after all. He often had the last line of his stories before he even began. "Tell me about the people in the hit-and-run," I said.

I waited for his remorse. I waited for it to spill from his eyes and mouth. But it was as if he had forgotten altogether. *It's been so long. You were young.* He made it into another story, a false story. I kept the pressure up, but he just went into his routine, spilling a package of Lola's cookies that weren't his to spill.

When I couldn't take another minute I ran out of the apartment, stopping at each landing to catch my breath. I fled down the block in a halting way. At first I didn't see the guys at the rehab center smoking their cigarettes with nowhere else to go except the ramp in and out of the building. One of them called, "Hey, come talk to me!"

"What's the hurry?" another yelled.

I kept going, and after three blocks I was hit with a side stitch and slowed. I thought of going to Nitro's. He didn't care what I showed up like or where I'd been or where I was going.

I didn't have my pack or wallet with me, so I had to hitch a ride along Clark Street. One guy stopped, and I held the door open, looking at the purple velvet interior of his car and the tattoo of a woman with a beat-up face on his neck. I really ticked him off when I said I'd changed my mind and felt like walking instead. He sat there for a while, window down, calling me a *cunt* as I moved up the street.

A woman who looked like someone's grandmother—not mine but somebody's—stopped and took me right to Nitro's door. The whole way she asked how I was doing in school and if I helped around the house, and I kept saying *fine* and *yes*, and finally she let me out with a solid scold about hitchhiking.

This time of day was early for Nitro. His hair was matted, and the stubble along his chin looked chewed up in places. He wore one of his shredded T-shirts, and maybe he didn't realize he wasn't wearing any clothes below this, his dick just hanging there. The place was cluttered even for him, and the jumbo screen was on with a frozen game.

Nitro pulled on a pair of jeans and dropped into his leather chair, watching me. I once heard him tell someone this was his LC3, his Le Corbusier, also known as a *cushion basket*. I found it offensive that he went on about it. To me it was a chair.

I cracked open a couple of windows and dropped onto his couch. Picking up the controller, I released the game and began to run through the village. He had this nostalgia for the '60s and '70s even though he wasn't alive then. So there I was, searching up and down the streets of Saigon, M16 in position, shooting whatever I had a chance to shoot. I had an arsenal of grenades to set off, and in the distance I saw the napalm drops. I heard screams. Plenty of screams hit the air, though I couldn't see anyone on fire. I knew that photo by Nick Ut of the girl struck by napalm running down the road naked, the guy in the background loading his camera.

I heard the choppers and ducked into a bar.

"Tell me what's going on," he said.

"Fuck if I know," I said, turning friendly fire on an ally. I was obliterated instantly, my score demolished.

Coming back to life, I started over.

"You usually text first," he said, "and later in the day."

"I think you need a new controller. Did you see that? I had my finger on the button."

"Are you on something, babe?"

"Fuck you," I said.

"Let me help."

"Nothing's going on. Just a few people blowing up, that's all. Do you have something to eat?"

"I could make you an omelet."

"I'm sick of your omelets."

"Okay ..." he said. Nitro was a patient guy, but he was reaching a limit.

The screen froze again just as I discovered VC hiding in the basement of a bar. "Goddamn it!" I yelled and stood up and threw the controller at the wall so hard the housing split apart and the batteries flew. A small patch of plaster chipped and fell.

Nitro jumped up and took me by the wrists.

"Let go."

"Not until you tell me what this is."

I squirmed, but he locked down harder.

"You really want to let go of me, dickhead," I said.

"And let you smash up the whole place?"

"I'm fine," I said, taking a breath. "I'm ready to tell you. As soon as you let me go." I looked at the floor, waiting. I counted. I looked up and smiled at him.

Slowly he loosened his grip. He reached over and pulled a strand of hair away from my face.

I hauled back and belted him in the gut.

"Jesus. Fuck."

"Don't ever pin me like that again," I said.

"Is this about your father? Because you just punched a man when he wasn't ready. You could cause a fucking rupture."

"I am. I'm causing a fucking rupture," I said.

He reached out as I walked toward the door but must have thought better of it.

On the way down in the elevator I could feel myself fill with heat. There was a high whine in my ears. I burst out onto the street and looked for a ride.

This guy who kept looking over at me like he wasn't sure I was sitting there in his car took me north. Along the way I felt dizzy, and my stomach clenched. I asked him to drop me off at the cemetery. He took me right there without asking for directions. Some people have a way of finding death.

The lake was iced over, and the only sound came from the cars fleeing around the curve. Looking across the gravestones and mausoleums, I saw some half-finished repair work. No one in sight, only a slow van on its way out of the main gate. In the warmer seasons the waves pound against the limestone break on the other side of Sheridan, and mist comes off the lawn as the morning temperatures shift. There have been reports of seeing an aviator out in the lake. The aviator has a routine where he struggles to stay afloat but ultimately drowns. Then his ghost hauls itself up out of the water, crosses Sheridan, and enters the cemetery, where it disappears.

I found the office, and inside a woman sat behind a counter, wearing three cardigan sweaters, one on top of the other. Her red hair was little more than a spidery wisp. An electric heater cranked by her feet, and she held a folded newspaper close to her face, squinting at the type. Without looking up she said, "Getting ready to close for the day."

"Is it too late to find a couple of graves?"

She peered over her bottle-thick glasses as I gave her my grandfather's name on my father's side. He had, my mother said, raised his son by knocking him down a set of childhood stairs until he toughened up. Mostly Dad made him an ogre and placed him in a broken-down castle in his stories, but last year Mom told me it was a house in Cicero, and my father's collarbone snapped when he landed the wrong way on the last step.

The clerk stood to her full height. She wasn't more than

four foot six or seven. Maybe it was this simple matter of height or the electric heating unit blasting away or too many fluorescent lights beaming overhead, but I began to feel unnaturally tall.

"Burial date?" she asked, looking at the file drawers.

I began to sweat and pressed a hand against my brow. It's possible I was floating a little. I was looking down not only at this tiny woman but somehow at myself—at my blue hair and my sudden concern with the ancestors.

I made a stab at a date, and she retrieved her glasses and set to work. She opened the first of many index drawers, looming in close to look at the cards, then slamming the drawers so fast I was amazed she didn't catch her nose. She flicked through hundreds of cards, each search followed by the hard smack. As she ripped along I could almost feel my head bump against the ceiling.

"Write this down!" she said, her eyes black dots now. "There's a pencil in the basket!"

In the basket of golf pencils were small slips of paper that she must have cut with a fingernail scissors, all the edges scalloped. She called out a number, and I wrote it down, my hands shaking. Then she pulled a laminated map out from under the counter and started to give me directions.

"Are you a Nazi hunter?" she asked.

"No, are there Nazis buried here?" I had a sick feeling, wondering if one of my family members ...

"Ghost tracker?" she said.

"Not that I—"

"If you're recording anything for film or television, you have to fill out a permission form. Do you need one of those?"

"No to film and television," I said.

"Don't forget to take a brochure as you go."

When I got outside the gravel under my boots tugged me back

to earth. I had begun to think I was going to take off like a helium balloon as soon as I hit the open air.

Moving toward the lake, I followed the map but couldn't find the number I had written down. I looked back at the office. The lights were off and there was no sign of the woman. I had hoped to talk with my father's parents, to ask why they had screwed up so badly. I had thought about desecrating their monuments. But when I looked again I saw I had written my own name on the piece of paper and there were no numbers at all.

I walked toward the road, picking up some snow and holding it against my face.

Ajay must have seen me from his windows when I got to the building. He stepped into the hall suddenly, shutting the door behind him. He put a hand against my forehead and then my cheeks.

"I'm fine," I said.

"I can see how fine you are," he said, taking my hand. "You're burning up."

I told him I was going to Cynthia's.

When we got there she had me sit on the couch, and she took my temperature.

"Almost a hundred and three," she said.

I believe we had a discussion about whether I should go to the walk-in clinic, but maybe we were talking about the walk-in closet. Words poured out like quick bursts of rain. If it was a clinic, my mother couldn't pick up those bills, and there was little I could do on my pay. I said I was staying put.

Ajay brought a glass of water and a bottle of analgesics. As I held my hand out Cynthia said, "You have the most interesting line in your palm between the Girdle of Venus and Line of Head. Sort of an accidental line."

I liked Cynthia, so I was patient when she went off on things. And when I considered this later I understood her way of making uncertainty into a game.

"She should drink something," Ajay said.

"There's orange juice. It's important to keep your electrolytes together," Cynthia said.

Ajay went off to the kitchen to rifle through the refrigerator. I asked Cynthia to take my phone and send a message to my mother saying, *Out tonight.*

A minute later she showed me the screen that said, *Have fun.*

Soon I was drenched in sweat and trembling. Cynthia pulled back the curtains to the walk-in closet and turned on a small lamp that sat on a wooden crate. She found a pair of PJs for me, and I slipped under the covers.

"I'm worried if I shut my eyes I'll start circling Calvary."

"You're okay," she said.

It was dark out when Ajay nudged me to move over. I sat up and let him try my temperature again.

I took a few sips of the cold juice he held out. "What's Cynthia doing?" I asked.

"I believe she's giving us *space.*"

I touched his shirt where the tattoo was drawn.

"I'm having it taken off," he said.

"Constantina," I said.

He gave me a funny look. "Yes ... we talked about her," he said.

He kissed my hot cheek, and I rested against him.

It took a moment to understand he was asleep next to me and Mr. Kapur was standing at the opening to the closet, railing at us in Hindi. My mother was crowded in next to him, trying to keep Mr. Kapur calm. She raised her voice in graduated decibels, asking him to stop shouting. Cynthia pushed in behind her, not wanting to miss anything. Ajay rolled over, mumbling something, and his grandfather reached out and swatted his legs. I thought this would wake anyone. In his sleep, or what appeared to be his sleep, he tried to bat his grandfather's hand away.

Finally Mr. Kapur yelled, "How could you mix yourself up with this *girl?*"

Ajay's eyes popped open. He looked at me and then over at the group filling the doorway.

My mother said, "Maybe if we all relax a little we can find out why they're here."

Cynthia rolled her eyes.

"Get up, you miserable boy!" Mr. Kapur yelled. Then he tapped Ajay on the bottom of his feet with one of his cowboy boots.

"Ahhh! Stop, old man. Stop," Ajay said as he sat up.

I began to shudder again, and my mother said, "Are you sick?" But instead of waiting for me to answer she nudged her way around Mr. Kapur and crowded into the tiny space. Leaning down, she felt my forehead and asked me to take my temperature again.

"What a wretched country," Mr. Kapur said. "Young unmarried people fornicating everywhere you look. No one with the slightest shame."

"We probably shouldn't jump to conclusions," my mother said.

"It's like *A Night at the Opera*, where people keep piling into that small cabin on an ocean liner," Cynthia said.

Mr. Kapur gave me a long, sorry look and said, "I do not know what I have done to deserve ... to deserve ..."

All of us watched Mr. Kapur. He seemed to have forgotten what he deserved. He cradled his head in his hands.

"Is he crying?" my mother asked softly.

"He just needs a minute," Ajay said and got up. He came back with a chair from the kitchen so his grandfather could sit down.

I handed the thermometer to my mother and asked if there was any ginger ale. Careful not to disturb Mr. Kapur, Mom went into the kitchen to search, and I heard Richard's voice move in the living room. I guess no one had bothered to close the front door.

"What's going on?" he said

"I don't want him here," I said.

"Is Mona okay?" he asked.

Ajay looked ready to take my father on if necessary.

"I'm making coffee. And I have some cognac," Cynthia said, as if we were having a social event and this was the time to make a toast to the New American family.

"She's fine," Mom said, stepping into the hall to address him. "I'll be up in a minute."

"If you're sure," Dad said. Then there was a long pause before his footsteps receded and the door clicked shut.

"He left Lola alone?" I said, starting to get up.

"She's on an overnight," Mom said.

"I better get my grandfather downstairs," Ajay said to me. "Leave your phone on."

As he slipped past my mother she stopped him and asked, "Is he ... has he become more forgetful?"

"Yes, I'm afraid so."

"That kind of temper, I saw it in my aunt."

"So far the progression is slow. But yes, things have changed," Ajay said.

"You talk about me like I'm not even here," Mr. Kapur said.

"*Daa-daa-gee*, we need to go downstairs now," Ajay said.

But this only seemed to get him going again. "I forbid you to see her."

"We can talk about that," Ajay said.

"How will you finish your schooling if you get carried away

and bring a child into the world? You will have to work instead, the way I work. I met your grandmother when the time was right. That was all. There was a dowry. My schooling was complete. Your grandmother was all I needed, and I married her, which is the proper way."

"Come on. I'll make breakfast," Ajay said.

As they made their way downstairs Mom came into the closet. Sitting at the end of the mattress, she touched my feet.

"Lola and I could stay down here until he leaves," I said. "Cynthia would be happy to have us."

"I could make the couch up or just give them my bed," Cynthia said, handing my mother a glass of ginger ale.

"At least you have a sense of humor when you're delirious," my mother said.

"It's up to you if you'd rather stay down here for a while. I realize how tight everything is upstairs. But no one's taking your room over, and Lola will be upstairs."

I sipped the cold ginger ale, and my stomach began to settle.

"If your temperature goes up again, I want you to call me. Call me anyway, okay? We'll talk about the rest when you're feeling better," Mom said and took off for work.

I remember turning on my side and Cynthia looming in at one point to say she had to go to work. "I like Ajay for you," she said. "Rest up."

The next time I woke up I took my temperature, and the lights on the wand flashed in a frantic pattern as if I were heading toward a runway. The numbers blurred together, and I drifted away again.

I was in Yellowstone, a crowd gathered in the parking lot. "There's a bear in that car," a tall, angular woman said. I pressed into the group of onlookers clustered around the vehicle—all those cameras and phones out taking pictures. Looking inside, I saw the black bear wedged behind the steering wheel. He was skittish from the flashing lights. A man in camp gear hurried over, grabbed my arm, and began to push me toward the passenger side of the car. "I want to get a picture of the two of you," he said. Everyone looked at me, waiting for me to behave. He opened the passenger-side door. "Slip in and put your arm around his shoulders."

I tried to untangle myself.

"I pushed the seat back as far as it would go," he said, "to make you comfortable."

The bear, tightly pinned, had had enough. He started to claw into the plastic-and-foam rubber visor and snapped off the rearview mirror.

"Go on!" a woman in a big pair of sunglasses called.

A man said, *"Chicken!"*

Clinging to the doorframe, I locked my arms and legs and arched my back to avoid the bear's reach. Beads of snot dripped from his nostrils, and his breath steamed the windows. He turned and looked at me. There were several people pushing me now. My fingers bent back, and I lost my grip and I fell into the seat next to him. But instead of attacking me the bear started waving for everyone to clear the path. He reached for the keys and fired up the engine. Traveling through the park, we followed a series of exit signs. I tried the door, but it was locked. The windows were jammed. I felt something touch my neck. My heart stopped when I saw Nan Kaminski in the backseat with her mother, Dorothy.

I reached back, and she dug something sharp into my palm. Her mother signaled to me by closing her eyes. She touched one of her eyelids as if to say, *Here.* The bear became distracted when we got to an elk crossing. I opened my fist and saw that the girl had given me a knife. It had made a cut in my hand.

"Go on," the mother whispered. She made another gesture, a quick sweeping motion, as if to say, *Hurry!* Wondering if I could ever forgive myself, I drove the tip of the knife into one of the bear's eyes. He bellowed with pain, and when he reached for his eye he drove the knife in further.

I sat on the passenger side of the car, watching the bear weep blood. The mother, who had become my mother, said to get out and pull the front seat forward. I did this, and she and Nan, who had become Lola, followed me out of the car, and the three of us ran into the woods. "Shouldn't I stop and call someone?" I kept saying. But they pulled me along, and when we had moved a few hundred feet from the car, there was an explosion that lifted us off the ground.

I felt like one of those Ambien poppers when I finally surfaced in Cynthia's closet. I was wearing a silk 1940s movie-star gown that was so long I had to hike the skirt up to walk. I found that all the hanging items in her closet had been thrown onto her bed or spilled onto the floor. Slipping out of the gown, I stood by the window in her bedroom and considered the uniform gray sky. Cynthia didn't believe in clocks, and she must have taken her laptop with her. My phone was out of juice. I was clueless about time. I borrowed a T-shirt and jeans and found my jacket hanging in the hall closet, my shoes by the door. She had left me a note with a few bucks *just in case* and told me I could stay as long as I wanted.

I walked over to Howard Street in a functional delirium. After running my pass through the turnstile, I went up the stairs to the northbound side of the L. There weren't many people. I began to think that if I had kept my father awake that day in the car, every last thing would be different now.

Framed posters told me to see a Gauguin exhibit at the Art Institute and get an advanced degree and not spit and report any suspicious activities and buy a fruit bouquet and submit my body to medical experimentation for which there would be modest compensation. Gradually moving to the far end of the platform, I leaned around a partition to see our building and the snow piled in our yard, the sculpture Mom was working on. There was a softness, a haze around everything. I got up to the edge of the platform and studied the rails as a train pulled away.

I felt hot again and opened my coat and looked out at our building.

My father's shape slowly filled my window, everything reduced to his outline. He was taking over. I wanted him to see me out on the tracks so he could understand what he was doing, what he had done.

I looked down the length of the platform. Only a handful of people stood under the sheltered areas, reading those posters, staring off into space. A boy sat with his mother on a bench. A woman with a black scarf had her hair tied up so that the thinnest strand wouldn't catch in the wind. A man coughed and coughed. When I looked at the rails, I was aware that the one farthest from the platform had 750 volts of electricity running through it.

Waiting until the next train took off, I jumped into the gravel between the two main rails of the track as I imagined Ajay had done. I walked north with great care until I stood in front of the yard. I looked at my father.

He was looking my way.

A man at the end of the platform yelled, "Hey, get the fuck off there!"

I heard someone else shout, "Call 911."

A guy in a hoodie and leather jacket started taking pictures of me with his phone. He seemed eager for blood sport, an image to send out to his friends. Maybe I had less than three minutes left. The wall that enclosed our yard came halfway up to the platform. The gap between it and the edge of the ties was six feet at most. I began to think Ajay used that wall to push off from rather than dropping straight down. When a strong vibration hit the ties, I looked up to see the headlights of an Evanston-bound train in the distance. It seemed early, but it was like all the trains that rode my days and nights—the ones that kept coming.

There was a raspy overhead speaker under the eaves of the platform that blurted something. I wondered if I could settle a score for Mr. Kaminski—if I could make his loss my father's loss. My mother would never have to find out about Dorothy and Nan, but he would understand.

It was when I tried to tell myself that Lola would be better off without me that I woke up. I saw him turn away from the window and disappear, and with only moments left I jumped.

There was a split second when I thought I was going to pitch over the wall or break on top of it. But I pushed off with my hands, my body torqued, my right hand dragged halfway down the wall, and I dropped into the underpass, going limp. The sound of the train rushing overhead.

I waited a minute or more for an alarm but heard nothing.

Counting to ten, I pulled myself up from a filthy, soaking-wet mattress and hobbled toward the break in the fence off Howard, the one behind the liquor store. I saw my hand bleeding. It's hard to say when I had felt that good. Not because of the blood, the abrasions, some mark of courage. I had no thirst for pain or combat with myself. But there was something I relished in that moment of pure flight from my father.

I was suddenly famished. Stopping at the coffee shop, I realized that it didn't seem out of the norm for a bleeding individual to drop into a booth for several cups of thin coffee before the next battle.

In the bathroom I saw what a mess I was. I washed my face and hands a few times and held a wad of paper towels against the cut.

Grabbing a spot by the window, I watched people coming and going around the L station. I considered the jeweler across the street. Cynthia had said his shop was nothing but fenced watches and fenced rings with the occasional necklace pulled off a dead person from a nearby funeral home. She said if he were a legitimate jeweler, the big clock over the door wouldn't be fourteen minutes off—that the guy even liked to steal time. It was one of her standing jokes. I had a bowl of soup, and whether it was one o'clock or one fourteen or twelve forty-six, I made my way back to Cynthia's.

I poured alcohol on my hand, timing this so I could cry out just as a train went by, and then I stopped being a child about it. I went through Cynthia's antibiotic cream as if it were body lotion and wrapped my hand in gauze. The line Cynthia called *the accidental line* was obliterated. My father and I both had our right hands covered in bandages now, but there wasn't anything I could do about that.

Richard

I woke to a series of mechanical noises that made me think of an old cash register or an adding machine. I had fallen back to sleep, and it was one in the afternoon. I found Liz working at the kitchen table.

"Hi, beautiful," I said and came around behind her and kissed her neck. "I think the gin did me in." I sat down, and she gave me a look I wouldn't call tender but maybe warm.

"You'll be rested for work tomorrow."

"What was going on at Cindy's this morning?" I asked.

"*Cynthia's*. Mona spent the night with the flu. And then it seems Mr. Kapur went looking for his grandson, and pretty soon the place was Grand Central," she said.

"What is it?" I asked, nodding at the contraption. There was a wheel on top containing the alphabet and the numbers 1 through 10 along with double and triple 0s. It had a large lever on the side like a slot-machine handle.

"Watch," she said. Sliding out a drawer, she fixed a small metal plate in a groove. She pushed this back into the machine and moved the wheel, drawing the lever down with each turn like one of those label makers. When she was done she pulled the drawer open and took out the metal. It was warm to the touch and had my full name stamped into it.

"It's a dog-tag embosser," she said. "Someone left it behind at one of my jobs."

"And you wanted this because?"

"An idea I'm working on. Go see how much I've done."

I grabbed my glasses, and from Mona's window I could see that Liz's sculpture was coming along nicely. It was hard to tell from that angle, but I guessed it was five feet high. She had cut and welded an array of metals, making something that looked both solid and fragile at the same time.

"Better than the Watts Towers," I said, joining her again.

"One of my inspirations," she said, looking pleased. "Help yourself if you want *breakfast*," she teased. "I'm going down to the basement to find a couple of things and switch the laundry. I have my cell if Lola calls from Alice's house ready to be picked up. If she uses the landline, come get me, okay?"

"Sure. I'm happy to help in the basement, you know."

"Everything's under control. When I come up we can talk."

I wasn't sure if she meant to sound stiff or if it was just the way she turned from the table, ready to tackle the next task on her list. Liz could be fiercely self-directed.

A train rattled through, and the cups under the cabinet did their dance. She grabbed one almost as if to stop it. Pouring a coffee, she slid this and the sugar my way and then started down the stairs with the next batch of wash. Maybe it was just the thick feeling in my head from too much sleep, but I could imagine a day when Liz would be able to stop working and devote herself fully to her artwork and keeping Lola on track. Mona might find her peace, I thought, once she was in school.

My first boss in the industry used to say, *People who buy insurance are pessimists, and people who sell insurance are optimists. So I think you know what I'm expecting.* I truly hated that man, but if ever there was a time to pull myself together and believe we'd find a way through things, this was it.

My cup was half drained when a pain opened up in my gut. Liz used to have Tums lying around so she could get her dose of daily calcium. I began a hunt and found two tablets at the bottom of a plastic bottle in the drawer by her bed.

Gazing into Mona's room, I went over to the dresser. Camera bodies and lenses and books on photography were everywhere. Mona had a slew of film canisters, photos, and negatives marked and labeled in boxes. Some were in Liz's handwriting. She had books on the desk and floor, in heaps and stacks. Mona had always been a reader like her mother. I wanted to pull all of the drawers open and rifle through the closet, thinking if I understood who she was now I could find some way to start a conversation, to work through and get beyond the worst. Her pack was on the bed, and it would have been easy to start with those compartments, but I knew I couldn't do that.

As I looked out the window I realized I had left my distance glasses on the kitchen table. But sometimes, unlike my precise, clear-eyed daughter, I actually enjoyed the blur. I couldn't drive at night or watch a movie without them, but in a funny way seeing the shapes of the trains move by gave me rest.

Mona's blind was off the window, and I wondered if it was broken or if she had pulled it down intentionally. Without curtains or blinds her window made a frame of the L platform and the trains. Maybe she saw everything in a frame the way Liz saw the world as weight and mass.

I spotted a workman out on the tracks, a lone figure, and I thought about what that's like, walking along the ties, watching out for the third rail, always out there under the elements. When I heard a clatter I turned suddenly, but I realized it was the holder for a woman's razor that Mona kept sticking to the tiles of the tub that kept coming loose and dropping against the porcelain. By the time I turned back the workman had moved on, and it was a good thing because a second later a train came through. I couldn't do that kind of work.

When Liz came upstairs I had showered and shaved and eaten lunch. I insisted on taking the laundry basket from her hands. I put it in the living room.

"Any word from the girls?" she asked.

I came over, held her around the waist, and whispered, "Not yet. Maybe we have a little more time." I moved my hands over her belly and down between her legs.

But she said she was dying of thirst. I let her go, and she poured a glass of water but didn't drink any of it. In fact she just stood there for a while, holding that glass. "I brought up some of my old dresses to see if they might fit Mona. I think the ivory one would look pretty if I took up the hem."

"You think she'll appreciate the time you put in?" I asked. I had my doubts. Mostly Mona seemed to wear black.

She gave me the oddest look. "I think Mona appreciates what I do. Absolutely."

"Of course," I said.

I sat down across from her in front of a pile of dog tags. "Mind if I keep working while we talk?" she said. "I'm getting behind."

"Go ahead."

"Last night ... I felt a little like myself again, you know?" She turned the wheel and pulled the lever down.

"Me too," I said.

"How to put this? Each of us is kind of spinning in our own orbits right now, and ..." She went on to the next number, pulled the lever, and tossed the completed tag onto a separate pile. "I'm trying to figure out how we're all going to get from here to there."

I thought she was asking for my help. So I said, "We'll look for a place to rent in Evanston in a couple of months. It might not be everything we want at first, but ..."

"That's not what I meant." She opened the little drawer and pulled out the fresh dog tag and added it to the pile. "Let me start over."

In all our years I couldn't remember a time she had seemed this uneasy with me.

"Lola is having a hard time fitting in at school. I'm afraid she's been picking fights."

I let out a deep breath. "Lola's always been headstrong. She'll adjust."

"And I've put four extra locks on the door," she said. "A couple of nights Mona's woken up on the stairs. She's getting worse, not better."

I wished she would stop working on the tags. "I'll be able keep her on my new insurance plan until she's twenty-six. Maybe if she went to one of those sleep clinics ..."

"I'll certainly explore that with her."

"I think the real problem is this boyfriend. He came over yesterday, looking for her."

"Okay. I'm not sure why you didn't tell me," she said.

"I didn't want to upset you. He's around forty."

"I see."

"He's a fashion photographer. He's arrogant. Smoked the whole time he was here even though I asked him to put his cigarette out. What's the word? Snide."

"If you got a separate place," she said, pulling the lever again, "for a while anyway, we could take our time and—"

"All of our money." Staring into the pile of bright metal, I said, "These are all addresses."

"Even if we had another bedroom, the girls need to adjust. If you had your own place, maybe we could start fresh."

"But you said you felt like yourself last night. Maybe if you could wait just a little on the next tag …"

She stopped and gathered and released her hair at the back of her head and looked at me. "We don't have any privacy."

"Mona said she wanted me to move out."

"You must feel ganged up on. But it would be good to consider a new arrangement."

"I plan to put in long days at the firm. I have to show them I can outperform the young guys. By the time I come home Lola will be just about asleep, and I'll get up and take my shower and be out of the house as early as you say so Mona can have her space."

"Richard," she said.

"On the weekends I can go down to the library and work, or into the office. Before long we'll be saving up money for her tuition—instead of seeing it go to two apartments. I really think we can make this work."

I could hear the refrigerator noises, everything else quiet.

"I'm a good man, Liz."

"Why would you say that? Of course you are."

"I mean, we all make mistakes, but you have to look at the whole person, and you have to admit …" And then I wasn't sure where I was going, and I began searching for something that would leave our conversation on an upbeat note. Just then the phone rang. It was Alice's mother. She was inviting Lola to stay over for dinner, and if that was okay, Liz could pick her up after dessert or stop in and join them. Depending on how Lola was doing, this seemed to leave another large window of time for us to spend together.

But Liz bundled up, asked me to think about things, and went back downstairs to weld.

When Liz took off to get Lola I went down to see the new work up close again. We would have that to talk about at least. The lights to the back stairs were out, but I made my way with the flashlight charging by the door. Downstairs, I beamed the light on her work. Liz had a way of keeping a vision going, no matter what life threw at her. I just had to convince her I was still part of that vision.

Even standing there, it was impossible not to think about Mr. Kaminski again. I began to wonder if he lived in the area still. I imagined he would be remarried by now and have a couple of little kids. They would probably be wrapped around his legs if I rang the bell and he came to the door.

He would look at me and ask if I was working for one of those environmental organizations. I'd see that he was staring at my chest, and realize I wore a T-shirt Liz gave me from an environmental group after making a donation. I would stumble worse than expected, saying something crazy or just *Sorry, I forgot my clipboard; I'll come back another time.* But maybe I'd find a way to look him in the eyes. If I apologized … if there really was something I could do … But I guessed that was thinking without oxygen.

When I heard someone on the back stairs, I realized Mona's bedroom light was on. I shone the flashlight upward, and there she was, carrying the garbage that I had tied off and meant to bring down with me. Liz had told me if we didn't make this effort nightly, the rats would be back, though she called them mice.

"Can you see okay?" I called.

"Not when you take the only flashlight in the apartment," Mona said.

"Sorry, dear."

I kept the light steady as she made her way to the bottom. On the last couple of steps she said, "Don't call me *dear*."

"Did your fever break?"

Again she iced me out, starting around the side of the building to toss the garbage into the dumpster.

"What happened to your hand?"

"Nothing," she said and dropped the heavy metal lid. "A minor darkroom thing."

"You sure?"

She said nothing, so I thought it best to proceed. "I realized after we talked," I began, "that all any of us ever really wants ..." The flashlight started to sputter, and I lost my train of thought.

"What?" she said and then more quietly, in the way that Liz gets sometimes when she has come to the end of her patience, "What do we *all* want?"

I felt like I was speeding through a tunnel of my own making, and the only thing I could hear was this shushing noise. The bulb on the flashlight fluttered again and went out. Pain traveled around my head, and I leaned against the rail.

"To get things right," I said.

She pulled the flashlight out of my hands and beat it against her leg too hard, and a faint glow appeared. "Then that's what you should do," she said.

She handed the flashlight back to me and told me to go first. So I did, and then I stood inside the door to the kitchen and listened until I heard her steps, worried that something might happen to her down there in the dark before Liz got home.

Mona

Evanston merchants had their shovels out the next morning as I slogged along in heavy boots, trying to wrap my mind around my life. If my mother had been with us that day I like to imagine she would have done everything in her power to save the Kaminskis, that her pregnancy would have made her fierce.

When I got to the studio Geary asked, "What happened to your hand?"

"Minor kitchen thing. I'm fine."

Before I had my jacket off he opened a book to a print of Marilyn Monroe by Milton Greene. "What do you see?" he asked. This was a ritual of ours, to start our day studying one image before we set to work. I began with the tangible, concrete facts.

"Marilyn sitting in a palm reader's window wearing a flared skirt, a Bohemian blouse dropped at one shoulder, plenty of necklaces and bracelets. A city street reflected in the windowpane."

"That *street* is on a 20th Century lot, and she raided the costume department for this shoot," he said.

"The way her palm is pressed against the glass, not far from the palm painted on the window, is overdone," I said. "And the light is harsh."

"The way Hollywood was to her, right? Maybe there were times

when she wanted someone to stop and read who she really was?"
Geary shrugged.

"So is this Milton's or Marilyn's obsession?" I asked.

"She seemed as engaged with the camera as her photographers,"
he said.

"There's one taken somewhere in Illinois in the 1950s where
she's lying on a bed asleep with one arm up. Plain white pillow and
sheets. I like that one."

"Different book," he said. "Eve Arnold. Hold on." He went
upstairs, and soon he was back and showed me the exact image.

"So what is it about this one that does it for you?" he asked.

"The light. The way the black edges hold her ... secure. And
the bedding illuminates her. Her humanness. The awkward reality
of her arm and the fact that it's half covering her face so you don't
feel like you're intruding. You can look at her without limit,
without embarrassment. The hand on her belly might be about
vulnerability. The dress makes me think of a series of hair ribbons
woven together. More than anything I love that Arnold caught her
at rest. Not performing, not used, not crushed, not over the top,
just still."

He snapped the book shut. "Are you printing your own work
today?" he asked.

"If you think there's time."

"We have some things to get out, but I think we'll be okay."

He had already printed the contact sheets on the job from the
day before, and he handed me those along with a marking pen.
When we had time he gave me first crack, and then he agreed or
disagreed and told me why. Sometimes he went along with one of
my choices just to illustrate what I hadn't seen with the loupe—
the small magnifying glass I held over the images against the light
box.

I circled one or another. "Have you ever worried if you did

something you felt was right, someone you love might suffer as a result?"

"Well, my family would have had a more comfortable life if I had been an attorney. But here I am." He laughed.

"No, I mean ..."

"Seriously? I would say ... I was arrested during marches. Beaten with a billy club once. And that scared my mother half to death. She was a widow and I was her only child."

My pen froze over the contact sheets. I had seen footage of Selma. I had seen the dogs, the fire hoses. "In the South?"

"Right here in Chicago."

"Did you take any photos?"

He said he'd dig them out but not today. "To put this in scale, Reverend King and Malcolm X had their houses firebombed with their families inside."

"I should let you mark the contacts today," I said, handing him the loupe.

Geary sometimes talked about the way speed is used in photography, which can be very different than motion. There's the speed at which we take in an image, how the eye moves from one point in the frame to another when we view a print. And there's the speed of the film, and that's something altogether different, though it's significant in the way it captures or seems not to capture motion. As I looked at the upper windows, branches moved by the wind, it was as if I were seeing something in time lapse. The trouble was I couldn't change my own speed to get in sync with them. I stood perfectly still as light and shadow streamed across the walls of the studio and the tears fell down my face and soaked my T-shirt.

"Now, here's a fact you don't know," he said, putting an arm around my shoulders. "My mother wanted me to be a Baptist preacher. So just for today, you and I could pretend I met that petition and that I've been sworn to a higher secrecy if you want to tell me what's going on." He let me go and pulled a couple of the prop chairs together and asked me to take a seat.

And so Geary became the second person I told the story of the hit-and-run to. I made this version considerably shorter than the whole coiled-up tale, stopping only when Lettie came downstairs to say she was off to see a friend. She refrained from asking me if I was okay but nodded as if to say she knew Geary would sort things out. We were behind schedule now, but he didn't seem troubled by this. Geary reached out and took one of my hands.

Then he let my hand go as if he were reeling out a line instead of cutting me free. Sitting back, he said, "Honestly, I don't know what I'd do. It's one thing for your father to pay for the consequences of his actions, but it's another thing altogether to see something go wrong for your mother and Lola and you as a result. You just don't know who might pick your father's story up on the news."

He suggested I give this more thought. He would too.

I stayed until I had developed and printed some of the Hasselblad film, and I made two or three more Lily prints. As I stood over the trays watching Lily's neighborhood children come to life, I found something I had never seen before. Lily didn't chase statements or moods. Maybe this came from an understanding that the world is overloaded with pitches and messages, or maybe it was simply her eye. But she allowed her captives to be flawed and temporal. She took what was there without finding an angle to interpret them or make them noble or worthy of pity. They were bald as winter trees.

When Lily's prints were dry I tucked them away.

I found Geary making out bills in his office. When I surfaced he asked to see my Hasselblad prints, and soon we had them laid out on a table.

"There it is," he said, singling out four shots he kept arranging until he found the best sequence. All of them were taken of my father the day he returned to town.

"You can see the regret," he said. "It's as if he was a powerful man once, or at least thought of himself that way."

We were both silent, listening to the print dryer ticking as it cooled.

"Nice," Geary said, folding his arms over his chest.

This was his highest praise, that single word, *nice*.

"I won't know where I stand unless you hit me between the eyes. I have times when I think I need to do something ... more practical, you know?"

"I believe you've heard me tell students they're starting to get a sense of composition because until that moment they hadn't understood composition at all and it's finally emerging in their work. Before that, maybe I told them their sense of balance or their affinity with their subjects was progressing because that's all they had and they needed to hold on to something to feel inspired. I'm telling you, you have competition-level photographs, and you have one week left to get them there."

"I don't know if this is the time," I said.

"I'll print out the blank application on Monday and go over it with you. Use these four shots. Nothing else. No essay, just a letter of recommendation from me. I'll get on it tonight. Smart to show the black edge of the negatives, mirroring the exposed man, even if Avedon already did it. Look, if I have to fill it out and send it in myself, I will. Meanwhile, you push through whatever it is that has you thinking the time isn't right."

"Thank you. You're..."

"Just leave the prints in my office."

I was happy not to carry my father around all day any more than I already had to.

A couple of guys in our park grumbled something at me, but they looked too wasted to do anything but cling to the fence, smoke, and hack their lungs up. One man wavered back and forth with a bottle wrapped in a brown bag and sang.

As I walked through the neighborhood I ran through the *Marvels* again. If the owner asked about my favorites, Cynthia said Silver Surfer or Storm were safe bets. But did her boss really want safe? I had crammed half the night so I could recall some of the better manga and name a few of the Italian as well. I couldn't call up more than two Alternative titles despite Cynthia quizzing me for a while, and I was totally weak on the Franco-Belgians. "Franco-Belgians?" I had said. She probably knew five hundred plus comic book series in all. If I got stuck, she told me to make something up. "*Be* the comic book," she said. "By the time he figures it out, you'll be hired."

Past the park now, I became aware of a noise like a pneumatic drill or machine-gun rounds firing off. I ducked as I turned. Constantina was moving my way at a fast clip, her high-heeled boots drumming on the pavement around patches of ice. I started to cross the street away from her when she called out, waving frantically. One of her ankles buckled, but she didn't let this stop her. I noticed that her hair, tightly bound in a ponytail, had an overload of bobby pins around the contours of her skull, as if she were trying to keep something in her head from slipping away.

"I've been looking for you everywhere," she said.

"You've been looking for *me*? Why not just watch the Auto-Tuned version? I have to get somewhere."

"I'll walk with you."

"No."

"So what did he say about my picture?"

I checked my watch. I was two blocks from an interview that was starting in five minutes. Despite my best efforts to pull away, I couldn't rest in my own body anymore and began to travel into hers. I felt the tightness in her chest and how cold it was when the air picked up and went through her jacket. Her stomach felt sour;

the button at the top of her jeans dug into her flesh. I felt the pinch and ache of her feet in those tall boots, all the toes cramped from the fit, numb from the cold.

"I haven't really seen him," I said as I snapped out of being Constantina.

"Hold this," she said and handed me her purse.

"Not today. I really have to go," I said.

"I'll be super quick," she said, and handed me her jacket. Then she pulled off a boot, and a tube of model-airplane glue hit the side- walk. She picked the tube up and placed it between her teeth, shift- ing about, trying to keep her bare foot from touching the icy pave- ment. The bottoms of her jeans were so tight they wouldn't yield, and I thought she was going to tip over. She wavered and put the boot on top of the pile I was holding and added the second boot.

Suddenly she unzipped her jeans.

"You don't want to do that," I said.

Ignoring me, she began to push them down her legs. That would have been the moment to run. But I was stopped somewhere between paralysis, fascination, and concern. As she stood on the bunched-up jeans, I saw that *Ajay* was written on one leg in a florid script near a cascade of marks. She must have used a razor blade to make dozens of 'A's up and down the insides of her thighs. "You'll never love him the way I do," she said around the tube.

Things spilled from my arms now, and I hurried to pick them back up. As I glanced around I wondered who was watching the woman stripped bare for love. The guys down at the park were too far away, but I could see neighbors looking from apartment windows. They didn't bother to peer through the cracks of blinds but stood boldly, in full view.

This wasn't an area where you had to worry too much about people calling the authorities. Nobody wanted to be known as someone who had called the cops, though sometimes people turned out for the battles that spilled into the streets and left someone unconscious or dead.

"I'm sorry," I said, not sure what else I could say.

The paint wrapping the glue tube started to flake, and some of that clung to her lips. I stood there as she began to pull her sweater over her head. I saw the tat of a small broken heart in blue and purple with a sword through it near her thin bra.

"Please stop," I said.

Constantina let her sweater drop back around her shoulders, took the tube out of her mouth, and said, "I'm going to stand out here all day and night without any clothes on until you find him and bring him here."

The wind picked up over the lake and pushed through the corridors and alleyways until it found us. She stood in the bitter air, waiting. Her scars reddened.

"I'll call him," I said, digging out my phone. She put her arms back in her sleeves.

"That's so interesting," she said. "You have the phone number of a guy you barely know and never really see."

When he picked up I talked fast, finally saying, "She's promised to get dressed if you hurry." Then I hung up. This seemed to satisfy her, and she struggled a little in the cold but was finally dressed again. As I handed her the boots I felt like a wardrobe person working on a B movie I didn't understand. Constantina wiped away the dark show of eyeliner, and I saw a newness to her as Ajay sprinted into view.

He mouthed something to me that I tried to decipher. Constantina made a careful study of this transaction and said, "I don't get it. What's so special about *this*?"

I was *this*.

I could see Ajay apply patience like slow pressure to a brake. "You're going to meet someone, Connie," he said.

"Did she tell you I wrote you a note to give to you, and she lost it?"

They both looked at me.

"And there's a photograph. She probably didn't give you that either."

Ajay asked me, "What happened to your hand?"

"A sledding thing. I'm fine."

"You can go now," she told me. She handed Ajay her glue. I guess this was the routine.

"You need help," Ajay said to her.

"You're my help," she said.

I took off at a sprint.

Some comic book stores sell lunchboxes, drug paraphernalia, and raunchy gag items, but this place was floor-to-ceiling series and action figures. They had a mass of vintage stock in original packaging with a section of graphic novels. Had Cynthia mentioned the graphic novels? I was fifteen minutes late.

Gator, the guy at the counter, was as lean and wasted as his boss, Peter, was round and robust. Peter wore a leather jacket that barely made it over his gut, and his skinny gray braid switched across his back when he got animated and made big hand gestures. He looked me up and down, adjusted a vintage *Rulah, Jungle Goddess* in its holder, and said, "Thrill me with how many Comic Cons you've been to, and please don't spare me about how you'll die if you don't get this job."

With a guy like that, I guess you just have to go for broke. So I said, "My mother's doing trashouts for a living, my father's a criminal, and I'm here to give my little sister a chance at normal. I think I've memorized fifty comic book heroes since last night. I knew two before that. I wouldn't go to Comic Con if you paid me, though E3 has some appeal. And I can't tell you dick about the Franco-Prussians."

Ajay appeared in front of the plate-glass windows just then. He was trying to catch his breath from running. I did my best to ignore him. Without looking over his way, Peter said, "That your boyfriend in the deep freeze?"

"Probably not," I said.

Ajay was doing a bad job pretending to read the signs in the windows when Gator spoke up, running his fingers against a couple of days' worth of stubble. "Cynthia says Mona here already knows how to run a register and she's a good photographer."

"Street stuff mostly," I said. "But I can do tabletop and portrait. I work as a photographer's assistant."

"If you photograph the store and a shitload of covers and stuff," Peter said, "so I can get some of this junk up on the web, you've got the job a couple of nights a week. But leave Tattoo Hero at home next time."

"You'll have to pay me five bucks over minimum if I use my own equipment," I said, taking a chance.

"Everyone's a capitalist. All right, show up on Sunday with your five-bucks-over-minimum camera and lights, and learn another fifty heroes by then, but don't go too heavy on the Anthros. When you're just hanging out at the counter, like gorgeous here, you get minimum wage, but I expect to see plenty of sales."

I looked around at the empty store and said, "No problem."

Ajay was eager to talk as we approached the building. He moved in front of me, trying to get me to stop. "I called her aunt the second I got your call," he said.

I wished I had a camera in that moment to rest behind. "I have a lot on my mind," I said.

I dropped down the three steps into our basement and unlocked the door to move a load of wash with Lola's dance clothes. Turning on the fluorescent lights overhead, I watched them go on in their usual pattern, illuminating a new stash of metal objects propped against the walls and stacked in the center of the room.

"Thank you for throwing her note out. I know it would have been like the other ones," he said.

"I didn't throw it out. I ate it," I said. "I think it made me a little sick to my stomach."

"I'm flattered?"

I stepped around a pile of grates. I had imagined, more than once, what it would be like to meet him in the basement some night. The sound of the furnace and the water heaters, the storage rooms with their open wooden slats, the way we would sit on the warm dryers, listening for footsteps, and the way we would stop caring about that and push closer, working on buttons.

He was tracking the things working inside me, but I turned away and got a load of wash out of the dryer. I put that in a plastic basket on the table and pulled the damp clothes out of the washer and threw those in, slamming the dryer door harder than I meant to. Then I went upstairs.

Geary and I didn't always agree on photographers. He was big on Fan Ho, someone I liked, but I found Cindy Sherman more interesting. He just shrugged. Maybe Sherman had started to shrug. She spent thirty years taking self-portraits in an unending stream of personas and identities. She did her own makeup, wardrobe, hair, sets, lighting, art direction, and the final shoot. In one image she was a medieval bishop, in the next she was a Hollywood starlet. High society heiress, waitress on the skids, clown, warrior. I once saw almost two hundred photos of her at an exhibit, and I was left with the dizzying sense that we are somehow part of every human being out there and that each one of us contains a million individuals that can be coaxed and teased out given the right situation, buzz cut or updo, no matter. My mother took me to see that show when I was fifteen. I had my first burdensome crush going then and had been reading about romantic versus courtly love in school. As I stopped at each photo the awareness that I was looking at one woman in various poses dropped away, and I began to feel as if I was in conversation with a stream of individuals. From the eyes alone you could imagine that some were more opinionated than others, a few quite shy, some haughty or boisterous, tragic or joylessly innocent, dead or lost.

I began to think about pure love as if I could get their opinions on this subject, and I felt a kind of silence in the room and turned around and looked at all the other Cindy Sherman rooms we had just passed through until one woman, Sherman as ingénue, laughed at my long, straight face. I had to sit on a bench for a while and shut my eyes.

I think Constantina held pure love where a lot of other people simply boast. But maybe that was all about glue and paint.

There were 86,350 hits on the SNAP video. I don't know why I bothered to check. In the comments, up toward the top, there were a couple of pseudonyms I was sorry I recognized, and very quickly I quit reading the *anonymous* posts.

Ajay and I exchanged messages as I made my way home from downtown the next day on the L. He had me laughing about everything and nothing. A couple of people looked at me like I was crazy, but I had already been exposed and overexposed and didn't care. I put my phone away and turned my camera on them.

Getting off the train four stops early at Loyola, I walked in the cold for a while. I was on my way back to the apartment when I was stopped short by a storefront. There was a giant palm drawn on the window, and shops and apartments across the street were reflected in the glass. Seeing the price list for having my fortune told, I got my camera out and took several shots in order to show Geary. I put on the polarizing lens to push past the reflections. I found an uncovered table and chairs.

Lifting my head, I looked into the lens again. A woman was staring me down. If it wasn't me, she was in every way like me. I don't mean the driver's-license version—height, weight, eye color, hair color—but my face and stance, my way of folding my arms across my chest. Only this version, this augur, seemed prepared to make up stories to explain things, while I was trying to record them before they disappeared.

I was pinned to the spot, studying her, studying myself, when she looked like she wanted me to come in and talk with her. Lowering the camera, I saw that same look in my own face in the reflection. It's hard to state this exactly, but I felt as if she was something in me that had burst from my head and found her way through the glass.

I took several steps backward, turned, and saw that the bus was coming. But when I looked at the store again, I clearly saw that I had been peering at a dry cleaner's, not a fortune-teller's. A series of hand-drawn bubbles advertised a special: *Clean TWO Pair of Pants for the Price of ONE.* I read the offer for winter storage and the headline for the Ultra-Lux leather jacket refurbishing. A woman was inside, but she was behind a counter with a customer, the overhead conveyor sending shirts and dresses and slacks round and round.

Maybe that's how my father saw what had happened. It shifted in his mind over time and became something else so he could live with it.

Once I was seated on the bus I realized I had hardly eaten and found an old protein bar at the bottom of my pack. While I ate it I tried to figure out where the hell I was going.

To have a terrifying dream without Nitro around wasn't the same. I was used to his dopey analysis.

I called him at three in the morning. When he finally realized I wasn't someone in Japan he got tender and listened.

"There's a particular sensation I have when I'm in a flying dream. I see the ground speeding beneath me," I said.

I told him about the windbreaks, the large industrial farms, the malls, the houses I saw in my dreams as I flew across the country. "Tonight the sky was a mix of rolling black clouds and bright patches of light that touched the earth at a slant. I jumped each time lightning brightened the ground in the distance."

"I can see that," he said drowsily.

"I keep going to national monuments. When I went to Yellowstone I saw this geyser called Screaming Mouth."

"Maybe that's what you want to have, a screaming mouth so you can tell your father where to go."

"I heard you stopped by."

"I see what you're up against."

"Do you think I should turn him in?"

"Yes. And no," he said.

"I know."

I listened to Nitro breathing, waiting. And then I hung up.

Richard

When I heard Mona come up from the yard, I opened the back door so she'd have enough light to make her way.

Liz and Lola came home, and Liz got on me about leaving the door open and letting all the heat out until Mona got upstairs with her bandaged hand.

"A minor lighting thing," Mona said. "I got a little too close to a lamp. I'm fine."

It seemed she had told me something different, but I was at loose ends and wasn't sure.

After dinner, which I couldn't eat—my stomach in a knot—I decided to put my things together for work the next day so I could be up early and out of everyone's way. Lola was asleep in Liz's bed. I sat on Lola's bed and considered that no one had asked how my first day had gone, as if they had forgotten. And maybe that was for the best because it hadn't gone as well as I would have liked with so much on my mind.

Liz started on the dog-tag machine again in the kitchen, and Mona joined her at the kitchen table.

"I don't know if I ever told you this," Liz said. "You remember my friend Tom Watts, the artist? The one who helped me with the architecture magazine? And then how he was in a motorcycle accident?"

I stopped what I was doing to listen to them.

"You showed me some of his ceramics," Mona said.

"I don't think I told you about the wake."

"Hmm, not sure," Mona said.

"A lot of our old friends gathered at a bar on the near North Side," Liz said, "and Tom's young girlfriend at the time, a slender blonde with anime eyes, arrived carrying a box."

"You mean she wore those black contacts?" Mona asked.

"What? No, it's just that her eyes were so large and round. Anyway, I told her, 'There's a case of champagne. Can I get you a glass?' Ignoring this, the girlfriend set the box down on the bar, and from its tissues she pulled one of the vases Tom had built. It was one of his best. The walls were so thin they were almost transparent when you placed it in front of a light. At auction, at the time, it would have sold for maybe ten thousand, God knows how much now. 'I remember when he made that,' I said, setting a champagne glass in front of her. The girlfriend said, 'It was one of his favorites.' With this she held the vase up high in the air.

"I almost reached out to grab it, you know, with this instinct to protect it. But then I thought this was her way of raising his art up for all of us to see. A moment later the girlfriend let the vase drop to the floor."

"You definitely did not tell me this story," Mona said.

"We watched it shatter like a crystal wineglass. As the room filled with voices she left the bar. I ran after her and caught her by the arm just as she was getting into a cab. When I asked if she was okay she said, 'No one loved him more than I did.'"

Liz described this woman's tragic face in the lights from the bar. The girlfriend was, it turned out, pregnant with his child. "She pulled the cab door away from me and sped off."

"And that was it?" Mona asked.

"I wrote, but she never answered. I heard she went home to Connecticut, where her parents live, to raise the baby."

"Good story," Mona said.

"People were upset that the vase was gone. But there's a funerary rite in some cultures. Something about breaking a pot and releasing the spirit. I kind of got it after I thought about it."

"Yeah, I can see that," Mona said. "But still ..."

How could that make sense? How on earth could that make any sense at all? There were times when they got together in their own little world and I just didn't understand.

I did what I could to stay on track, but the week went from bad to worse. I couldn't figure out one of the main programs at work and had to keep asking an admin for help. It didn't help that one hand was bandaged up, making it harder to type. I managed to lose the key to the office, and then I forgot on Thursday night to wash out another shirt, so the one I had to wear had a stain that my tie didn't cover. I kept my head down. On Saturday, after Lola's dance class that I couldn't say I was encouraged to attend, I asked Liz if I could borrow her van.

She thought over what she had to do and asked if I could be back in a couple of hours, three at the most.

"Don't worry about the new sound," she said. I started down the stairs, keys in hand.

"What new sound?"

"You'll know soon enough. I'm losing a heat shield."

It turned out to be a noise somewhere between the air being let out of a balloon and the whistle of ordnance being dropped from a great altitude. I wasn't sure if it was coming from the engine or a wheel, but maybe she was right. Maybe she had hit a pothole recently and the undercarriage had been torqued, loosening a shield. I got out and looked, but I couldn't tell.

I took a different route than our old one but found Euclid Avenue and drove over to Arlington Racetrack. The park was closed for the season and wouldn't open until May. I went past the fence, gazing at the stables and the wide parking lots, where the snow had been plowed and mounded here and there. I pulled over onto the shoulder. The main building in the distance housed the Million Room and the press boxes, the private suites and the wagering windows, but from the paddock side it was just one large white building with plenty of glass, and I couldn't even see the track.

Arlington was a Polytrack now—with its artificial turf and fine wax coat—making it a consistently fast track. Horses took the turns differently than they did when I used to go, when clods of dirt and grass flew up against the jockeys if the surface was wet, sometimes causing a horse to go down. Now if they went down, I think it was more about steroids. I listened to the sounds of cars going by on the Northwest Highway for a while, and when a security car approached, I drove away, taking the more familiar route this time.

I thought I had missed the restaurant at first. All I could remember was the red-and-white interior and the framed pictures of cows. I was about to give up when I spotted a building with boarded-up windows. Large sections of plywood had graffiti on them. When I looked into a gap in the wood, I saw the old interior, untouched, beams of light coming down from skylights. I imagined Mona sitting in one of the booths. I recalled how excited I was to tell Liz about the money I'd won, and I knew taking my time and getting a solid meal and plenty of coffee would make me fit for the road.

I let this go and got back to the van and that high-pitched sound. Past the hedges and fences and empty swimming pools. The toboggan run was busy. At this point I slowed into the right-hand lane and let any car that came up behind me speed ahead. The water tower was still there, painted in its familiar bright colors. I pulled off and sat there for a while, looking at the ladder going up the side, wondering how my high school buddies and I had ever been brave enough or stupid enough to climb it.

I drove off again and knew the exact place I was looking for because I remembered the name of the road we had turned off on that day to get to a phone booth. I found an easy opening in the traffic and did a U-turn, driving over the double yellow line to the other side of the road. I let the car rest in the dirt and gravel and blackened snow. When I got out to look there was no giant pole with a sign at top that turned with an advertisement. What I did find was the square of concrete with a rusting circle of metal embedded in the center where the pole had been sheared off.

The temperature kept dropping. I pulled my jacket in at the lapels and recalled the way our car had angled into theirs. I looked up and back on the road and across to the other side and placed our cars in position. I got out and walked around a little, going into the surrounding forest, my boots breaking into the crusted leaves and ice where water had pooled in the late fall.

I wanted to find something. A ring or hair tie, a piece of bone or fabric from one of the seats, a door lock. I listened for Dorothy Kaminski's voice. In my mind's eye, the face I had once seen with exact clarity had become a combination of her face and Mona's face and Liz's face. And the little girl, she was beginning to look like Lola.

I saw the smoke fill the car, Dorothy Kaminski beating on the window, begging me to help. Her little girl crying, the mother trying every lock, all the windows. I hurried and rifled around in my trunk until I realized I had used the crowbar to pry something open for Liz, some crate, and hadn't put it back in the car. The tailgate was jammed and wouldn't open. I saw nothing, not one thing to smash the windows.

As I turned to leave the wooded area, a branch came down, maybe fifty feet away, heavy with snow and ice.

I got back in Liz's van and sat there for a minute, trying to catch my breath. Turning on the engine, I drove to the spot where I had tied the fender up that day. I understood the angle at which I had traveled back across the road and how poor the visibility was from there. It would have been so easy to get into a second collision that evening. There is always some traffic on that road. Someone, more likely many someones, must have seen the accident. If so, they had passed by after the impact. Surely people had seen the car wrapped around the pole. But no one had been willing to stop and help or act as a witness.

I got out of my car again, walked back, and sat on that cold square of concrete. I had stopped at a store on the way there and bought some of those things people place by roadside accidents: a cluster of plastic flowers, a Mylar balloon, and a stuffed animal. I arranged these at the site. I asked for forgiveness.

There was only a trickle of traffic, and it was easy to cross the road without stop signs or lights. The walk was a little longer than I expected, but the sun would be out for another hour. I had the short winter jacket I used to wear when we went down the toboggan run years ago and a wool scarf that Liz had given me.

Once I was a couple hundred feet from the water tower I stopped and took it in. I had forgotten my reading glasses, but I did my best to make out the warning sign on the fence. Other than STOP and CAUTION, the letters were blurry shapes, but it looked like the same sign my buddies and I had ignored in high school when we climbed to the top. I went through a break in the fence and slipped in freely.

The ladder was cold but not icy. A glove wouldn't fit over my bandaged hand, but I had put a fresh gauze wrap on that morning, making it extra thick, and this was held together with white medical tape. I wore a glove on the other hand.

I started up the ladder. It wasn't like back in the day, when we egged each other on and called the stragglers *chicken* and kept climbing. I stopped more than once, and when I realized how high I was getting I felt surges of panic. Several times I thought I couldn't make it up another rung, but finally I got through the opening at the top and clambered around and held tight to the railing while I stood on the walkway ringing the tower. I circled the tank once, feeling light-headed and scared and at the same time a devotion to Liz and what we once were that had my heart bursting.

Reaching the door that opened to the water supply, I gave the handle a tug, and just as it had when I was a teen, it opened. Inside was the dark cavern filled with all that quiet water. I remember my friends and I, calling into that tank, our voices echoing.

I closed the door, stood back, and took everything in. There was Liz's van. That's where the pole sign once stood. I became aware of the houses edged close to the tower. Anyone in the surrounding area would have to be standing in their backyards practically looking through a pair of binoculars to catch sight of me. I saw a backyard fireplace going, a group of kids horsing around, one man smoking a cigarette in a lawn chair in the snow.

The light was starting to turn. I couldn't read the face of my watch, but I had a different sense of time at this height. There had to be a way for Liz to understand that over my entire lifetime she was it. She was the person I set my life to. She was the reason I thought about the future.

I became intoxicated with the colors spreading across the tank and the plains as I held tight to the railing.

I heard a siren on the road, a strong breeze picked up, and my scarf flew off into the air. In a moment of light and speed and the full impact of pain, I reached out toward the ladder and started to descend.

Mona

Mr. Kapur handed me an envelope with my name in thin letters, some with long, sweeping tails. It appeared to be written with the kind of ink that comes from a well. Inside, I found a dinner invitation for that evening. The cream-colored paper stock had turned yellow at the edges, and I imagined it was his wife's or daughter-in-law's stationery that he kept in a box of things he was unable to toss.

I looked at his hopeful face and thanked him. "Are you going back downstairs, Mr. Kapur? I was just heading that way."

"I will accompany you," he said and took hold of my arm. "My grandson tells me your father is a menace. And that your family must lie about where your sister goes to school because he has put you in a bad state."

"All of her friends are at the other school," I said.

"I understand. Did I say I would tell anyone?"

"No, I didn't mean ..."

"The world can be very cruel, very harsh. Ajay lost the best of fathers too early, and you have a father who is alive but does not act properly. I am sorry."

Mr. Kapur stopped, took a handkerchief out of his back pocket, and dabbed at his eyes. "Ajay tells me you are an accomplished photographer. So you study the way things are arranged. It is the same in mathematics and engineering. My son, he was an engineer. A brilliant fellow."

"I'm sorry you lost your children," I said.

"This is a terrible country," he said. "I would not have lost him if we had stayed in India."

We were both quiet for a moment, stopping between the third and second floors.

"Ajay told me just this morning that a family who cannot afford to buy a home must pay a greater percentage of their earnings to the government than a family who can. And now it seems this less fortunate family is supposed to pay for the homeowners who need to save their homes because the miserable bankers made them think they could purchase them with no money in their pockets and nothing in the bank. My grandson tells me the very rich can own several houses and pay no taxes at all. So we are paying for everyone. Things have always been backward here."

"The government should go after Wall Street," I said.

"Exactly. This should be so."

Mr. Kapur seemed pleased that we were in agreement. We continued down the stairs. "Maybe Ajay will buy you a home someday," I said.

"He told me he would design and build a home for me. He might have to make it a well-designed funeral pyre at this rate. But he is a smart boy. Maybe he will manage things. Do you like to photograph people or objects?" he asked.

"People mostly, street photography."

"You should go to India.

"I would love that."

"You are not like that other girl. She vexed me terribly. All she wanted was romance, romance, romance. She never left my boy alone when he had to study. She told me she wanted to marry him.

But Ajay must establish himself before he turns his eye to family. Now, you will come to dinner tonight. And someday, when the time is right, you and the man who is right for you will have good jobs, and then you will get married and have an excellent family. Perhaps it will be my grandson. In any case, there is an order to everything," he said.

I wanted to say there isn't really, that order fled long ago. But I didn't want to depress Mr. Kapur.

I put on a vintage ivory dress Mom had given me and a pair of cowboy boots. Lola came into my room, wanting to use my closet to dress in her PJs. I finished getting ready while she hid behind my hanging clothes.

"Look in the yard," she said.

Mom's sculpture shimmered in the lights from the L platform. I couldn't see much with the backlight still out.

"She's making it for me," Lola said.

"Then she'll put a plaque on the base with your name on it. This is very special, Lola."

I thought of Ajay when I tied up my hair in my bedroom mirror, leaving a few wisps to fall against my neck. It's possible, for the first time outside the world of dreaming, that I had begun to feel an honest machinery work between us. I thought of taking a series of photographs of him that I would hang up in the darkroom just to watch the chemicals drip from the edges of the paper. It was becoming more difficult to push him away.

As soon as my lipstick was on Lola popped out in her PJs and said she wanted to come too. I told her maybe next time. She could, however, use her stamp kit in my room as long as she did her work on the floor and put newspaper down.

Richard came home a short while later. After saying hello he asked if we'd mind if he took a shower. Mom said she should probably take the first one since she had to get dinner started and no one wanted bits of metal in the meal. He seemed to take this with good humor but I could see his look. He had become that person who was chronically in everyone's way, filling up space no one had, using supplies no one could afford to replenish. Even Lola, who loved cuddling with Mom in the evenings, wanted her bed back.

Mom got in the shower, and I knocked to come in. She stuck her head around the shower curtain. She looked tired, but I knew that pervasive mood when things had gone well with her artwork. This was a good tired.

"That dress looks great on you," she said. "Where are you off to?"

"The Kapurs invited me to dinner. Thanks for taking it in."

"Do you think they're making Indian food? I would die for some good Indian food."

It's possible she was reconciling to the idea of Ajay.

There was something about her use of the perfumed body splash on the tub's edge, the eyeliner out on the counter. I thought she had stopped using these things altogether. Maybe I had forgotten to see my mother as someone separate from her obligations. Sitting on the toilet, I said in a low voice, "You aren't in love with him again, are you?"

There was a long pause as the shower continued to run, and I was about to repeat myself, thinking she hadn't heard me, when she said, "I think I'm trying to find out."

I opened the door and heard his low, rolling voice. Lola had started to listen to another one of his stories. She had red and black ink on her hands, and this time she was almost pressed against his side. He had his arm poised to hold her around the waist. I watched as Lola got sleepy and entranced. I did not need to fly into her small frame, into her complicated heart to know how she felt. She would stand there, rocking back and forth, until he got to the scariest part, and then she would wait breathlessly until the hero appeared by inexplicable magic. I had been Lola once.

Lola and Richard were glued to a pulp talk show when I walked in late from the studio the next night. She was stretched out on her bed, and he sat on a kitchen chair next to her. Her school worksheets were spread out along the floor as if they had cascaded from her fingers. Nothing had been started. On the TV a woman in a blonde wig belted a sad little man in the face, appearing to break his nose. The bouncers moved in. I hit the off switch and the screen went cold.

He leapt to his feet. "Lola and I were watching one of her kid shows. The other program just came on."

"Lola, I want you at the kitchen table right now doing homework. Where's Mom?" I asked.

"You can see her from your room," he said.

"I want to see," Lola said, rushing ahead of me.

I looked back at him and said, "Lola gets a snack and does her homework first thing. And then she plays with her toys or reads. She has dinner, and after that she has a bath and is read to. She is asleep every single night by eight p.m."

He looked confused, though I didn't understand why, and he said, "I'll get it down."

From my bedroom Lola and I spotted Mom in the yard with her welding torch. She had a studio light rigged up again.

"Did you have your snack yet?" I asked Lola.

"I'm really hungry," she said.

I took my sister's hand and we went into the kitchen, where I put a plate together with fresh apple slices and peanuts. "You can nibble while you work. Cookies tonight for dessert *if* you get started by the count of ten."

Lola rushed into the living room, gathered her papers, and

spread them out on the kitchen table. I told her I'd be back up to check her work shortly. I raced down the back steps despite the shaky handrails that gave me the feeling I might plunge forward without anything to break my fall. Downstairs I found Mom on her haunches.

"Do you have any idea what they were watching on TV?"

She turned the flame down and tipped her face shield up.

"Hi. What?"

I told her about the woman who punched the man.

Her cheeks reddened. "I'll talk to him. Did he get her a snack?"

"Of course not. That's what I'm saying. Her worksheets were scattered all over the floor, untouched."

She shook her head. "I see."

"Do you? Do you *see*?"

She turned off the torch and stood up. I turned to look at the tiny altarlike structure that Lola had made in one corner from the bits and pieces of metal Mom had found that were too small for her own work. I could see that Mom had done some welding to anchor it. When a breeze picked up, the dangling metal moved.

"I have to get this section welded before the whole thing collapses," Mom said. "Fifteen, twenty minutes at the most."

"Some of us are worried about Lola's *life* collapsing."

"Ease up, Mona. I'm a sculptor, not a permanent trashout person. I have my first commission in two years. This means money for us. You know I would never do anything to put Lola in jeopardy."

As I looked away from her I realized that her sculpture was almost done. She had made a tree with leaves that shimmered in the slightest breeze like a quaking aspen. I moved closer to it and saw that she had used dog tags to make the leaves, each one stamped with an address.

"You have a commission?"

Examining her work with some insecurity, she said, "They've come out to see it once, and everyone's very pleased, so ..."

"What are the addresses?" I asked.

"Foreclosed homes," she said. "I've only done a small portion of the ones I know about, but if I put any more on the whole thing will topple."

"How will you move it?"

"The gallery will do it. Carefully. In sections."

We stood there for a while, and then I walked around it to consider it from different angles. She said, "I've asked your father to get his own place."

I didn't say anything. He would still be able to see Lola. He would still pull on Mom.

"I know there's something else," she said, trying to tease it from me.

"I have to get upstairs," I said.

"I'm here whenever you're ready."

"I know."

I began to climb the stairs. The way the handrail pushed back and forth, it was like a bone starting to pull from a socket.

I sat in my room and traveled back to the night of the accident and my old bedroom. I had counted the glow-in-the dark moons on my ceiling, hoping to fall asleep. When that didn't help I had lifted the blind on the window by my bed and gazed out at the lawn. I don't know how long I was like that before I fell asleep and saw the smoke from the car again. Instead of streaming upward from the hood of the car, it was sucked back into the engine. The woman waved us off, and the little girl's tears traveled up into her eyes. We drove backward to the restaurant where we had stopped so my father could have coffee while I had a malted, then along the edge of the road with the water tower, returning to the winning ticket, the Clubhouse at the race track, the drinks, the paddock, all the way to the dress my mother had laid out for me on the bed that morning as if she were setting it out for a funeral. Finally it was the morning before the accident, and I said to my mother, *My stomach doesn't feel right.* And she said, *Would you rather stay home today? You could certainly do that, love.* But that never happened, and the blue station wagon rode my life. When a second explosion occurred the roof of the car blew off, and Dorothy Kaminski, holding Nan in her arms, flew into the air so hard I thought she was going to crack the sky in two with her skull. Her daughter was ripped from her at the last, and they began to fly.

Richard

Liz and I used to sit at the kitchen table and read the newspaper. There was the morning she read about an accident on that stretch of road between our home and the racetrack.

Liz was in the eighth month of her pregnancy and often preferred to stand so she could breathe better. "It wasn't far from the water tower," she said. "Did you see anything?"

"It must have happened after we went through," I said.

The spoon I was stirring, her words, the pain, all of it went in slow motion as I tried to look normal.

"The husband was home waiting for their return from a shopping trip," she went on. "I can't imagine what that man is going …" Her voice faltered.

"Try not to focus on sad things," I said.

"It's just that … there are times …" She trailed off.

"What?" I said.

"Times you wish you could save the entire world."

That's what she said.

"Maybe after the baby comes and things settle into a routine," she went on, "I can start volunteering at the senior center again. I've been collecting ideas for new art projects."

"We could both do that. I could teach them something

about buying insurance, how to balance accounts, that kind of thing."

"I think they'd love that."

I cleared my throat and said, "Listen, before I forget to tell you, we stopped the car off for the tune-up."

"I thought that was next month."

"No, right on time. I decided it was easier to just leave it overnight so it would be the first car on the hoist. I've got a loaner."

"Oh, make sure they check the brakes. I've been hearing that sound again. And we really have to replace the back tires."

"They might keep it an extra day if they get stacked up. I'll be putting in more hours at work after the baby comes. We should be able to cover things without using the credit card."

I wanted to say something more, some small suggestion that she really shouldn't worry. Because she had been so anxious when Mona was pressed into her ribs, one night asking what if she had a stillborn or ... a baby with vestigial wings. I told her that's the trouble with having an overactive imagination. And she told me I needed to work on my sense of irony.

I will always wonder if, as we sat there at the breakfast table, Liz thought that it could have been us, that we could have swerved and hit a pole while she was home sculpting. That we could have been blown to kingdom come.

I was about to ask if Mona had already had her breakfast when I looked up and saw her creeping from behind the kitchen door.

I'll never know how long she had been there, how much she heard.

I didn't say anything, not one thing—but I asked Mona again with my cloudy eyes never to tell anyone, especially her mother.

The thing is, you live a decent life, you treat people well, you strive and work hard, you do everything you can to take care of your family, to protect them, to see them through, and then one day something terrible happens and that's it. From then on that's all you are—the man who did the terrible thing.

You try to erase it by leading an even better life than you thought you were leading before, but there it is, sitting on your head, waiting for you.

You come into this world with a good heart, and in a split second it stops.

Mona

Two nights after I came home to find Richard educating Lola on how people punch one another on TV, he didn't show up after work. He didn't call.

When Lola asked if she could sleep in her own bed now, Mom said he was working late and she would figure out the bed situation very soon.

Mom tried his cell a few times before she dropped off.

Geary was the one to see the late news. He hurried down to his office and pulled my photographs out of the box. He showed them to Lettie, who had followed him through the dark studio. They waited on the line while I woke my mother and we found the end of the story on another news station.

Mom gasped when she saw Richard escorted to a police vehicle. He didn't even bother to cover his head with his jacket. He looked like his life had flown away from him like a hat the wind had grabbed.

"He turned himself in." I began to hyperventilate.

"What? What are you talking about?" Mom said, getting up to find a paper bag.

"Dorothy and Nan Kaminski," I said.

She had no idea what I was on about. She unfolded the lunch bag and handed it to me.

When I had told her everything, my mother did not list what might have happened to me as a result of childhood trauma. She didn't go into the shower to break down out of sight. Instead she held me and let me weep. I think she was relieved to recognize something she had known was there but could never quite make out, something that required a different type of lens.

The next morning Mom took Lola to school the way she always did, but when she got home we sat at the kitchen table together and she called her brother on speakerphone. He had just arrived at his office.

"It's good you called me first," he said. "I've been thinking about Lola's *plight*."

I watched my mother restrain herself. *Plight?* she mouthed.

"It's possible that Lola's living out of district could become problematic now," he said as if she were stepping onto an ice rink with loose skates.

My mother said, "I'll be making enough on my current commission—and another I've signed a contract on—to find a place in Evanston if you're willing to advance the money. The gallery is about to crate the first one up, so I'm almost there."

My uncle arrived in his lemon-yellow Mercedes and watched over it nervously from the living room windows, worried it would be stolen and chopped. When he glanced around long enough to take in our condition he shook his head. Mom was dressed in her best suit and heels with her hair up. She looked like a high-end model who had been dropped into a bad urban scene for a fashion shoot.

That afternoon she grabbed a modest rental one block from a good neighborhood in Evanston in Lola's school district.

Money can be an impressive thing despite the tastelessness

and greed that can travel with it. My uncle paid for the movers. This was a midmonth winter move, so he had no trouble finding a company. They wrapped our small life into lots of tissue paper and labeled everything.

The gallery crew crated and moved the foreclosure tree while Mom supervised. By late afternoon we were ready to go. I dropped down to see Cynthia for a few minutes while Mom made sure nothing had been left behind. We had no intention of cleaning.

When she was finished with aftercare, I picked Lola up and took her to an early dinner at the pancake house so Mom could get a few things in place. Lola was a little dizzy and chatty from an overload of syrup as I drove her to her new life. The movers had even assembled her bed.

She inspected everything as if the floor might drop away or someone might leap out from a cabinet door and snatch it all back.

That night Lola showed the first sign that she'd picked up our inability to sleep. Mom and I tried everything. Finally Lola crawled into bed with Mom and I got in with them. Our mother looked weary but glad to have us close. An old foreign film was going with the volume on low, Jean-Paul Belmondo's voice the only thing that seemed to work on us. If I had photographed the moment, I would have shot it through the filmy TV screen, the edges of the frame blackened out, the center aglow.

It had warmed to sixty degrees for three days running when Lola mentioned Richard for the first time. She and I had taken a walk near the lake to a park she liked.

"He'll keep you in his heart," I said.

We sat down on adjacent swings. Lola kicked at the wood chips.

"Have you cried?" she asked me.

"I think I will eventually," I said.

"Me too," she said. "Eventually."

I pushed her on the swing for a while, doing a couple of underpushes. Afterward she went down the slide several times while I got out a snack. We sat on a bench and looked out toward the lake.

"I saw you from the living room windows," she said, "when Mom's TV woke me up."

I wasn't sure what she was saying at first. "At the old apartment?"

"I'm going to walk on air someday," she said.

Maybe this is how loss puts things together—that feeling of being suspended out in space. Lola had a book on the circus, and I thought she might be thinking of tightrope walkers. Or maybe when the lights were on in the living room and the curtains were open her reflection looked as if she were walking on air.

Mom lined Lola up with the counselor at school, and she went for a few sessions of play therapy. It was the counselor who finally said, "More than anything, Lola needs play dates and social exchanges with her peers." This was not easy for a girl whose father was sitting in a holding facility for a hearing that would take more than a year to happen. It had, after all, become a news item. The counselor reached out to a couple of the mothers she thought might be receptive. She explained that Lola's parents were in the final stages of a divorce, that she would not be seeing the father again. And that Elizabeth was an exceptional artist who had donated a work to the children's museum.

I stopped in to see Cynthia before one of my shifts at the comic book store. She told me that Anna Lily had been taken away in an ambulance and never returned.

"What happened?"

"I don't know," Cynthia said. "After a month the super cleaned out the apartment and loaded up the dumpster with a ton of photo boxes, and then there was a *For Rent* sign outside. What a miserable way to go."

I felt sick. "You pulled them out, right?"

"The boxes?"

"The photographs, the negatives!"

"I looked at some of them. They were just a bunch of down-and-out people. I guess the camera wasn't empty."

"Do not tell me they came and emptied the dumpster."

"Weeks ago."

"I need the super's number."

"Now?"

"Yes, now."

Cynthia dug it out of a drawer, and I called while she got dressed for a party.

The super took the opportunity to crab about the way we had left the apartment. I made some vague sound, not wanting to get into it with him, and asked if he knew anything about Anna Lily— if he had saved anything.

He said, "I got a couple hundred bucks for the cameras. If you find her, I'll send her a check."

"A couple hundred bucks?"

I didn't say he had destroyed Anna Lily's life's work, that irreplaceable vision. I didn't say he had squandered thousands of dollars of honesty machinery. I didn't say anything before I hung up.

I had the prints I had made. That's all that was left.

Richard

I lift the receiver and look at her for a long time through the plexiglass. "How was the motel?"

"Cheap," she says.

"And the drive?"

"Flat. You know ... Illinois."

I take a seat in the booth and look up to where a fluorescent bulb buzzes, a surge of light washing over us. She has made sure not to wear a sundress, a hat or cap, a skirt two inches or more above her knees, or a sleeveless blouse—just jeans and a T-shirt that doesn't say a thing in the world, all according to regulations. She's left her phone in the van, another rule, and this means she can't photograph me in this state of wildness. I have paced for months in a few feet of space, sometimes slamming my body against one of the walls, hoping to break through.

"Are you ever out of your cell?" she asks.

I try out different thoughts to locate one that might put her at ease. A full visit is forty minutes. I'm determined not to waste it. I tell her, "Yes. Most days." I don't say that my lower extremities have gone numb except for an occasional tingle in the balls of my feet and even out in the yard the air smells like an open toilet. I don't talk about what goes on here. Despite everything my hair is clean and neatly run through with a comb today, my uniform pressed.

"Tell me about Lola," I say, stretching one leg out and then the other.

"I brought a drawing of a funny three-legged horse she did the other day. The colors are wonderful. And a book Mom said she liked."

"Did she ask you to bring it?"

The question hovers for a moment but goes unanswered.

"And I brought a carton of unfiltered cigarettes," Mona says. "I probably won't be able to drive down this winter. Not until the van is fixed. Let me know when you need something."

"I thought I kept that a secret from you," I say, maybe more to myself than anything.

"What? I don't—"

"My smoking."

"I used to steal your cigarettes," she says.

I want to appreciate her ingenuity instead of harping on her, so I laugh a little.

She removes her sunglasses. Maybe she got up too late to put on makeup. I think she looks prettier this way, more comfortable somehow.

"When I get back on the highway, I'm going to drive down and photograph the ruins of Cairo."

"You'll have to show me next time you come."

"I try ... I try to imagine what it's like for you, unable to tell your stories to anyone," she says.

I don't say that I tell them to the people who crowd into my cell at night. I don't say that she's one of them. I move the phone to my other ear to catch something in her voice that might signal love, not just pity.

"How can they make the only time eight twenty on a Tuesday

morning down in nowhere Illinois?" she says loud enough for the guard with the small mouth and long jaw to hear—as if he set the rules and built the walls and added the concertina wire in thick coils several deep around the entire perimeter. "There must be other people ... plenty of relatives who live in Chicago who want to come down. It's a six-hour drive if you stop at all."

"But then the guards would have to deal with a whole lot of visitors," I whisper. Maybe this particular guard won't get annoyed by Mona's remark. He's young and fairly new, keen to impress the assistant warden, but he will talk to one of the other guards about this exchange if he's asked, and the seasoned guard could come after me for insolence, looking for any small privilege left to take away. I worry often that I could lose my lined paper and my pencil, my envelopes.

"Is this your second visit or your third?" I ask. She's been my only visitor so far. The oddness, that I'm not sure, stops both of us.

"Third," she says.

"Maybe I told you I'm reading the dictionary. The whole thing starting with A. Did you know that *fluorescence* is about blooming or flowering?" I crane my neck and look at the bulb as if it might be a manifestation of something divine, permitting me to see my daughter in different lights: now the hard one, now the softer one, now the one that might finally have a chance to bloom.

"All I want is a photograph," I say. "I have one of you and Lola. I'd like one of your mother. Maybe you could catch her when she's at her happiest?"

"There's one of the two of you in Muir Woods. You always liked that one."

"Yes." I nod. "If it's unframed and you crop me out, that should be okay."

Mona

From the sky it's more about seeing patterns: the way a river snakes out into tributaries; farmland threads into quilts. It's different seeing things from the road. I am content to ride for miles, stopping to photograph some of the natural wonders. But mostly I focus on the state of ruin in the small towns, the people trying to get by. Ajay says I have become a self-appointed WPA photographer.

We put a check in a notebook by each monument we explore. Ajay made reservations to see Keet Seel. This means a nine-mile hike in and back. The Ancestral Puebloans or Anasazi built their homes into the earth, and ears of corn and pottery shards are still scattered on the ground. Some people believe the Anasazi disappeared, he says, but they probably migrated and joined other tribes.

We spend a night at the Grand Canyon, sit out on the deck of the North Rim Lodge with drinks and talk about Ghost Ranch, what it would be like to descend into the canyon.

"I can't take it in," I say.

"Right?" He reaches down into his daypack to hand me the Nikon he's added to his weight.

"Where would I even start?"

"Helicopter ride?"

"No, I like that I can't take it in. I like this idea of awe."

"Awe it is," he says and puts his feet up.

Anywhere I can find an Internet café, I Skype with Mom and Lola. Ajay talks with his grandfather by phone. He's staying with an old friend while we're away, and his truck has become Ajay's truck. Sometimes we talk about how much we'll have to deal with when we get home.

Two weeks after we hit the road we pull into Joshua Tree National Park. We have a site at Indian Cove. Driving around in the thick air we find our numbered spot with a fire pit and picnic table. We arrive at a place hotter than a Chicago summer.

Spreading a tarp, we set up the tent, unroll the pads and sleeping bags, and drop the pillows on top. We get out the wood we bought at the last gas station and arrange it in the fire pit so it will be ready to light. I wash down the table from our five-gallon water jug and set up the stove. Ajay puts the cooler and dried goods in the iron lockbox.

We have some light left, and I suggest we walk one of the trails to get away from the other campers and the noise of the generators. The trees are mysterious with their waxy resin trunks and small knife-like leaves. The sun starts to drop, making Ajay's face almost golden. The short chopped hair, the markings on his arms and chest. I wish I had my camera with me in this moment, but we left our valuables locked in the truck.

Soon it gets dark and peaceful, and we follow the lights of the campfires.

We're starving as if we haven't eaten for days, and I light our fire first thing. Ajay cuts up vegetables and cooks them with potatoes and fried eggs over the fire, and then we put our feet up and eat under the stars.

After the dishes are washed and put away, the food stored again, we get into the tent. It isn't cool enough yet to be under the sleeping bags with the campfire going, though I know it will get cold soon, the way the desert changes at night. We lie on top of the bags for now, watching the fire. I've lived off grief too long. Both of us have. We curl into each other and feel our ribs expand and contract.

When I drop off I travel east toward the light. A thermal lifts me over abandoned warehouses, razed lots and speedways, empty rodeos, vacant strip malls. Some towns are half missing, and *closed* signs are tacked up like quarantine notices.

A wind pulls at me until I hover over the Grand Canyon, feeling for a moment like a young girl, the way my father would hold my body afloat in a pool when I first learned to swim.

In the walls of the canyon I see the layers of earth I studied in the national monuments book to prepare for the big family trip. Kaibab Limestone, Hermit Shale, Bright Angel Shale, Vishnu Schist. I get lost in naming them. Earth and pine smells fill my head. The Colorado River looks small beneath me, though I can only see a portion of it. I fall end over end through the shade.

Acknowledgments

To my daughter Sienna Haines who gives so much love and support to my heart and work, always willing to offer sage advice. My special thanks to her for creating the new website for my books. To my stepdaughter Charis Haines for her love and inspiration. To the agent of my dreams Esmond Harmsworth and his remarkable insight, faith, generosity and joie de vivre. To Fred Ramey, brilliant publisher and remarkable ally, as we celebrate our third book together. I am filled with gratitude for his impeccable editing, trust and immense care with every detail of this book. To Greg Michalson the other half of the amazing Unbridled Books. To Lee Pelton, Michaele Whelan, Robert Sabal and Maria Koundoura for the gift of their support. To the Emerson College Writing, Literature and Publishing faculty and our talented students. My thanks to Ragdale and the Virginia Center for the Creative Arts for much needed space and time to write. To my friends, especially Megan Marshall, Kerry Tomlinson, Rick Kogan, Pamela Painter, Richard Hoffman, Jennifer Freed, Mike Steinberg, Elizabeth Searle, Lane Stewart, Lyn Kustal, Jinx Nolan and Bob Livermore for their generosity. To my Chicago family, including Suzanne and Barry Cooperman, and Sandy Blau for their encouragement, support and help with research. To my aunt Alice Kay who brought life to books during her many years in the publishing industry. She will be greatly missed at the launch. To my grandfather Charlie Kay and the print shop he owned and ran for many decades in Chicago's Printer's. Row. To Alex Ebel for his help and wit. My thanks to the writing community and its Boston anchor, PEN New England. Thanks to Read To A Child for the reminder that it all begins early with a shared love of books. To Chicago my first home, Santa Barbara my second, and Boston my third.